"The ghosts of hard-boiled legends such as John D. MacDonald ...and—yes—Dan J. Marlowe himself haunt these pages. Pure pulp pleasure."   —Wallace Stroby
Author of *Shoot the Woman First*
and *Kings of Midnight*

"Author Jed Power has the...touch...it doesn't get much better..."
—Charlie Stella
Author of *Rough Riders*
and *Shakedown*

"...Jed Power channels the tough-as-nails prose of Gold Medal greats Peter Rabe and Dan Marlowe."
—Shamus & Derringer
award-winning author
Dave Zeltserman

"Fans of Dennis Lehane will revel in the settings and atmosphere ...an absorbing read...a hard-charging plot...Boston nitty-gritty."
—Charles Kelly
Author of *Gunshots In Another Room*
a biography of crime writer Dan Marlowe

Praise for *Th*

"Power's work, already cover-t
better. Boston has never had a better P. I."

—John Lutz
Edgar & Shamus award-winning
author of *Single White Female*
past president of Mystery Writers of America
& Private Eye Writers of America

Jed Power

HONEYMOON HOTEL

a Dan Marlowe/Hampton Beach Novel

Dark Jetty Publishing

Published by
Dark Jetty Publishing
4 Essex Center Drive #3906
Peabody, MA 01961

Cover Artist:
Brandon Swann

ISBN 978-0-9858617-6-6

10 9 8 7 6 5 4 3 2 1

ACKNOWLEDGEMENTS

Again I would like to thank my editor, Louisa Swann, for her continued excellent work on the Dan Marlowe series.

Also thank you to my wife and first reader, Candy.

Chapter 1

IT WAS MIDAFTERNOON when he stepped through the front door of the High Tide Restaurant & Saloon. I was behind the bar, holding court with a half-dozen customers spread out along its length. He spotted me and plopped himself down on a stool at the end of the long L-shaped mahogany bar.

I was surprised to see him. He'd never been in the bar area of the Tide that I knew of. He had jet black hair combed straight back and eyes the same color. He had a dark brown complexion. The man was Pakistani or Indian, I wasn't sure which. I did know his first name was Peenell and that he didn't drink. That's why he'd never been in the bar before. And that's how I knew something was up.

I walked down to greet him, placing both my hands on the bar in front of him. "How are you doing, Peenell?"

He shook his head slowly. "Not so good, Dan," he answered. His English wasn't great, but it was much better than my Hindi or whatever the hell it's called.

"What's the problem?" I knew the second I said those words I might regret them.

Peenell fidgeted around on the bar stool like it was his first time sitting on one, which it probably was. "I have big trouble, Dan."

My heart sped up and I got a bad feeling about what was coming. Still, I didn't hesitate about listening to his story. I knew the man only slightly. He owned a small hotel on Hampton Beach's Ocean Boulevard and as far as I knew was a hard-working businessman. I'd seen him many times coming or going from his hotel or hurrying along the strip. We'd exchanged pleasantries a few times. I'd never heard a bad word about him. Being a bartender at Hampton's most popular watering hole, I would have heard such a word had there been one. So you see, I had no out. I left my hands on the bar.

"Would you like something?" I asked.

Peenell's eyes drifted over the liquor bottles stacked along the back bar like he was actually contemplating making a selection. Finally, he said what I'd expected, "A ginger ale, please."

When I returned with the soda and placed it on a cocktail napkin on the bar in front of him, he touched my arm. "Dan, I am in *very* big trouble."

His black eyes looked watery and bloodshot. I thought for a moment the man might cry. I cleared my throat. "Peenell, I get off work in a while. Why don't you wait and we can talk then."

He nodded, then sipped his soda through a straw.

When my relief arrived, I gave Peenell the high sign to follow me into the restaurant section of the High Tide. It was still a bit too early for the supper crowd so all the booths were empty. I carried two sodas with me. We sat opposite each other in a booth beside a long plate glass window that looked out onto Ocean Boulevard and the Atlantic Ocean beyond.

"Okay, Peenell. What's the problem?"

He pursed his cracked lips, dragged some ginger ale through the straw, and looked at me with desperate eyes. "Dan, terrible things are happening to me."

I won't bore you with all the details, we'd be here all day, but he ran the entire story by me. It seemed Peenell was being harassed. A gang of teenagers had been hassling his guests as they came and went from the hotel. The front of the building had been spray painted with bigoted slogans during the night. Then someone had snuck in when the front desk was unoccupied and had hidden dead fish in various places around the establishment. Peenell was still trying to get the stink out of the building. On top of that, someone had papered his car with political bumper stickers from roof to tires and hood to trunk. I knew from personal experience just how hard those things were to get off.

And it hadn't ended there. Just a couple of nights ago someone had placed a large pile of papers and rubbish against the back of his building and set them on fire. Fortunately, a passerby from one of the bars had discovered the fire and doused the flames before the building caught.

I figured that was it. Enough for anybody. But that wasn't all. He looked at me with those black eyes. His lower lip quivered as he said, "They call on phone, Dan. Say they will kill Peenell if I don't leave beach."

I tried not to show my alarm. I didn't want to frighten him more than he already was. "What do the police say?"

"Nothing. That's why I come to you, Dan. People say you can help me."

I knew what he meant. In the past I'd been involved with clearing up a couple of unpleasant situations on the beach. Some people thought I had a knack for it. I knew better. It had been just dumb luck. Still, I kind of enjoyed the reputation and Peenell coming to see me was one outcome of having this rep. So here he was and I had to keep listening, keep talking. Besides, I had that damn code of mine. The one I'd sworn myself to. The code that said I'd never back down from anything ever again, just out of fear. Otherwise, how could I be sure it wasn't just my anxiety condition ruling my actions? I couldn't. And so far, I didn't see a reason for me not to hold to that vow. Except fear, that is. And like I said, that wasn't an option for me.

"The cops must've said something, Peenell."

He tapped the fingers of both hands on the table. "They say they are investigating. I tell them some kids' names. They can't do anything yet. They must catch them doing something first." Peenell leaned across the table toward me. I could smell his breath. There was an odd aroma to it that I couldn't name but associated with an ethnic restaurant I'd been to once. "By that time, I will be out of business. People are afraid to stay at my hotel. The summer has just started and already I have lost guests. You know the beach, Dan. It is only a ten-week season. That is all there is. If I lose that, Peenell is done."

I knew that was true. Hampton Beach, New Hampshire, has a season that only extends from the end of June until Labor Day. You do have the Seafood Festival the following weekend, but that's it. Except for a couple of restaurants like the High Tide and some motels that cater to the down-trodden "Winter People," the beach closes up tighter than a clam. So, yeah, that was it for ninety percent of the beach businesses—ten weeks to make your dough or you're dead.

"I'm not sure if I can help, Peenell." I didn't like saying it but I was being honest.

His eyes scanned my face. "Dan, you know everyone on the beach. You could ask people, find out something. Why they do this, maybe? If I ask, some of them . . ." He bowed his head but I could still see a flush come to his dark skin.

I knew what he was embarrassed about and he was right, to a degree. Some people on the beach, like everywhere else, didn't like immigrants too much. A bartender hears everything—piss-colored, rag-head, sand jockey, and worse. And you have to keep your mouth shut when you hear it. It's part of the job. A real bad part.

"What cop did you talk to?" I asked.

"Steve Moore," he answered.

At least that was good. I knew Steve Moore. We were friends.

"All right, Peenell, I'll see what I can do," I said, adding quickly, "but I can't promise anything."

He smiled, showing teeth as white as those of a Hollywood actress. "Oh, thank you, Dan. I knew you would help Peenell."

"For now, why don't you hire some security," I suggested.

"I cannot afford it, but I will have to."

We stood and he shook my hand before hurrying out of the restaurant. As I watched him go, I realized I had absolutely no idea if I'd be able to help the man. But I was going to give it a shot. What choice did I have? Like I said, I promised myself a long time ago that I'd never back out of anything ever again because of fear alone. I'd done that enough in reaction to the panic attacks that had dogged me ever since I'd sworn off cocaine. No more.

As I gazed out the window onto Ocean Boulevard and the bumper-to-bumper traffic on the one-way street, I hoped I hadn't bitten off more than I could chew with this Peenell problem. My hand dropped to my jeans pocket. I fingered the prescription bottle of Xanax. I didn't take them very often. Still, I lugged the pills with me everywhere. Just like a child with a security blanket.

Chapter 2

THERE WAS ONLY one place I could go to find out about Peenell's problem—the Hampton Police Station. I made a phone call and found out my friend, Steve Moore, was on the premises. I didn't have far to walk. The one-story cinderblock building was located a few blocks from the Tide, behind the Casino, on Ashworth Avenue.

Inside, I knocked on a door marked "Detectives."

"Come in," I heard Steve shout. I entered, closed the door behind me.

Steve Moore was seated behind a metal office desk littered with papers. He had a brown buzz cut, sport shirt, and tie. He looked at me and I saw dark circles under his eyes. He motioned for me to sit. I settled in one of two folding chairs in front of the desk.

The room smelled of cigarette butts and stale coffee. It was pretty dreary too. Windowless with a few filing cabinets against one wall. On the opposite wall were a half-dozen framed photos of high-ranking police officers I assumed to be past chiefs of the Hampton department. Above them, in a larger framed photo, was a picture of President Clinton. I grimaced.

Steve and I went over some personal history for a bit, then we got down to business.

"I haven't seen you in a while," he said. "Not that I don't like to see you, but you've never been here on a social call before. So what's up?"

"Do you know Peenell? Owns the Waterview Hotel up on Ocean? He . . ."

Steve waved his hand. "Enough said. I already know the whole story. What's been going on. And we're looking into it. We haven't been able to prove anything . . . yet."

I shifted around in the uncomfortable metal chair. "It's a short season, Steve. This poor guy can't wait long. He'll be out of business."

He gave me a disapproving look. "How the hell did you get mixed up in this anyway?"

"He came in the Tide, asked me to look into it. I don't know what I can do. I thought maybe you could tell me something that might help him."

Steve peered around me at the closed door and lowered his voice. "I shouldn't tell you anything. But I know this Penile guy has a good reputation on the beach."

"Peenell," I corrected.

"Whatever. Because of that *and* it's you asking *and* I know it won't go anywhere else . . ."

I interrupted. "That goes without saying."

Steve pulled a green file free from near the bottom of a stack on his desk. He didn't open the file. He did pick up a pen, clicked it rapidly, and said, "Leo Karnack."

Leo Karnack. I knew the name, not the face. It wasn't a good name on Hampton Beach. In fact, it was one of the worst. Karnack ran the Honeymoon Hotel. It was located on Ocean Boulevard, a couple of buildings from Peenell's Waterview Hotel. That was the only connection that came to mind. Other than that, they were about as dissimilar as two beach hotels could be.

The Waterview was kept in tip-top condition inside and out. Its reputation was one of the best on the beach. Not so the Honeymoon. It was one of a handful of third-rate dives scattered around the beach, the type of place that during the summer season the owner rents rooms to kids who get so drunk, you're surprised a few don't go over the balcony every year. And in the off-season, the rooms are occupied by alcoholics, drug addicts, and those just plain down on their luck.

"That scumbag?" I said. "He owns the Honeymoon, right?"

Steve shrugged. "Well, he's the manager of record anyway. We figure because the economy's not so good he's trying to drive out his closest competition."

Now it made sense. A little. It appeared there was more to Peenell's troubles than teenage vandals. "Sounds like something Karnack would pull," I said. But there was one thing that troubled me. "The type of tourists who frequent the Waterview wouldn't be caught dead in the Honeymoon. They'd sleep on the beach first, wouldn't they?"

"I dunno. Maybe Karnack figures it's better if they don't have any other choice."

"Maybe," I said, but I was sure that I'd choose the sand over the Honeymoon if I was ever faced with the choice. On the other hand, I'd seen tourists spend money on some odd things through the years.

"So . . . ," I said, hesitating a bit, "if you know all this, why . . . ?"

Steve interrupted by tossing his pen down. It bounced around on the desk. "He's a slippery character, that's why. He's got some young punk kids all jacked-up about Penile and . . ."

"Peenell," I interjected.

Steve fluttered his hand. "Yeah, yeah, whatever. You know—racist slurs, terrorist stuff—that kinda crap." He opened the file for a moment, glanced at it, and slammed it shut. He didn't speak for a short minute, then a little more calmly said, "He's got his nephew, the kid's maybe twenty-five or so, doing the dirty work for him. We know we can get the young street kids the nephew's using to rat on him, but we aren't sure he'll finger his uncle. He's scared to death of Karnack. And he's the one we . . . *I* . . . want. We'll get him. But it's going to take time."

"He hasn't got time, Steve. If he loses even a few weeks, it'll kill his business."

Steve sighed, shrugged his shoulders. "I know all that. I also know that these things take a while. Believe me, I hate seeing a dirtbag like Leo Karnack pushing around decent beach people as much as you do."

I knew Steve well and I knew that was true. He was a good man and we'd been through a couple of hairy situations on the beach together in the past. A thing like Karnack was trying to pull would bother a person like Steve. Personally. He couldn't always separate himself from his work. Leave it at the office when he went home at night. That wasn't good for a cop. But like I said, he was a good man. Maybe too good for his job.

"How'd you find this out?" I asked.

Steve gave me a sly grin. "We have our ways."

We were both silent for a bit before I said, "I'm going to look into this."

Steve frowned. "I *knew* you were going to say that, but I wish you hadn't told me. Should've just done it."

"Told you what? I didn't tell you anything."

Steve smiled, then stopped. "Gant's on this too, Dan. You know what he thinks of you. And of me for that matter."

Sure I knew what Lieutenant Gant thought of me and it wasn't nice. I'd had problems with him in the past. I also knew he wasn't a big fan of his underling being a friend of mine. Gant had caught Steve giving me a helping hand before. He hadn't liked that. But because we'd been lucky, and we had resolved the unpleasant beach happenings in a positive way, Gant had reluctantly not pursued action against either of us. If Gant was on this case, both Steve and I would have to be extra cautious.

"I'll be careful, Steve. I won't do much. I'm not even sure what I can do." I thought for a moment, came up with nothing, except . . . "If I need your help, can I . . . ?"

Steve made an ugly face. "You would ask that."

Anyone else would have taken that as a no. I knew Steve well enough to know a disguised yes when I saw one. "Thanks," I said.

Steve shook his head, an exasperated look on his face. "Just don't make a bad situation worse, will ya? Please."

I chuckled, pushed myself up and out of the chair. "You don't have to worry about that."

"Sure," Steve said, looking up at me and rolling his eyes. "I've heard that before."

"Talk to you later," I said, turning and heading for the door.

"And don't get arrested, either," Steve said to my back. "I'm not going to bail you out."

Just before I left the room, I thought of something and looked back at Steve. "Where's Karnack live anyway?"

"Seabrook."

"Figures."

"Nooo," Steve said, shaking his head. "He's over in the ritzy part. The beach."

"Still figures," I said before walking out of the office and the building's front door into the late June sunshine.

On the walk along Ashworth Avenue to my small cottage in the Island section of the beach, I had time to think. It didn't do me any good. I couldn't figure out my first move. Find Leo Karnack's address and try there? Or go right to the Honeymoon Hotel—not that I could be sure he'd be about. Or something else?

Chapter 3

I ARRIVED AT the Tide at ten thirty the next morning, my usual time. I opened for business at eleven. That gave me a half-hour to set up the bar—cut fruit, get ice, restock beer and booze, make the waitress banks, and a couple of other things. It was tight, but I always finished in time. I had it down to a science. I should have. I used to own the High Tide.

I was running Peenell's problem through my mind as I worked and the time went quickly. When I was done with my chores, it was only minutes away from eleven. I went to the big front door, unlocked and swung it open, expecting to be greeted by Eli and Paulie, two of my morning regulars. Instead, in through the door came an old-timer named Cliff Ingalls. He looked like someone's grandfather. I guess you could say he was a semi-regular. He owned a small gift shop on the beach. Once every week or two he'd show up, have a draft beer. But never at eleven in the morning. He was a mid-afternoon man.

Of course Eli and Paulie trooped in right after him. Cliff stood watching as both men made beelines for their customary stools, Eli near the draft beer spigots located at the center of the bar, and Paulie at the L-shaped end in front of the large picture window that looked out onto Ocean Boulevard. It didn't surprise me that Cliff went and took the last stool at the other end of the bar. Most people in the know stayed clear of Eli. And Cliff would have had to do his drinking in the kitchen to be any farther away.

For the second time in as many days, I had a feeling something bad was in the wind. It wasn't just my anxiety level either, although that was accelerating nicely. I quickly came around the bar, poured a draft Bud for Eli, and placed it on a cocktail napkin in front of him. He was dressed as always—dirty white painter's shirt and pants. Cap, too. I knew the paint stains were mostly old. He was a good sixty and didn't work much anymore, although he'd never admit it. A Camel cigarette was stuck in his mouth, ash as long as the butt itself. He nodded and grunted something. He wouldn't say much until he'd killed his first beer. Then you couldn't shut the man up.

Down near the window, I gave Paulie his Miller Light, no glass. He was friendlier. He brushed his long brown hair off the shoulders of his mailman's shirt as he thanked me. He worked the graveyard shift. I didn't hear the next few sentences. If they'd been anything new, I'm sure I would have noticed. I was anxious to get down to the other end of the bar, so I excused myself and did.

If there was ever a man more uncomfortable looking than Cliff, I hadn't seen him. He stared around the bar like he'd never been here before.

"Draft, Cliff?" I asked.

"No, no thank you," he said, a slight quiver in his voice. "Way too early. Coke, I guess."

I went to the tonic gun, then returned with his drink. He looked at the glass sitting on the bar in front of him, then up at me. He said, "Dan, I've got a problem."

Twice in two days? What the hell was going on? I almost stepped outside to make sure there wasn't a sign out front announcing, "Dan Marlowe, Private Investigator." Instead, I held up a finger for a moment, turned to look at my two other patrons. Paulie, at the other end of the bar, was looking directly at me. He was blowing large perfect smoke rings as he watched. Eli stared straight ahead at the bar mirror. He didn't fool me though. I could actually see his head tilted a bit toward me, ear cocked.

I grabbed a clicker off the back bar shelf, turned up the volume on the TV over Cliff's head. I walked down to Paulie and did the same thing with the clicker and overhead TV at that end. The same inane game show that was on every day was on both TVs. I heard the announcer shout, "Come on down."

When I returned to Cliff, I repeated myself for the second time in two days. "Okay, Cliff. What's the problem?"

It seemed his granddaughter, who'd just turned seventeen, was holed up with some older junkie. The girl had lived with Cliff and his wife for years; her parents were out of the picture. I didn't ask why. Cliff said he'd tried to get her away from the man but with no luck. I could believe that. Cliff was frail, and if he wasn't at least seventy, I would've chugged a bottle of tequila. The police had been no help either. She was a good girl, he said, and he was sure it would end up badly. He assured me the character his daughter was tied up with was harmless, even though he was a known drug addict. I was wary. I'd heard statements like that before—the harmless part that is. Those statements didn't always turn out to be true. Then he asked me if there might be something I could do.

My heart started to speed up and I fingered the prescription bottle in my front jeans pocket. I wanted to say no. But something stopped me cold and it wasn't just that damn promise I'd made to myself. Years ago Cliff had helped me during the tail end of a bad cocaine run. I was behind the bar. What I must've looked like, I don't want to think about. I'd been so strung out I'd imagined every customer who came through the door was a cop. It had been as real to me as a schizophrenic's hallucinations. Things would've gotten real ugly if one of the waitresses hadn't asked Cliff to take me home. Instead he took me to his house. I stayed there three days. He and his wife helped me down. I didn't feel close to normal until over a week later.

So between that and my oath, what else could I say now but, "Where are they staying, Cliff?"

His answer surprised me and didn't surprise me—if that were possible. "The Honeymoon Hotel. Room number 210."

So there it was again, twice in two days. If I didn't know where I was going next, I probably was drinking too much beer.

I told Cliff the same thing I'd told Peenell the previous day. "I'll see what I can do."

"That's all I ask, Dan," he said, nodding his head rapidly. "Thank you. Thank you. And please be careful."

Why he said that last part, about being careful, I didn't know. Especially when he'd said the boyfriend was harmless.

Maybe it was just a figure of speech. It didn't matter. After all, *Careful* was my middle name. Or at least I liked to think it was.

Chapter 4

IT WAS FIVE o'clock when my shift ended and I turned the bar over to my relief. I left by the front door for a change and started walking north on Ocean Boulevard in the direction of the Honeymoon Hotel. The weather was good and the streets fairly crowded for the month. By July the strip would be like Times Square on New Year's Eve. A real madhouse. A lot of year-round people didn't like the crowds. I did. It was great for people watching and I liked the action. Besides, I'm not sure there is anything more dark, desolate, and depressing than a summer resort in the off-season, especially the winter. How people could prefer that time of year on the beach, I couldn't fathom.

The smell of the salty sea air was a nice change from the cigarette-and-beer odors I'd been subjected to for the last six hours. As I walked by the old faded-gray Casino building, my ears were blasted by the shrill sounds of the shooting gallery and my nose was filled with the aroma of fried dough and foot-long hot dogs. The two-story building is two blocks long so it took me a couple of minutes to get past it. When I did, I didn't have far to go.

When I reached the Honeymoon Hotel, I stood on the street, just off the sidewalk, hands on hips, looking up at the front of the building. Why I was checking it out, I didn't know. After all, I was sure the place hadn't changed much in the more than half-century it had been standing there.

The bottom floor of the building housed the standard T-shirt shop and an ice cream joint. The T-shirt shop carried the same cheap crap as every other shirt joint on the beach. The ice cream stand dispensed a third-rate brand I didn't really consider to be ice cream. Only a couple of ice cream businesses on the beach had top quality product. I knew this because I was an ice cream connoisseur, or maybe an addict, depending on which way you looked at it. Anyway, a glass door separated the two businesses. It had the word *Enter* stenciled on it and the glass was cracked from top to bottom. Above the ground floor were two floors of rooms for rent. The ones on this side of the building all had small balconies that faced the ocean. What a waste, I thought.

I stepped over to the hotel's door and removed a loose Xanax from the change pocket in my jeans. I quickly tossed the pill under my tongue and noticed the familiar medicinal taste as it dissolved. I took a deep breath, let it out, and pushed on through the door.

I trudged up the skinny staircase in search of Room #210. The odor of disinfectant reminded me of trips I'd made to Boston's Combat Zone when I'd been at my worst back in the day. The paint on the walls was peeling and the stairs were as rickety as they could be without collapsing. How they ever passed a building inspection was beyond me. A moron could see why only kids seemed to be interested in staying here during the summer.

I reached the second floor and found Room #210. The number 2 was loose on the door, hanging upside down. I cleared my throat and knocked forcefully.

"Yeah, who's there?" The voice was loud and aggressive.

"A friend."

"Get lost, friend."

The next thing I said wasn't original either. I hoped it would work though. "Sure. But I'll be leaving with the hundred bucks I was going to give you to answer a couple of questions."

"Questions? Questions about what?"

"The girl. Her grandfather just wants to make sure she's okay. And find out if she wants to come home." I could hear the girl's voice too, low. They were going back and forth.

I stood there for a long minute. Finally, a deadbolt clicked and the door opened. I stepped inside. As I had expected, it was your standard bottom-tier beach rental. One that could accommodate both low-end tourists in the summer and a rough, down-on-their-luck crowd the rest of the year. There was the customary backbreaker of a double bed, a small sink with a tiny hotplate on the counter beside it, a three-foot high refrigerator plunked in a corner, and a red Formica kitchen table with four mismatched plastic-cushioned chairs. There were also two easy chairs and a love seat squeezed into the room.

There was one good feature on the far side of the room—a floor-to-ceiling sliding glass door that overlooked the Atlantic Ocean. The door was open and ugly brown drapes moved with the breeze. Beyond the glass door was a wooden balcony that appeared crooked and rickety. I wondered how it could support more than a couple of drunken teenagers partying on it in the summer.

There were two people in the room. They both looked like they belonged there.

"Let's see the money, Pops."

When you're my age you can still ignore that kind of name calling and I did. After all, the punk who tossed it at me was just that—a punk. I didn't need the services of Stella, the beach psychic, to tell me that, or that he was the junkie Cliff had told me about. The punk stood near the open window and was so skinny I wondered why a gust of wind didn't bowl him over. He was tall though—taller than me and I'm six-feet—with long black hair that looked like he'd forgotten that you were supposed to wash it every so often. He wore wrinkled black jeans and a black long-sleeved T-shirt with some hard metal group's logo on the front, something to do with the devil. His face was pockmarked. Steve had said he was about twenty-five. He looked ten years older, with a face that could have been used on an anti-drug poster.

He held out his hand. The sleeve of his T-shirt rode up, displaying an arm as skinny as a pipe cleaner. I thought I saw something else there, too. He rubbed thumb and forefinger together so fast, I was surprised I didn't see sparks. "The money. The money. Where's the money?"

I ignored him and glanced to my right. Sitting on a sagging bed was Cliff's granddaughter. She looked like he had described her, except younger than seventeen. I knew that wouldn't last long. She was pretty and petite, with short blonde hair. She wasn't much older than my own daughter, I realized. She looked awfully scared and strung out. She couldn't sit still. She was bouncing around like the springs were poking her. I knew the poor kid could've used one of my pills, but at this point that would've just made her situation more tolerable. I figured the more uncomfortable she was, the more likely I was to get her out of this dump.

And again, I didn't need Stella, the psychic, to tell me what drug they were doing. I could smell it in the sickening sweet body odor they gave off. And even though they both wore long-sleeves, I was sure they were shooting it. I'd seen it before.

I took out my wallet, removed five of the six twenties I had in there. The punk took a step forward. "Not yet," I said, shoving the bills in my pocket.

"Whattaya mean?" He looked at the girl on the bed then quickly back at me. "You can see she's good."

I had no idea whether he really believed that or not. And I didn't care. "I told you, I have to ask her something."

"Ask it. Leave the bread. Then get the hell out."

I turned to the girl on the bed. "Your grandfather wants you to come home."

"She don't wanna go home," the punk interjected.

"I wasn't talking to you," I said. I kept looking at the girl. "He's worried about you. He sent me to bring you home."

"Nobody's goin' home."

I looked over at the punk. Tics were doing a little dance on his face now. "You let her answer."

She looked from me to the boyfriend, back and forth a few times. Like I said before, she was strung out. Bad. It was going to be tough to get her out of this hellhole. I knew that. But I also knew I had to get her out.

My heart was pounding and if the pill hadn't kicked in, I'd hate to think what I would've been like. I kept picturing my daughter and what if that was her sitting on that bed and someone else was in my shoes and that someone just walked out and left her here. I couldn't do that. No one could do that. At least no one who was decent and had any balls. And wanted to be able to look at their face in the mirror the next day. So there it was, my old promise to myself again—never back out of any situation because of fear alone. I couldn't break the promise. It was about all I had left.

For a moment though, I thought I might have an out. Wouldn't a bust be a good thing for the girl? Get her away from this creep? But then I realized that any police raid was unlikely to have consequences that would lock up the punk for more than a night. After all, I could see these two were so bad that any dope they got was up their arms and gone the minute they got it. The cops would have to be awful lucky to catch this guy with any significant amount.

I walked over to where Cliff's granddaughter sat on the bed. I knelt down. Her blue eyes were pinned and when I touched her arm, she jerked. "Honey, I can take you out of here, back to your grandfather. No one'll stop us or bother you." I looked at the punk; he smirked. I turned back to the girl. "Come on. It'll be all right." She was shaking and I could see she probably couldn't even speak. I didn't think she'd leave now if Jesus Christ came through the door and took her by the hand.

When I stood, the punk said, "I told you so. Now how about my money?"

"I want to use the can first."

His tics started dancing faster. "This ain't a bus station."

"You sure of that?" I started for the only other door in the room. I was almost hoping he'd try to stop me. He didn't.

Once inside I closed the door behind me. The little bathroom had a toilet, sink, and shower stall. All were filthy. I wouldn't have used the toilet even if I'd had Montezuma's Revenge. I looked around. The girl was leaving with me—that was for sure. Whether the boyfriend would try to stop us, I couldn't be sure. I was sure that Cliff had been misled somehow about the punk being harmless. I knew a sleazebag like that could easily pull out a gun or a knife. I had to find a weapon. Even the odds up. I kicked myself now for not going back to my cottage and getting my .38 revolver before I'd come here.

I quickly went through everything before I found a small pair of scissors. The blades were only a couple of inches long and they were rusty. Maybe used by a previous tenant to trim a mustache. I grabbed the scissors with my right fist so that the sharp point of the closed blades protruded between my index and middle fingers.

I put that hand down behind my thigh, opened the door, and stepped back into the main room. The punk was standing where I'd last seen him, and of course, the girl was still nailed to the bed. She wasn't going to be for long.

I strode across the room in the girl's direction. As I passed the punk, he said, "What about my money?"

"I'll mail it to you." I said to him. To her, I said, "Come on. You're going with me to your grandfather's."

She just looked up at me with frightened blue eyes, the pupils as small as a grain of sand. She wasn't going to move unless I made her. I grabbed her hand, pulled her to her feet. It was easy. She was awfully thin and didn't weigh much. I made one mistake though. I turned my back on the punk.

"You motherfucker."

Something popped into my upper left arm, stinging like I'd been touched with a hot iron. I let go of the girl and spun around. I don't know where he'd gotten it from but the punk was standing there, wild-eyed, a small steak knife in his hand. There was red on the blade. I glanced at my arm. All I could see was a tear in the material of my beige shirt. There was a small amount of blood.

"Get away from her and get the hell out of here," he shouted. "Or you'll get it worse."

Like I said, I wasn't leaving the girl behind. He must've seen that in my eyes, because he jabbed the knife in my direction and started moving toward me. I'm not a great fighter but I didn't have to be. When he got within arm's length, he jabbed again, harder this time and at my stomach. I pulled my midsection back and he missed me by inches. He pulled back with the knife, and as soon as he did, I took one step forward and shot my right fist out, the small scissors protruding from between my fingers. I aimed for his face; nowhere special on it. When I connected, I felt the pain in those two fingers that held the scissors just as much as I'd felt the stab wound to my shoulder.

The scream he let out was one you might hear on a battle-field. The steak knife bounced on the floor and his hands shot up to cover his face. He started to move like a jerky marionette in the direction of the balcony. "My eye, my fuckin' eye." He got caught up in one of the floor-length drapes and started to spin around, trying to free himself. Streams of blood flowed between his fingers.

He finally shook himself free of the drapes and stumbled along like a drunken Frankenstein. I could see where he was going and I guess I could have stopped him. But I thought better of it. I let him finish his dance.

He went over the side of the balcony in seconds. There was a scream, cut short with the sound of a sickening thud that came up from the street. Brakes squealed and people shouted. I didn't feel bad. Instead, I felt relieved. I looked at the girl beside me. I could tell she felt the same.

Chapter 5

"YOU DON'T WASTE any time, do you, Dan?" Steve Moore said. "Even for you this sets a record for getting in trouble fast."

I was seated on one of the kitchen chairs in Room #210. Steve was standing, looking down at me. He was on duty, had a holstered gun on his hip. There were four or five uniformed cops—a couple standing around, the others rummaging through the premises. The girl was perched on the bed. A female officer sat beside her, her arm around the girl's thin shoulders. I had my shirt off and two rescue personnel dressed in navy blue were just finishing tending to my arm. It was swathed in a wraparound dressing.

"You're going to have to go with us, Dan," the older of the two said. It's a small beach. Locals know locals. "Stitches."

"Hold on," Steve said. "Can I talk to him for a minute before you put him in the meat wagon?"

The older guy shrugged. "I guess so. It's not deep. Looks like he was just trying to scare you."

"He did," I said.

The two rescue men walked to the balcony to give us some privacy. They looked down on what I assumed was a crowd below.

Steve leaned his backside against the kitchen counter. "I thought I told you to leave this Penile thing alone, Dan. Let us handle it."

"Peenell." I shook my head and glanced at my bandaged arm. "This doesn't have anything to do with that."

Steve looked at me like I had two heads. "Do you think I'm *that* stupid?"

"I don't think you're stupid at all." I proceeded to tell him about Cliff and his granddaughter. After a few seconds he stopped me, removed a pen and small notebook from his shirt pocket, and began taking notes. He flicked the pen often as I spoke.

When I was finished, he shook his head. "If it was anyone else, I wouldn't believe this. As far as coincidences go, this takes the cake."

"Coincidence? What coincidence?"

"You really don't know? That kid you threw out the window is Leo Karnack's nephew. Shawn Fredette. The same one's been hassling your friend at the Waterview."

"I didn't throw him out the window," I said before I started to absorb that info. "He stumbled and went over the railing himself."

"I suppose he went crazy and stabbed himself in the eye, too," Lieutenant Richard Gant said from the hall doorway. He wore a blue shirt, red tie, and dark slacks. An expensive black leather car coat hid the pistol I was sure he had beneath it. His silvery gray hair was combed straight back. He was Steve's superior and he didn't look too happy to see me. I wasn't jumping with joy either.

Gant stepped into the room. He looked at Steve. "What have you found out?"

Steve barely finished one sentence concerning what had taken place when Gant interrupted him. "I know all that." He glared down at me. "Why isn't this man in cuffs? His arm doesn't look that bad."

"We think it was self-defense, Lieutenant," Steve said. "This Fredette kid came at Dan first. Stabbed him."

Gant glared at Steve this time. "*Dan*, huh? Can't you keep this professional? What about the mess on the sidewalk? The kid throw himself over the balcony?"

"That's about it," Steve responded. "After he stabbed . . . ahh . . . Mr. Marlowe, Mr. Marlowe poked him with a small pair of scissors. It looks like Fredette was so disoriented he just went over the side."

"Ha! Anyone else tell you that fairytale besides Marlowe?"

"The girl." Steve nodded in her direction. "Same story."

Gant looked suspiciously at the girl, then at me.

Just then the two rescue personnel returned from the balcony. "We have to get going, Steve. We got to take him now."

Steve looked at Gant. "All right, take him away," Gant growled. Then to me he said, "But don't think this is the end of it, Marlowe. You been a lucky son-of-bitch in the past. You may not be this time. I'm going to look into this personally and see what the hell you're involved in now."

I ignored Gant, stood, and spoke to Steve. "You'll get her to her grandfather?"

"I'll take care of it," he answered. I knew he would.

The two rescue men escorted me down the stairs and out into the Ocean Boulevard sunshine. There was a huge crowd milling around and we had to push our way to the rescue truck. Two fire engines and numerous police cars were parked haphazardly on the strip. A young woman with a *Hampton*

Union I.D. hanging from her neck snapped my picture just as I was being placed in the back of the rescue truck.

One of the attendants told me that it looked like Shawn Fredette had escaped his fall with not much more than a broken arm. He also had a nasty cut on his face. I'd missed his eyes with the scissors. I was glad of that.

On the ride to Exeter Hospital I had plenty of time to think. The girl was all right. Steve had assured me he'd take her home. The punk, Shawn Fredette, wasn't all right. I was fine with that. It didn't bother me a bit. Cliff's problem was solved. Not like I'd expected, of course, what with me being stabbed and jabbing a man in the face with scissors and him taking a swan dive off a Honeymoon Hotel balcony and splattering on the sidewalk below. And now me taking a ride in an ambulance. And worse, having my old nemesis, Lieutenant Gant, making threats.

And then I remembered—what about Peenell's problem? I hadn't done anything about that. Or had I? With Fredette now on the disabled list, maybe that would put an end to the harassment. Still, one thing troubled me. It was awfully strange that Shawn Fredette, the punk making trouble for Peenell, was doing the same to Cliff. Just in a different way. Steve had called it coincidence. I wondered if he was right. Or was there something else going on?

Chapter 6

THE MINUTE I stepped through the back door of the High Tide and into the kitchen the next day, they were all over me like flies on shit. Dianne dropped the knife she'd been using to dice carrots on the speed table, brushed her black hair out of her eyes, and rushed up to me.

"Dan, are you all right?" Her eyes moved around, checking me out for wounds, I guess. The bandaged knife cut on my arm was covered by a long-sleeved shirt.

I held up my hands. "I'm fine. Fine." The wound hadn't been deep and except for some moderate soreness, I was telling the truth.

Guillermo, the head chef, raced around the speed table from the fryolators where he'd been working. His black hair was dusted with flour. "You hurt, Dan? I hear. I worry."

"I'm fine. Fine," I said again.

Dianne's observations—and my statement—must have assured her I hadn't been injured too badly, because the concern left her voice. It was replaced by irritation and a touch of anger. "Where were you last night? After I heard about what happened, I called and called."

I grimaced. "I took a couple of the pain pills they gave me at the hospital when I got home. Disconnected the phone so I could sleep."

"I hope you didn't have any beer with them," she said, a stern look on her pretty face.

"Just one," I lied.

I don't know whether she believed me. She was just about to say something when the swinging doors that led into the dining area shot open and Shamrock Kelly burst into the kitchen. He was dressed in his usual restaurant whites. Same as Guillermo.

"For the love a Mary, what the hell happened, Danny?" he asked. "Are you all right, my friend?" He came right up to me and gave me the once-over, two or three times, just as Dianne had. He looked just as concerned, too.

For the third time in as many minutes, I said, "I'm fine, Shamrock. Fine."

"From what I heard, I thought you were cut up bad by that guy you threw off the balcony."

That did it. If Shamrock had heard *that* story, others probably had too. There was nothing I could do about the others but I had to make sure Shamrock and Dianne, at least, knew the truth.

"Can you all come out there?" I nodded in the direction of the dining room. "I want to tell you what *really* happened."

Shamrock spun on his heels and headed back the way he'd come. Dianne removed the stained white apron that was tied around her waist, dropped it on the speed table, and followed after Shamrock. I knew Guillermo wouldn't join us. He rarely left his domain, the kitchen, and his understanding of English was such that he sometimes had trouble following complicated conversations. Not to mention there was an air of mystery about his immigration status and I knew that made him leery of getting mixed up in anything that might be trouble.

Still, I invited him.

"No, thank you. I work now," he said. He dashed back to the fryolators and resumed whatever he'd been doing when I'd first come in.

I waited a minute and pulled my thoughts together before going into the restaurant. I knew where Dianne and Shamrock would be—in my office. It's not really my office. I didn't have one here anymore. The real office at the back of the building hadn't been mine since I'd sold the business to Dianne. It was hers now. What was jokingly referred to as *Dan's Office* was the back booth over in the bar area.

Once out in the dining room, I walked around the wooden partition that separated the restaurant section from the bar area, glancing at the well-stocked aquarium that sat on top of the partition and ran almost its entire length. When I came around the other side, there they were—sitting in my office. They both faced me, oddly sitting side by side on the same bench. I walked over to the booth, sat across from them. I realized now, by the way they were both staring at me intently, that they'd sat this way so they could watch me as I told my story. Apparently, one of them had had sufficient time to stop at the coffee pot and get three cups because there was one in front of each of us. I took a sip. Two sweeteners; just how I liked it.

Before I could say anything, Shamrock gestured excitedly. "Don't you worry, Danny. Dianne and I know that lowlife got what he deserved. He must've tried to kill you with that knife for you to throw him off the balcony. There's no one any good at that Honeymoon Hotel."

I was exasperated, but before I could set them right, Dianne jumped in.

"What were you doing there, Dan?" she said. "That's a terrible place. A horrible clientele."

"Aye . . ." Shamrock began.

I held up one hand like a cop stopping traffic. "Will you two let me tell you what happened?" I looked from one to the other, then added, "And not interrupt?" I raised my eyebrows at Shamrock. A little red seeped into his freckled cheeks.

I told them the story. At least everything I thought was important. Cliff Ingalls, his granddaughter, the Honeymoon Hotel, Shawn Fredette stabbing me, me poking him back with the scissors in self-defense, and then Fredette, apparently disoriented, doing a swan dive off the balcony. When I was done, I looked from one to the other. I wasn't surprised who spoke first.

"Sweet Jesus, Danny, you're lucky to be alive," Shamrock said. "And I'm glad you told us. That's not the scuttlebutt going around the beach." He brought his thumb up, tapped it rapidly on his chest. "Of course, I didn't believe a word of it. The part about you throwing him off the balcony, that is."

Dianne pursed her lips, then turned them into one thin line. "What the hell were you thinking going up there like that? You could've been killed. You know what type of place that *hotel* is. You should've had the police handle it."

"Dianne, I couldn't. Cliff had already tried the cops. They hadn't done anything." I could see that she was mad at me. I didn't like that. Still, it didn't excuse me from playing the pity card which is what I did next. "If I hadn't gone up there, Dianne, that young girl wouldn't have lasted much longer. She was strung out bad. He had her injecting it in her arm."

I wasn't surprised when Dianne's anger faded a bit and she looked resigned instead. "Still, why did you have to be the one to go up there and get her away from that man? You were lucky, Dan."

"Aye, he was," Shamrock said, nodding his head sagely.

We were all silent as we sipped our coffees.

Finally Dianne spoke. "Well, I guess—if this is the end of it—we might as well be glad you weren't hurt worse, and that the girl is back with her family and away from that horrible man."

I should have just shut up right there, let it lie. But I couldn't. There was still something I had to deal with. And there were only three people I could talk with about it. One, Steve Moore, wasn't here. But two were here and they were both sitting across from me.

Dianne must have picked up on something because she looked at me warily and said, "What?"

I didn't like it but I felt I had no choice. So I began. Told them about Peenell's visit to the Tide. About the harassment he'd been suffering. How I'd told him I'd look into it. How Steve Moore had said Leo Karnack and his nephew might be behind it.

On that, Shamrock broke in. "Leo Karnack? He's the one owns the Honeymoon."

Dianne turned to look at Shamrock. Her large green eyes were larger than usual. "*He* owns the Honeymoon Hotel? Are you sure?" She must've realized immediately how unnecessary those questions were. After all, if anyone farted the wrong way on Hampton Beach, Shamrock knew about it. Without waiting for him to answer, she turned to look at me. "Oh, Dan."

"And Fredette is Leo Karnack's nephew," I added reluctantly.

"Oh, Dan," Dianne said again. The tone of her voice and the look on her face both signaled pity. And maybe a little worry, too. Or maybe more than just a little worry.

"Steve says it's probably just a coincidence," I said quickly.

Dianne looked doubtful. Shamrock's shoulders sagged. "There hasn't been a coincidence on Hampton Beach since I got here," he said, looking off into the distance like he was remembering that very day.

"You're not going to do anything with this Peenell thing are you, Dan?" Dianne asked. "Especially with Leo Karnack and the Honeymoon involved? Not after what happened."

I didn't answer, just looked around, tried to think of a way out of the jackpot I'd gotten myself into.

"Maybe with the Fredette kid in the hospital," Shamrock said, "Peenell's problem is over."

"Maybe," I said. "But . . ."

"Dan!" Dianne interrupted. Her tone was anything but friendly. "I want you to promise you won't do anything else. I'm sure it's all over."

I wasn't. But before I had to take any vow, I saw my out, even if only temporarily—the clock. It was close to eleven, opening time. "Hey, look how late it is," I said, feigning surprise. "I got to get this place going."

Shamrock and I both jumped up and stepped out of the booth. "I got work too," he said as he strode away in the direction of the restaurant area. He glanced back over his shoulder. "If you need any help on this, Danny, don't be afraid to ask Michael Kelly."

"Shamrock!" Dianne shouted.

Shamrock grimaced and disappeared behind the partition.

"I'll see you . . ." I started before Dianne interrupted.

"Wait a minute." She slid along the bench, came out and up from the booth. She stood close to me.

"I don't want you getting involved in this. And I'm *serious*."

"I know you are, honey." I wrapped my arms around her waist, pulled her close, tried to kiss her. She turned her face away.

"Don't *honey* me. I want you to promise you'll forget this Peenell predicament. I'm sure you resolved it." She furrowed her brows, let me know she meant business. "And if somehow you haven't, let the police handle it."

I was trying to think of a way out. It didn't help my ingenuity any that we were flush against each other and that we fit like two halves of a clam. And that it felt awfully good.

She must have felt it, too. "Good god, Dan. Can't you think of anything else? Now promise me."

Someone banged on the front door. I had my out.

"Jesus, customers. I'm late." I pecked her on the cheek and fast-walked toward the door.

I was glad that I hadn't had to deal with the promise Dianne had asked me to make, but as I unlocked the big front door, I wondered if I'd regret dodging that bullet.

Chapter 7

IT WAS NO surprise who barreled in before I had the Tide's big wooden front door all the way open—Eli, with Paulie right on his heels. The outer screen door we left unlocked.

"You're late," Eli grumbled as he pushed past me. "It's quarter after eleven."

I glanced at the Bud clock, the one with the Clydesdale horses and wagon, above the bar mirror. It was only a couple of minutes past eleven. I didn't say anything though. With Eli it wouldn't have done any good.

Paulie nodded as he walked by, a knowing grin on his face. "Dan."

They both went directly to their respective stools. I came around the bar quickly, set both men up. Eli gulped half his glass of draft beer down like he'd just returned from a desert march. He let out a long, "Ahhh."

Paulie, on the other hand, didn't touch his beer right away, as was his custom. Instead, he lit a cigarette, blew perfect smoke rings toward the ceiling. That was his custom too.

I ran around the bar like a machine, making up for lost time. Ice, fruit, restock beer and booze, clean the bar top, place ashtrays along it, make the waitress banks. A dozen little things that I usually did every morning before the bar opened. As I worked, Eli piped up.

"We wasn't sure you'd be here today, Dan," he said. "After what happened. Ain't you gonna show us where you got stuck?"

I stopped what I was doing. Looked at Eli. He was staring at me with his grizzled face. I glanced down at the other end. Paulie was eyeballing me, an inane grin on his face. "I'm okay," I said, patting my bandaged arm. "It was nothing."

Eli jerked up straight. "Nothing! I heard you poked out a kid's eyes with a sword and then threw him off the roof of the Honeymoon Hotel. *And* you got stabbed with one of them mean-looking knives they sell on the beach."

I threw the dishrag I'd been wiping some dusty liquor bottles with into a sink. I was going to have to explain again what really happened. If Eli and Paulie got to repeating what they'd heard, half the people on Hampton Beach would hear *their* version before the next high tide.

"Listen, that's . . ." I began. Paulie interrupted me.

"Dan, can you turn those down?" He nodded twice, up in the direction of the overhead TVs I'd just turned on.

He was right. I wanted to make sure that they both heard the true story of what went down at the Honeymoon Hotel. I probably wouldn't get a second chance. I used the clickers, brought down the volume of the game show on both televisions.

I stood about halfway between Eli and Paulie, leaned my ass against the back bar, and folded my arms across my chest. "You heard the story wrong. What really happened was . . ."

Just then someone banged open the screen door and marched directly up to the bar. I'd seen him around the beach. Never knew who he was. Even still, I had a sinking feeling it was Leo Karnack. I had no idea if Eli or Paulie knew him. But they soon would.

"You Marlowe?" he said, glaring at me. He was about my height, a little older maybe, and built a lot thicker. He wore jeans too and had on a tight black short-sleeve polo shirt. His upper arms were all muscle and I could see a tattoo peeking out from under one shirt cuff. His face was hard and he didn't look like he'd need help dealing with any Honeymoon Hotel deadbeats.

I cleared my throat. "I'm Marlowe." Eli had sunk down low on his stool. He was hunched over his beer with both hands squeezing it like he was the Boston Strangler. I knew Paulie was blowing smoke rings like crazy at the end of the bar because the damn things were sliding by in my peripheral vision like the cars of a freight train.

"You dirty son-of-a-bitch," Karnack bellowed, his face red. "I oughta break your fuckin' face."

I had no doubt he could do it. I glanced below the bar, only slightly reassured to see the Georgia toothpick under there. I hoped I wouldn't need the baseball bat we kept—and had never used—for incidents like this.

"Whoa, whoa, whoa," I said, holding up my hands. "Hold on now. You must've heard the wrong story too."

"Wrong, asshole? You stabbed my nephew in the face. Almost blinded the poor kid. Then you pushed him off the balcony . . . *my* fuckin' balcony by the way. Busted his arm. You coulda killed him."

I spoke fast. "He came at me with a knife. Stabbed me in the arm when I wasn't looking. Sure I stuck him with a tiny pair of scissors in self-defense. I guess he went into shock or something. He stumbled out onto the balcony and went over the side. By himself."

"Bullshit! You're a liar."

"The girl saw it all too," I added quickly.

"You're both liars."

Eli leaned so far to his left—away from Karnack—I was worried he'd fall off his stool. Smoke rings were still floating past me, drifting up to the ceiling, and then exploding. A waitress—Ruthie, judging by the red head—peeked around the restaurant partition and quickly disappeared.

"Hey look, you can believe what you want, but I'm telling you what happened," I said, hoping I still had a chance to appease him.

He headed toward the end of the bar. I was sure he was going to come around after me. I glanced down at the baseball bat. Just as Karnack reached the end of the bar and I reached for the bat, there was a shout.

"What the hell are you doing?" It was Dianne. She stood, hands on hips, near the end of the partition. I figured Ruthie had tipped her to what was going on. "Get away from that bar and get out of my restaurant. *Now.*"

Karnack stopped, turned, and looked at her. He didn't move. Dianne raced up to him, got right in his face. "Out!" she said, pointing at the front door.

Karnack looked stunned. I walked down the bar, without the bat, and stood on the other side of Karnack. He looked back and forth between Dianne and me.

Finally he looked at me and said, "I'll see you some other time, Marlowe, when you haven't got your protection around. Pussy!" He turned, squeezed past Dianne, who didn't move an inch, and walked out the door. The screen door slammed shut behind him.

"Dianne, he . . ." I began before she waved me off.

"Don't start, Dan. I don't want to hear it. I knew something would happen. Stay away from his stupid hotel." She turned quickly and headed back for the kitchen.

"Wow!" Paulie said. "What the hell was that?"

I walked back down behind the bar, stopped near Eli.

"Ya had nothin,' to worry about, Dan," he said. "I had your back the whole time." He tapped the rim of his empty beer glass. "Now fill this, will ya?"

I did, then went through the motions of waiting on the trickle of customers who started coming in. My mind kept going over what had just transpired and what I was going to do now. After meeting Leo Karnack, I was less sure than before that Peenell's troubles were over. So I still had the promise I'd made to Peenell—see what I could do about his harassment problem. Of course, that led right to the Honeymoon Hotel again. *And* Leo Karnack. Not a pleasant thought. Because if I did follow up on that, it could mean big trouble for me with Karnack. I'd seen firsthand he wasn't hesitant about using violence. Keeping my promise could also cause problems for me with Dianne. That I didn't need either.

I would have dropped it right then like a hot casserole dish, except for one thing—that vow I'd made to myself. To never give up on something just because of fear. And if I gave up looking into Peenell's troubles, would fear be the reason? Maybe. Probably. I couldn't be sure. So I was stuck.

Before I wrapped up my shift I made arrangements to meet Shamrock at his favorite watering hole—The Crooked Shillelagh. I hated bringing him into this. But I had to talk to someone about it. And he was my best friend. Besides, if I didn't go over it with him and he found out I was still sticking my nose into the hornet's nest and hadn't asked for his help, I'd never hear the end of it. Shamrock was that kind of a friend.

Chapter 8

"SO WHAT CAN we do to help Peenell?" Shamrock asked.

We were seated at a corner table in The Crooked Shillelagh at the south end of the beach. Shamrock had left his restaurant whites home; he was dressed beach casual now—T-shirt, baggy shorts. His red hair and blue eyes, not to mention his brogue, made him fit right in with the Emerald Isle decor. The Irish band had just stepped down for a break. We resumed the conversation we'd been forced to stop during the band's last set. Irish music is very loud, to say the least.

"I'm not sure," I answered.

"Let's go right up and tell that Karnack arse to lay off the man." Shamrock took a hefty swig from a mug full of dark Guinness beer. "Ahh," he said, banging the mug down on the table. "We'll tell him to stop bothering good beach people."

I grimaced. "That might not work with this guy. Karnack's a hot head and a tough guy. *And* he's not a big fan of mine."

"He doesn't scare Michael Kelly." Shamrock pointed a thumb at his chest. "We just go up there, read him the old riot act, Danny. That'll stop him."

I shook my head. "I don't think it'll be that easy with this character. I think we have to come up with something else." But I knew there was nothing else. I'd run it through my head a hundred times already. Confronting Karnack was the only way I could see. A very dangerous way.

I was just about to lie to Shamrock. Tell him I was dropping the whole thing, then go on up tomorrow and visit Leo Karnack on a suicide mission all by myself when Shamrock whispered, "Ahh, for the love a Jesus. Look who's coming."

Before I could turn around, they were at our table. Two small-time beach hustlers I'd had the misfortune to have had dealings with in the past—Eddie Hoar and Derwood Doller.

"Hey guys, you mind?" Eddie said. Before we could answer they sat down at the two open chairs at our table.

Derwood had a black eye and a banged-up face.

"What happened to you?" Shamrock asked.

"He walked into a door," Eddie said quickly.

I doubted that. It looked like a beating. And I'd seen Derwood in action before. He was good. If someone had thumped him like that, they must've been a lot better.

Eddie looked around, saw the waitress. He pointed to my Heineken and held up three fingers, then pointed at Shamrock's beer and held up one finger.

"Thanks," Shamrock said reluctantly.

I said nothing; it was too early for that yet.

"So what's been shaking with you guys?" Eddie asked, a grin on his pockmarked face. He looked at me, then at Shamrock, then back at me again. "Stayin' out of trouble? Heh, heh, heh."

"We should be asking *you* that, Eddie," I said. "Especially with . . ." I nodded toward Derwood and his busted-up face.

"Ahh, nothin' serious," Eddie said. "Just a misunder-standing."

"Took someone a while to realize it, huh?" I said.

Just then the waitress brought the four beers, with glasses for our two new friends, and placed them in front of us. She stood there, looking from Derwood to Eddie and back again. Nothing, of course. Finally, she looked at me. I shrugged. "Put it on my tab."

Eddie smiled as he poured his beer into a frosted mug. The waitress rolled her eyes and walked away.

"Thanks, Dan," Derwood said. He brought the mug up in a big hand and had no trouble slurping the beer through swollen lips.

"Oh, yeah," Eddie said. "Thanks. Nice of you."

Shamrock was, like most beach people, no fan of these two men. "Don't you two have *any* money?" he asked. "Haven't you still got your *business* going?"

Eddie sat up in his chair. Looked around the room. He was dressed like it was still the disco era. Polyester pants, wide white belt, print shirt open halfway down his chest, and a gold chain around his neck. A look of worry came over his thin face. "That's kinda what I wanted to talk to you guys about."

"Don't talk to *me* about it," Shamrock said in a loud voice. He leaned toward Eddie and said in a much lower tone, "I still remember that time you sold one of my countrymen that so-called ounce, Eddie. It was mostly oregano."

Eddie raised both eyebrows and held up his hands. "I don't remember that. You must be thinking of someone else."

"You weren't on the beach for the rest of the summer. And he wasn't the only one looking for you, either."

"Well," Eddie said, "just a difference of opinion over quality. A misunderstanding."

"Another one of your damn misunderstandings."

Shamrock was getting hot. He never forgot when someone took advantage of one of his Irish friends or any of his friends for that matter.

I could see Eddie's wheels spinning like he was one of the pinball machines up at the Funarama Arcade. Before he could say the wrong thing to Shamrock, I said, "So what do you want to talk to us about, Eddie?" I figured the faster he got whatever it was he wanted to say off his chest, the faster he'd leave. Especially once he realized I wasn't going to spring for any more free beer.

What passed for a serious look came over Eddie's face. "Well, Derwood and I got a little trouble." He pointed his thumb at the big man beside him. Derwood didn't seem interested, just worked on his beer. "Seein' you guys helped us out of a tight spot before, and you know a lot of people, Dan. And you," he looked at Shamrock, "bein' a Mick and all . . ."

"Why you . . ." Shamrock started to get up from his seat, his calloused fist all ready to go.

Eddie shot back in his chair. "What? What? What'd I say?"

I reached over and grabbed Shamrock's arm. "Forget it. He doesn't even know what he's saying." Shamrock remained half-standing. "Besides, you don't want to start any trouble here." Shamrock grudgingly sat back down.

Then I looked at Eddie. I should've told him to leave but I was curious as to what he had to say. My inner radar was going off. I wanted to know why. "What is it you want to say, Eddie?"

He looked quickly around the room with his beady little eyes. He seemed jumpy enough to be high, but with someone like Eddie it was hard to tell. He was a squirmy character even when straight. "Well, like I said, we got a little trouble. We was hopin' you could help us out for old time's sake."

Shamrock said it before I could. "You're kidding, right?"

"Naw, I ain't kidding. We helped you guys with that problem you had a while back, didn't we?"

Derwood rolled his eyes.

"Helped us?" Shamrock said. "If it wasn't for Dan here, you two would have had a brick of firecrackers shoved up your arses."

"He's right, Eddie," Derwood said. "They saved our lives."

"When I want shit from you, Dumwood," Eddie said, "I'll squeeze your head."

"Don't call me that, Eddie," Derwood said, standing up from his chair. "You know I don't like it."

Eddie pushed his chair away from the table. "Can't you take a joke, for Chrissake?"

I pointed at Derwood's chair. "Sit, will you, Derwood?" He sat. I looked at Eddie. "Come on, just spit it out, will you please?"

Eddie looked relieved that I'd called off his partner. He pulled his chair back to the table. "All right. Well, Derwood and I had a good little business enterprise going on the beach. We—"

"The oregano business," Shamrock interrupted.

"Please, Shamrock," I said. "The sooner he finishes, the sooner he's gone. No offense, Eddie. Just finish your story."

Eddie looked like a hurt little boy. That didn't last long. As soon as he restarted his tale, he began to look more like a low-rent carnival barker. "Well, we *did* have a good business going, 'til some tough guys came around. They want a piece of our business." Eddie adjusted the front of his rayon shirt, sat up in his chair. "The business I built into a thriving enterprise."

"Ha!" Shamrock said. Derwood rolled his eyes again.

That someone would want a piece of Eddie's business didn't make sense. I figured a guy like Eddie probably didn't limit his wares to just ditch weed. Still, Eddie couldn't keep it together long enough to build up a decent drug business. Everybody on Hampton Beach knew that. Including the local police. Eddie was so small-time that when the cops had bothered to devote the money and manpower to catch him, he usually had had such small amounts in his possession that the sentences he'd received were negligible. In addition, Steve Moore had hinted to me once that the police weren't totally against having incompetents like Eddie and Derwood bumbling around the beach. They could easily keep an eye on the pair, and occasionally, through their observations, get intelligence on higher ups in the seacoast drug trade.

The alternative could've been a group of more organized dealers who might have ambitions to start a thriving summer tourist trade. Bothering the tourists was a big no-no on the beach. Eddie and his partner weren't capable of that type of business. Their *Winter People* persona would have tourists running in the opposite direction. So why would someone think Eddie was worth shaking down? I'd never heard of anyone trying to muscle in on low-level dealers like Eddie on the beach before. Maybe someone not much higher on the criminal ladder just wanted a bit of what Eddie had. If that's what it was, I knew they were in for a big letdown because it wouldn't be much.

I offered the obvious advice. "Pay them," I said.

Eddie looked around nervously. "It ain't that easy. They want more than we make."

"Ha!" Shamrock said again. He turned, signaled the waitress to bring a beer for me and him only.

"Eddie?" I said doubtfully. "Don't be a chiseler all your life. You're going to get hurt. Pay them and chalk it up to a business expense."

"He ain't lying, Dan," Derwood said. He licked his lips nervously. It was unusual to see the big man that way. "These guys want more money each week than we make in a month. Even a summer month when everybody's gettin' high."

"Yeah," Eddie interjected, "that's our most profitable season. We do some summer kids."

"I'm sure," I said. I decided to offer a little more advice only because Eddie was a beach person and had been for as long as I could remember. Beach people stick together. Because of that, I didn't want to see him hurt. At least not badly.

"Tell them what you make, Eddie. *Really* what you make. Then offer them a generous chunk of it." I didn't know much about this type of shakedown, except what I'd read in the newspapers and crime novels, but common sense told me that people like this would rather have some money as opposed to no money.

Eddie looked at me. There was desperation in his eyes. I felt a little sorry for him. "We already tried that, didn't we, Derwood?" Derwood nodded. "See," Eddie said. "They want us to pay them more than we got or we gotta get off the beach. If we don't . . ." He glanced around the bar like he was on the FBI's ten most wanted list.

I shrugged. "I guess there's only one thing to do, Eddie. Leave the beach."

"Oh, great," Eddie said, throwing up his hands. "That's a big help. Where would we go?"

That was a legitimate question. Where else would two not-too-successful small-time beach hustlers like Eddie and Derwood be tolerated for more than a few days? Nowhere, that's where. They were only put up with on Hampton Beach because they'd been around forever. Everyone knew them, and for better or worse, they were one of us. In a way, they were icons.

I remembered something else. Unfortunately, that's when the barmaid came up to the table and plunked a Guinness down in front of Shamrock and a Heineken in front of me.

"Hey, you forgot us," Eddie exclaimed, pointing first at himself and then Derwood.

"How much we owe you, lassie?" Shamrock asked.

She looked at the check, told Shamrock the amount, and before I could reach for my wallet, he'd dropped some bills on her tray. "Keep the change," he said, smiling and looking right at Eddie.

"Thanks, Shamrock," she said. She looked at me, gave me a wink. "Have a nice night, Dan." I was distracted for a moment. She was a very good-looking redhead. Young, though. Twenties somewhere, I guess. I shook my head and forced my mind back to reality.

"You still want two more?" she asked Eddie.

He looked irritated. "No never mind. We gotta leave anyhow." She walked away, disappearing into the noisy bar crowd. I turned and watched her go.

Then I turned back to the table and brought up what I'd remembered before the barmaid arrived. "Eddie, why did you say Shamrock being Irish might help you with this?"

"Because the two thugs was Irish," he answered. "Well, at least one was."

Shamrock furrowed his red brows, looked hard at Eddie. "How do you know that?"

"How? How?" Eddie said. "Because he talked like you. But worse. I could barely unnerstand him. Oughta make these immigrants learn English before they let 'em in our country."

I could see Shamrock's rosy face turning rosier. "He doesn't know any better," I told him again. I don't know why I bothered, but I looked at Eddie and said, "That's a brogue. Their accent. Like someone from down south. It's all English."

"If you say so," Eddie said. He made a face and added, "And one had a flat little hat on. He looked like he had a plate on his head. It sure wasn't no fashion plate." He snickered nervously.

"Scally cap, right, Shamrock?" I asked.

"Aye."

"And I think they're from South Boston too," Eddie said. "I heard them saying something about it to each other."

"That isn't good," Shamrock said warily.

"But they're livin' on the beach," Eddie said as if that would make the problem solvable somehow.

"On the beach?" I said. "Where?"

"The Honeymoon Hotel," Eddie answered.

The Honeymoon Hotel.

Shamrock and I exchanged glances. It seemed all roads on Hampton Beach, at least the troubled ones anyway, led to the Honeymoon. I remembered what Steve Moore had said about coincidences. I wondered if he'd still stand with that theory if he knew what I now knew. Something was going on here. What, I had no idea, except that it wasn't good. By the expression on Shamrock's face, I could tell he felt the same way I did. We both grabbed our beers, took big swigs, set the glasses back down.

"Well, can you guys help us or not?" Eddie asked, looking back and forth between the two of us. "Me and Derwood'll owe you a favor big-time if you do. Right, Derwood?"

Derwood nodded, a pained look on his face.

That these two could ever do a favor for Shamrock and myself was very doubtful. What was less doubtful was that they could easily get us into a pile of trouble like they'd done in the past. I was just about to tell them this when the band returned and took their places on the stand. I stalled for a minute, long enough to save me from answering Eddie. The female fiddler stomped her foot and the band started playing at a loud and furious volume. It was impossible to talk above the music.

So I was off the hook as far as making a decision about Eddie and Derwood's problem—for now. I wasn't off the hook as far as thinking about their problem though. Or about Peenell, the Honeymoon Hotel, Leo Karnack, and the two Irish thugs.

I drank beer the rest of the night and wondered what the hell it all meant.

Chapter 9

THE NEXT DAY I had off. I awoke with a slight hangover. Not too bad, I'd had worse. While waiting for it to recede, I had a small breakfast—bagel and some fruit. Then I went out to the porch, sipped coffee in my rocking chair. I could smell the salt air as it rolled in from the ocean over the dunes. A beautiful day, only a wispy cloud here and there.

My cottage was located down at the south end of the beach in what was known as "The Island" section. It wasn't really an island, just a small group of streets surrounded by Ocean Boulevard on one side, the Atlantic Ocean on the other. Some of the homes had ocean views. Mine didn't. Still, it was a nice place. I'd been left with it after the divorce. It had a living room, kitchen, bathroom, and three bedrooms. All very small. But it was fine for me—I was alone. Sure, I was with Dianne but we'd decided not to live together for now.

Of course, that was my fault. I'd had a relapse over the winter. Winters on Hampton Beach are very dark, desolate, and depressing. As I've said. At least for me. One night after too many beers mixed foolishly with rum, I'd stumbled down to a dump I knew from the old days. Nothing had changed. I got what I needed. Went berserk for a couple of days.

Fortunately, I was able to pull out of it before anything irreversible happened. It goes without saying that I missed work and Dianne found out why. She nixed the idea we'd been toying with to move in together. I couldn't blame her. At the time, I wouldn't have lived with me, either.

To top it all off, Sandy, my ex-wife, heard from one of her spies that I was back on cocaine. I tried to convince her it was just a one-time slip-up, which it had been so far. She didn't buy it. The kids wouldn't be coming for a while, she told me. At least until I'd proven myself—*again*. I couldn't blame her for that either though. I'd screwed up good—again.

I took another sip of coffee and tried to peel myself off my pity pot by getting my mind back on everyone else's problems. That's when I remembered a little note I'd jotted down at the Shillelagh sometime the previous night. Occasionally when I have a brainstorm, or what I think is one, I'll write it down. I've learned from experience if I don't, it'll usually be gone the next morning especially if drinking is involved.

I dug into the pocket of my jeans, uncrumpled the piece of paper and read last night's drunken cursive. *Steve said Karnack manager Honeymoon. Is he owner too?*

Now I remembered. During my conversation with Steve at the police station, Steve had said something about Karnack being the manager of record. I didn't think much about it at the time, but could that mean that someone else *owned* the Honeymoon? Even if it did, what difference did it make? I didn't know that either. Still, I figured if I was going to help Peenell at all, I'd better find out if I was dealing with the top man.

I decided to take a little trip. Before I did, I called Peenell. He told me there'd been no trouble since he'd put a security man on the premises twenty-four hours a day. He also said the cost of that security was breaking him. Before he had a chance to ask if I'd accomplished anything, I told him I was working on it, to hang in there and be careful. His voice cracked when he said he would.

After I'd hung up with Peenell, I grabbed my keys and jumped in my little green Chevette. It wasn't much. That's because I didn't have much, what with the child support payments and trying to hang on to the cottage. Still, I was lucky. On the beach you didn't really need great wheels. Work was within walking distance and so were the beach watering holes. I only needed a car for occasional jaunts like this one, so I didn't need anything terribly reliable.

My drive took me up Ocean Boulevard and past the two-block-long Casino building. The Seashell Stage, which hosted nightly entertainment during the summer season, was on my right. It was only around ten o'clock and the traffic hadn't started to build up yet. It would—in a couple of hours. Always did on great beach days like today.

I kept going until I reached the Hampton Town Hall on Winnacunnet Road. I parked and went inside to the Assessor's Office. Behind the counter was the same cotton-headed woman who was always there. I didn't know her name.

"Hello, Mr. Marlowe," she said. I hate it when someone knows your name and you don't know their name.

"It's a beautiful day out there today, isn't it?" I said lamely.

"Oh, yes," she said. "And no humidity. I hate humidity. 'Specially as I get older."

"I know what you mean."

She beamed at me. "Well, Mr. Marlowe, what can I do for you today?"

Not only did she use my name again, she was one of the most pleasant civil servants I'd ever met. Her face was as smooth as a baby's behind.

"I'm just trying to look up the owner of a property." I gave her the address of the Honeymoon.

"Going to get back in the restaurant business, I bet."

I didn't want to go down that road, so I didn't respond.

"Let's see." She opened one of three large books that sat on the counter between us and pulled a pen from her hair. She flipped expertly through the pages, stopping when she found what she wanted. She used the back of the pen to run down through the listings. "Here we are." She turned the book around and pointed with the pen.

I put my cheaters on and read. The hotel was owned by something called the *Claddagh Realty Trust*. The only other information I could see was that the trust had purchased the property less than a year ago.

"Hmm," I said. "I've never heard of them." Not that I should have. There were more real estate trusts in Hampton Beach than grains of sand.

"They're fairly new around here," the clerk said. Then she leaned toward me and lowered her voice. "Bought another property on the boulevard in the last year or so, too."

I doubted she was supposed to be telling me this, but I wasn't going to look a gift horse in the mouth. "Oh? What else?" I looked at the pen in her hand. She pulled a piece of paper from a small pad, wrote something, and handed it to me. I put the paper in my pocket. "I wonder whose trust it is?" I said, hoping to get lucky again.

She just smiled at me like she was my grandmother. "I don't even know that. Some fancy-pants Boston lawyer handled everything. Tremblay, I think."

Hmm, I said again, this time to myself. Fancy-pants *Boston* lawyer. "Well, thank you for all your help."

"You're welcome, Mr. Marlowe. Any time."

I wanted to tell her to call me Dan, but under the circumstances that would have drawn more attention to the fact I didn't know her name. Instead, I smiled, nodded, and slithered out the door.

Back in the car, I just sat there for a few minutes. Had I really gotten anything out of this little trip? Sure, now I knew the Claddagh Realty Trust owned the Honeymoon and at least one other spot on Ocean Boulevard. But that really told me nothing. For all I knew, the real owners could have been the Easter Bunny and Santa Claus. Or Leo Karnack.

I decided to head back to the beach and see where the address the clerk had given me was located. I didn't have any better ideas, and besides, I was headed that way anyhow.

As I drove, I made a mental note to find out the nice clerk's name before I visited again.

Chapter 10

I KNEW PARKING would be tough on the beach so I didn't even try. Instead, I returned my car to the cottage and walked back uptown. As I walked, I removed the paper the clerk had given me. I was surprised by the address. When I reached the High Tide, I went in. I was just in time to catch Shamrock before he left. He usually came in early in the morning, cleaned the place, did his thing, then left. Many days he returned in the late afternoon to handle the dishwasher along with other chores during the dinner rush.

I told him where I was headed, asked if he'd like to come along. He said he would.

The two of us started walking north on Ocean Boulevard, Shamrock in his restaurant whites, me in shorts and a *Hampton Beach* T-shirt. With the band's noise and the beer last night, Shamrock and I hadn't been able to discuss what Eddie and Derwood had told us. I figured now was as good a time as any.

"You got any idea who these Irish guys moving in on Eddie might be?" I asked.

"None. But I can certainly put a feeler out if you like."

I could smell the exhaust of the bumper-to-bumper traffic as we walked along Ocean. It smothered the salty aroma of the sea like a rug thrown over a flame. "Tread carefully. They sound like two hard cases."

"Aye. Two Irish thugs. Not the best example of my countrymen." He gave me a quizzical look. "You really want to help Eddie Hoar?"

We were passing the Casino, walking in the street, dodging people as we went. A shrill onslaught of noises came from the shooting gallery.

"I'm really more curious as to why they're staying at the Honeymoon."

"Probably just Irish bums, Danny. Where else would they stay?"

I could think of a dozen places. A few on Ocean, lots more down on Ashworth Avenue. Places where they'd probably fit right in. "I guess so," I said. "It's just between that, Cliff's daughter staying there with the same punk who was hassling Peenell, *and* the punk's uncle being the manager—I dunno."

"Karnack's the *owner*, right?" Shamrock took a pack of cigarettes from his shirt pocket, fired one up as we walked.

"Not sure. I was over at Town Hall. The Honeymoon's owned by something called Claddagh Realty Trust." I said the gh as a hard g.

"*Claddagh*, Danny," Shamrock corrected, making the g silent. "That's an Irish ring, you know."

No, I hadn't known. I asked Shamrock if he thought it might mean something.

"Maybe that the two Irish tough guys are the owners of the Honeymoon?"

"I doubt it," I said. "From what we've heard about them so far, they don't sound like innkeepers."

Within a minute we were there. The address was a dilapidated one-story building on the same block as the Honeymoon and Waterview. It contained a mishmash of beach businesses catering to the tourist trade. One caught my eye. Apparently caught Shamrock's, too.

"Hey, that place is new," he said, pointing a scarred finger toward a skinny storefront in the middle of the building. The black sign with white lettering on the top of the facade read *Smoking Accessories & Knives*. Certainly didn't leave any doubt what was for sale inside. Pretty brazen for the beach. Shamrock and I walked up, perused the window displays.

The window to the left of the open entrance held smoking paraphernalia. And I don't mean for tobacco. Pipes, bongs, and some things even I didn't know what the hell they were used for. The other window contained knives of every size and shape, from swords to razor-sharp throwing stars. Shamrock and I looked at each other, shrugged and walked in.

Inside, the store seemed to be laid out the same way as the window displays. There was a long aisle that ran down the middle to the back wall. I could see a door marked Do Not Enter back there. There was a gaggle of young kids down at that far end. Someone behind the counter—who I couldn't see—was assisting them. The left side of the aisle had glass display cases full of pot-smoking devices. The display cases on the other side of the aisle held the more lethal objects. Shamrock and I naturally gravitated to the left. We both had some experience with these types of wares. Little to none with the other.

We stuck our noses over the cases. There were pipes for smoking marijuana in every conceivable size and design. The colors on some were bright, to say the least. There were what looked like everyday tonic and soup cans, but these ones had screw-off bottoms to conceal contraband inside. The section with a huge, varied assortment of cigarette rolling papers was the most innocuous of the items offered for sale. Everything was expensive.

"Hey, look at this," Shamrock said. I moved up to the case he was staring into. The first thing that caught my eye were the straws, short metal and plastic ones in different colors, along with small glass vials with tiny silver spoons attached by thin chains to their caps. There were grinding devices about the size of a small woman's fist and little clip spring scales that could weigh up to an ounce. Everything else in this display case was in the same category. I knew what it was all used for. My bowels did too.

"I thought they couldn't sell any of this stuff, Danny," Shamrock said, not taking his eyes off the case.

"A gray area, I think," I answered. "They can't in Massachusetts. Up here, it goes back and forth. I guess it's back now." I pointed at the display cases on the other side of the aisle. "Same for that stuff, too, it looks like." From where we stood we could see every size blade from a jackknife to a samurai sword. The bigger weapons were displayed on the wall behind the cases. The cases also held nasty-looking military-type combat knives, nunchakus, blow guns and darts, and other implements that looked like they couldn't possibly have any other use but to damage the human body. New Hampshire was certainly a strange state in many ways. *Live Free or Die* was its motto.

Just then there was a voice behind us. Apparently, the clerk was done helping the kids, but I couldn't make out a word he said.

Shamrock and I turned. The kids who'd been in the back squeezed past us, heading for the door. A couple of them held bags at their sides. They all looked like they'd just bought their first prophylactics. None looked over fifteen.

The man said something else I couldn't understand. His brogue was so thick it made Shamrock sound like he was an old Yankee.

Shamrock had no trouble with it though. "We're just looking," he said. "Checking out your store."

Shamrock and I pretended to peruse the items in the display. The clerk stepped behind the case, watched us.

He was a big guy and he didn't look like he would or had to take any shit. From anyone. I thought he looked about as much like a shopkeeper as I looked like a MacDonald's worker. A longshoreman or ex-con, maybe. Then again, you couldn't look like Mr. Rogers if you were going to sell this kind of merchandise. He wore a scally cap on his head. Scally caps were about as common on Hampton Beach as snow was in July.

I waited a couple of minutes, then said, "You just opened up, huh?"

I caught what he said this time. "Yeah."

I didn't like asking another question. Didn't want to appear too nosy, but I was here, so I did, reluctantly. "You the owner?"

"Nah."

I was surprised and dismayed when Shamrock, going a little too far, piped in with, "Who is?"

That was enough for the plug-ugly. "What's with the questions?" Now I could understand him perfectly and he'd said it in the unfriendliest tone I'd ever heard a beach storekeeper use. And I'd heard some pretty bad ones.

"Nothing, just curious," Shamrock said.

"Shamrock and I thought we'd just check out your new business." Even though he must've known Shamrock's lineage from his accent, I was hoping the use of his Irish nickname would mellow the man. It didn't.

"Shamrock, huh?" he said with a smirk, looking my friend up and down. "Whattaya work in a mental hospital?" He chuckled and not in a nice way.

Shamrock turned red and I thought we might have trouble right then. Shamrock wasn't against using his fists. He was pretty good at it, too. But by the looks of this guy, probably not good enough.

I knew it was a long shot, but since Shamrock had already opened the box I had nothing to lose. After all, this guy didn't look like the shiniest shell on the beach.

"I bet this is pretty profitable merchandise. I might like to buy a bunch for a friend of mine who has a shop up in Old Orchard," I lied. "How do I get in touch with the owner?"

Unfortunately for me, Scally Cap wasn't *that* dumb. "You a cop?"

"No, a bartender," I said inanely.

Scally Cap put on a face that would terrorize most people, including me. "Then why don't you two get outta here and back to your bar apron and looney bin."

Time to grab Shamrock and beat a hasty retreat.

"Marlowe!"

I turned to look. Leo Karnack walked into the place like he owned it. Maybe he did. He bulled his way up to me, got in my face, then looked at the clerk. "Don't say nothin' to these two. He's the one threw my nephew off the balcony."

"Oh, yeah?" Scally Cap lumbered out from behind the display case. "I knew they was no good. Been askin' questions. Wanted to know . . ."

Karnack held up his hand. "No. Don't say anything else." He glared at me. "You keep buttin' into other people's business, you might find yourself going around the beach on crutches."

Scally Cap started to move toward me. "I can make *that* happen now."

Karnack stopped him again. "No, you fool. We don't want any trouble here." Then to me he said, "You're lucking out again, Marlowe. Just make sure you and your Irish clown stay out of my business or it won't be pretty."

I don't know why I said it. Maybe I was sick of the insults. "Shamrock's not a clown, but *he's* sure a gorilla." I pointed at Scally Cap.

He was black Irish, with dark hair and eyes, and his face grew dark, too. "Why you fuckin' piece a . . ." He moved in on me, and Karnack had all he could do to hold him back.

"Not here, not here," Karnack shouted. He was in front of the bigger man, blocking him.

"You ain't my boss," Scally Cap said, "I don't take orders from you."

"Be quiet," Karnack said. He lowered his voice, but I distinctly heard him say, "He wouldn't like it either."

Scally Cap stopped trying to get at me. He was just as mad though. He was breathing through his nose like one of those furious bulls on a cartoon show.

"Get the hell out!" Karnack shouted.

Shamrock and I headed toward the entrance. I didn't like being tossed out by this bum. As we reached the door, I said over my shoulder, "I hope all this stuff's legal, Karnack. You know, in case the cops get a complaint about it."

"Screw you."

Out on Ocean Boulevard Shamrock and I walked south.

"Well, that wasn't pretty, Danny," Shamrock said. "What do you think?"

"I think we were lucky to get out of there in one piece."

"Aye. That Irish boyo's a mean one. His type's a disgrace to my country."

"I was surprised to see Karnack show up, though. He seems to have a finger in everything."

"Do you think he's the owner of that place, too?"

"I don't know. Did you hear the other guy tell Karnack he wasn't his boss?"

"Maybe one of them figures of speech, Danny?"

"I don't think so. I heard Karnack saying the boss wouldn't like it either. Meaning the real boss."

"I didn't hear that."

"Karnack didn't want me to hear it either. But I did."

As we approached Blink's Fry Doe, Shamrock grabbed my arm. "Hole up a minute, Danny. I'm hungry."

I waited off the sidewalk while Shamrock stood in the short line, then ordered. I checked out a couple of the more attractive sights walking by, but even that didn't get my mind off of what had just happened.

When Shamrock had his big chunk of fried dough, we resumed walking. His treat was smeared with chocolate sauce, red jelly, and had white powder on top. He ate as we walked and talked.

"Any ideas, Danny?" Shamrock said with a mouthful. He had a line of red jelly down his chin.

I had one. I hated to mention it. It could be dangerous. But it was so obvious I knew Shamrock would bring it up sooner or later anyway. "The Irish thug at the knife store.

He's got to be one of the two who are shaking down Eddie and Derwood." I pointed at my chin. "You got some jelly."

He wiped his chin with the back of his free hand. "Aye. There for certain aren't many like that lad walking around the beach."

"So I was thinking—"

Shamrock interrupted. "You don't have to say it. I'll ask around. There isn't an Irishman within fifty miles I don't know about. I don't want that bloke spoiling my record. I'll find out about him and his friend, too. You can be sure of that."

"Okay," I said warily. "But Shamrock, you have to be very discreet and careful. These guys are dangerous. That much I know."

"I told you before, my middle name's Discreet. I'll get the whole ball of wax on them."

"All right. Just be careful."

When we reached a side street near the Tide, Shamrock gave a wave. "I'm heading home, Danny. Will I see you tonight?"

"I don't know. I might have to do something."

"All right then. Later."

I watched for a bit as he walked down the lettered street toward Ashworth Avenue and his small place. I hoped he'd be careful as he'd promised.

On the short walk back to my cottage, I mulled over everything that had happened. There was a lot of it. Cliff and his granddaughter, Peenell's harassment, Shawn Fredette, the Honeymoon Hotel, Karnack, the two Irish toughs who were trying to shake down Eddie Hoar and who also just happened to live at the Honeymoon *and* seemed to know Karnack personally, a mysterious boss that Karnack had mentioned and . . .

That was plenty. I was confused enough.

Chapter 11

EVEN WITH A bellyful of beer, I'm a light sleeper. That's why my eyes popped open at the sound of steps in the sand outside my open window. I just lay there at first, listened. On the beach, especially in the summer, footsteps outside would usually mean nothing. Could be kids—drunk, stumbling between cottages, trying to find their way home. Or maybe young lovers with a blanket, heading down to the dunes for some fun. Certainly not like the off-season when the area is deserted and footsteps at that hour of the night could mean house breakers taking advantage of the vacant cottages.

Being summer, I didn't think anything of it, except the inconvenience of being awakened, the headache I had, and the thought that I might have trouble getting back to sleep.

The sound of the steps stopped. The next thing I heard was the sloshing and splashing of liquid. Water? Odd. Was I still half asleep?

I was awake enough though to know the smell that came drifting in through my bedroom window—gasoline!

I jumped from the bed. My feet had barely touched the floor when there was a frightening whoosh! and my room lit up like the Fourth of July.

Outside someone shouted. I didn't bother with pants. I had jockey shorts and a T-shirt on. I dashed outside, down the porch steps, and around the cottage to my bedroom's side. Flames danced up that section of the cottage. I ran up and using both hands, I scooped up sand, threw it on the burning building. Frantically, one scoop after another. I could feel the heat from the fire on my face.

In the moonlight I could see my neighbor from the adjacent cottage dash up and join me. We threw sand like demons. It didn't extinguish the flames, but it did seem to keep them from spreading further. I could smell the burning asphalt shingles as they bubbled.

Just then two more men ran up. They each had a couple of large sand pails. They tossed one each to my neighbor and myself. The four of us scooped up sand like madmen and threw the sand onto the burning cottage. In the distance I could hear the wail of fire engines. None of us spoke, we just worked like machines.

We didn't put the fire out, but we kept it from making any headway. About the time my arms felt like they were going to fall off, the first fireman hurried around the corner of the building. He had a water canister on his back, a hose in his hands, and aimed a stream of water onto the flames. Other fireman with the same equipment quickly joined him and did the same thing.

In no time it was all over. Inky black smoke hung over everything, but the flames were done.

"God, Dan. You were damn lucky."

It was the first neighbor who'd joined the fire fight. His cottage was actually on the next street over. But because ours were both the rear cottages at their respective locations, both buildings backed up to each other and were only separated by a few feet. It was tight on the beach. The Island was no exception. Still, I only knew him by sight, not his name.

"I heard something," he continued. "Looked out the window just as the bastard was lighting it. Jesus, you could've been killed. I never seen nothing like it."

My heart was beating so fast it hurt and I knew my voice cracked when I asked, "Could you see who it was?"

He shook his head. "No. T-shirt, dark pants. Hair kind of long. I never saw his face. He took off like a bat outta hell."

"Which way?"

"Toward River Street. I couldn't see exactly from this angle. And boy, was he moving. He had the gas can in one hand . . . and there was something about his other arm."

"What about his other arm?"

"I couldn't see it. It was like he was holding it close to his chest or something. Burned it maybe."

"Or he had a cast on."

It wasn't a question but my neighbor didn't know that. "Yeah, guess it could've been. I hope he burned it though. He deserves it. Pulling something like that."

I turned back, stared at the scorched side of the cottage. The entire half of the rear wall near my bedroom was a grayish black. The smell of smoke, gasoline, and fumes from the burned asphalt shingle siding was strong and nauseating. Police meandered back and forth among the firefighters. A fireman and a cop asked if I was all right. I just nodded. The strobe lights of the fire engines and police cars bounced off the cottages. I stood there, trying to catch my breath. Not only from the flames I'd helped put down but also from my anxiety—that was flaming, too.

Neighbors mingled, chattering among themselves. "What happened?" "What did you see?" "Was anyone hurt?"

Police kept them from getting too close to the building. There were men, women, and children. Women and children! I was in my underpants! I hurried around the cottage, heading for the front porch. Hopefully, it was dark enough that my attire went unnoticed. Of course that was doubtful. Inside, I switched on a light, threw a pair of jeans on my legs and a Xanax in my mouth. I was just about to head back out into all the commotion when there was a bang on the door. Before I reached it, it opened.

Steve Moore came in, closed the door behind him. It didn't keep the noises out. "Dan, are you okay?" His words came out in a rush.

I assured him I was. He looked me up and down, probably checking to make sure I wasn't lying about my condition. "What the hell happened?"

The pill hadn't kicked in yet, so my voice shook. I lamely tried to make light of it all. "I guess someone didn't like the asphalt shingles on the side of my cottage. They are kind of dated."

"This is no joke, Dan. Someone tried to burn your cottage down with you sleeping in it. You were sleeping, weren't you?"

The flashing lights of the cruisers and fire engines coming in the windows gave Steve's face a washed-out look. I wondered what mine looked like. It couldn't be pretty. We both just stood there. "I was 'til I heard someone prowling around out there."

"Did you get right up?"

"No. You know what it's like around here. I figured it was just kids passing between the cottages."

"Then what?"

"I heard something being splashed around outside. Then I smelled the gas."

"*That* didn't get you out of bed?"

"You're not kidding it got me out of bed. But by the time I did, the whole side of the cottage was on fire."

"Did you go right outside?"

"I didn't even put on my pants."

Steve half-smirked but only for a moment. "I heard about that."

I scowled. "He was already gone. But the whole side was on fire. The neighbors and I threw sand on it 'til the engines showed up. That's about it."

"You didn't see anybody?"

"No. But my neighbor did." I jerked my thumb in the direction of his cottage. "Saw the guy running away."

"The cottage right behind you? The white one? I'll want to talk to him. What'd he tell you?"

"Nothing, but plenty."

"Don't play games, Dan. What the hell did he say?"

The pill was kicking in a bit, but under the circumstances a double dose probably wouldn't have hurt. "The guy had his arm in a sling, Steve."

Steve brought out his pocket notebook and pen. He clicked the pen a few times. "He told you that?"

"Not exactly."

He wrote something in the notebook, then looked up at me. "What? *Exactly?*"

"Kind of long hair. Dark pants, T-shirt. He had the gas can in one hand."

"And what about the sling?"

I wished I could've lied, but I couldn't. After all it was Steve, and he'd talk to my neighbor anyway. "He said the guy had his other arm in front of him. Up near his chest. Like in a sling."

"He said that last part?"

"No," I admitted grudgingly. "He said like maybe he might've burned it."

"That makes more sense to me. If he burned it good, he'll be easy to catch. He'll have to get it treated."

"Wait a second, Steve. Don't you get it? Leo Karnack's nephew. Shawn Fredette. He's got a broken arm. It must be in a sling."

"How come I knew you were going to say that? For Chrissake, it could've been anybody. Nobody said anything about a sling. You told me that. It's just your imagination. And I told you to stay out of this. That there'd be trouble if you didn't. Was I right?"

I was just about to defend myself when the door flew open and in blew a hurricane. Lieutenant Gant. He looked like he'd just woken up. Instead of his steel gray hair being combed perfectly back on his head, parts were up in little spikes here and there like maybe he'd joined a metal band. His eyes were bloodshot. He had on his leather coat, but his shirt was hanging loose out of his pants.

He walked right up to me. "What the hell happened here, Marlowe?" His breath was bad and I thought I detected booze along with some type of cold cuts.

"Maybe someone tried to burn down my house?" I said.

I hadn't meant it to be sarcastic. Gant took it that way though. "Don't get fresh with me, sonny." He glared at Steve. "You question him yet?"

He said it like I'd lit my own house on fire.

"A little," Steve answered. "He's told me all he knows. Didn't see anybody."

Gant harrumphed. "*That's* no surprise."

I didn't like what he was implying. "My neighbor saw the guy who did it running away."

Gant's eyes narrowed. "We'll look into that. But even if there was a guy, which I doubt, he could've been working for someone. Like you, maybe."

I was incredulous. There was no love lost between us, but this was pretty far out even for Gant. I wondered for a moment if he was drunk or just angry because I'd gotten him out of bed.

"Wait a second, Lieutenant," Steve said. "Dan was in his bed when this happened. He could've been burned alive."

"In his bed? Got any witnesses to that, Marlowe?"

"I live alone. You *know* that. Someone tried to burn my house down and you're accusing me?"

Gant backpedaled a little. I didn't think he wanted to but the man wasn't a fool either. "Don't worry. We're going to look into all angles on this. Including the trouble you're causing on the beach."

"Trouble?"

"I call throwing someone off a hotel balcony trouble. Wouldn't you?"

"I thought that was all taken care of. He stabbed me with a knife and then stumbled over the railing himself."

"After you stuck him in the face with a pair of scissors."

"It was self-defense."

"We're still investigating that."

"What's to investigate? The girl told you the same story."

"And what about this?" Gant pointed toward my bedroom. "You could've burned down half the beach."

Now I was mad. I raised my voice, and even with the pill in me it shook. "*I* could've burned down the beach? Are you serious? There's an arsonist loose around here who might be torching the Casino while you're standing here like a freakin' idiot, accusing a victim."

"And you may be that arsonist." Gant's eyes bugged and his face reddened. "I'd call an ex-junkie who blew his business, lost his wife and kids, and is probably involved in every shady thing on the beach, a good suspect. Wouldn't you? How much insurance you got on this place, anyway? Plenty I'll bet. Check into that, Moore."

"Look, you goddamn—"

Steve stepped between us and put his hands on our chests. "Whoa, whoa, guys. This isn't getting us anywhere. Nobody wants any trouble."

Gant snorted. "Guys? I'm not a *guy*, inspector. I'm *your* superior. Get outside. I want to talk to you *now.*" Before they left, Gant turned back to me. "I'll talk to *you* later."

Chapter 12

LATER THAT MORNING, I talked to Steve on the phone. No one had shown up at the hospital with arm burns or any burns for that matter. He said he'd spoken to Karnack's nephew. The kid had an air-tight alibi. Steve was going to continue investigating. He warned me to stay out of Gant's way. The man was still convinced I was behind the arson. He also advised me to drop the snooping and keep my nose clean. He asked me for a promise on that one. I didn't give it.

I couldn't. How could I? I might've been killed in that arson attempt. And there was something worse, something that gave me chills when I thought of it. My kids could have been with me, visiting. If anything had happened to them, it would have been the end of my world. So I couldn't let it lie.

And that's why I found myself sitting at a patio table at Hampton Beach's premier biker bar that evening. It was still light out. Seated across from me was a mountain of a man. He went by the name of Tiny. We went way back. I won't get into details, but he'd helped me before with some unpleasant situations I'd found myself involved in.

I was hoping to recruit Tiny into helping me put the fear of God into Shawn Fredette. I didn't want a repeat of what had happened the previous night. It wasn't that I was scared of the skinny junkie. Why should I be? I had my .38 revolver in the back waistband of my jeans, covered by a thin windbreaker. But that was just in case. I didn't want to take the gun out unless I had to. I was worried I might lose my temper and shoot the guy. I didn't want that. And without the gun, I wasn't sure I had the demeanor to intimidate the lowlife enough to make certain he'd never try anything again. That's why I'd come to Tiny. He could back down a Hell's Angel with just a look. I'd seen him do it before.

"Wench, beer," Tiny roared as the barmaid passed us, heading back from serving the other patrons scattered in tables along the patio. "Kraut for him."

"Wait your turn, Tiny." She flashed him the finger.

I gulped. Tiny roared with laughter. "She's a good broad," Tiny said. "Nice chick."

He'd been sitting with a couple of other bikers when I'd walked up. He'd jumped up, given me his customary bone-cracking bear hug, and told the others to give us some privacy. Naturally, they did. We did some quick reminiscing about the old days. Then dropped it when the unpleasant memories almost took over.

"How's Dianne?" he asked. He knew her from way back when. She was one of the few sane people who would have anything to do with us.

"She's doing great."

"You two married yet?" Tiny gave me a sly grin.

I shook my head slowly. "No."

"You still got a thing going though, right?"

"Oh, yeah." I smiled.

Deep lines formed on his wide forehead. "What the hell's the matter with you, Dan? You ought to tie her up. That's one beautiful woman. Great chick, too. And she's always had a hot thing for you. Even when you were still with Sandy."

"I don't know, Tiny. I guess we're both gun shy."

"Bullshit. She'd marry you faster than I can chug a beer. And you *know* how fast that is. Gotta be you, you chickenshit. The only reason she wouldn't would be if you were . . . Hey, you ain't doing the nose candy again, are ya?"

I put a shocked look on my face. Probably looked ridiculous. "Of course not. Are *you?*"

"No way, Jose. Long time now." Tiny picked up the empty beer bottle, shook it. "This is it for me nowadays." Then, "Hey, by the way, where's our beer?"

Just as he looked around, the barmaid hurried out to the patio with a tray of drinks. She placed a Heineken in front of me and a Bud in front of Tiny.

"Thanks, beautiful," Tiny said. "I got it."

I noticed she was fairly good looking, and the tight jeans showed off a nice lower figure. Her face did have a little wear and tear though. I guess that was an occupational hazard, dealing with people like Tiny day in and day out.

Tiny must have been running a tab because she didn't ask for any money, just gave me a little smile and headed for another table.

Tiny put the beer up to his lips, killed half with one big swallow. He placed the bottle down on the table, wiped the back of his hand across his full black beard. There was more gray in that beard than the last time I'd seen him. I probably had a few more strands decorating my head, too.

Tiny expanded his massive chest and let out a huge sigh. "Jesus, that was good and cold." Then he looked at me with the only small thing about him—his black eyes. They fit his name. "All right, Dan. Let's have it. You never come down to see me here unless you got your balls in an uproar about something. Tell me a story."

So I told him the story. At least some of it.

When I was done, I thought he was going to jump up from the table right then and there and march up to the Honeymoon Hotel. His face was dark with anger and his breathing deepened. "That skinny little piece of junkie shit. You want me to bust his ass up, Dan? I know all about him. He's pushing powder to freakin' kids for Chrissake."

I tried to defuse him quick. "No, no. I'm just wondering if you could be backup for me. I got something I'd be bringing along." I reached back and touched my jacket near the concealed gun.

"You? With a piece?" He looked genuinely shocked. "What do ya need me for then?"

"I don't want to even show it unless I have to. He's not playing with a full deck. If he made some crazy move, I might have to use it."

Tiny harrumphed. "You might have to use it anyway, Dan. You're a nice guy and all, and I know you can handle yourself. I seen that a couple of times." He chuckled. I smiled. "But you ain't gonna spook a punk like that with *your* mug."

"I know, so I was wondering . . ."

He slammed his hand down on the table. "Honeymoon Hotel? Let's go."

He started to rise. I reached over, grabbed his arm. "Wait. I don't even know if he's there."

"He's there. Junkies like him leave to score and that's about it."

"He won't let us in, Tiny. I have to figure a way to get us in."

"I'll bull the door down," he said so loudly a few people at other tables looked our way. When they saw who'd spoken they quickly turned away.

"No, no, no. We can't do that. Somebody'd call the cops in a heartbeat."

Tiny's voice lowered. "I don't need that." He sat back in his seat.

We both sipped beer. Neither of us spoke.

Finally Tiny said, "Hey, I got an idea." Before I could ask what it was, he yelled toward a large group of both men and woman sitting at a table on the far side of the patio. "Hey, Janine. Get your buns over here, girl." Everyone on the patio turned to look, and again just as quickly, they all looked away.

A cute biker chick got up from the table and walked over to us. It was hard to tell her age—late twenties, maybe. Her blonde hair hung below the blue bandana she wore on her head. Jeans and a tight Harley T-shirt that barely constrained her ample breasts rounded out her wardrobe.

"What's up, Tiny?" She seemed friendly, not nervous at all.

Tiny pushed out a chair. "Sit down here, girl. How would you like to do your old friend Tiny a favor?" She took the seat, but now she looked leery.

"Last time I did you a favor, Tiny, I had that insurance guy on my ass for months."

Tiny's face, at least what I could see behind the bushy beard, reddened. That was unusual. I could count with one finger the times I'd ever seen him show embarrassment.

"Well, I squared it all away, didn't I?" he said indignantly.

"I guess you did. The cops showed me the pictures of him in the hospital when they came to question me. He didn't look good. Lucky I'm a woman or they would've tried to hang it on me."

"Ahh, nothin' ever came of that. It's old news. Forget about it. You want to make some quick money?"

Money? I hadn't mentioned money.

"Maybe," Janine said warily. "How much and what for?"

"You know Shawn Fredette?"

"The junkie? I used to see him when I was dancing over at the Slipper. Cheap bastard'd sit at the stage and *never* toss out even a buck." She made a sour face. "Creepy looking guy, too."

"Would he know your name?" Tiny asked.

"No. I didn't use my real one."

"That won't work then," Tiny said.

"He'd remember my roller skates though."

"Roller skates?" I asked.

"Yeah, that was my gimmick. I did all my dancing wearing roller skates. Man, I could zip around that little stage. The guys dug it, too."

Tiny beamed. "Now that'll work."

And Tiny told her what he had in mind.

Chapter 13

IT WAS AFTER dark when the three of us—Janine, Tiny, and myself—trooped up to the Honeymoon Hotel. We walked along Ashworth Avenue and didn't cut up a side street to Ocean Boulevard until the last possible moment. That was a wise move. We would have stood out like sore thumbs walking the crowded strip on a summer night. Well, at least Tiny would have with his huge size and intimidating appearance. Janine, too, now that I think of it. Males would've been bumping into each other when they turned to check her out. On the way I had discreetly popped a pill and let it dissolve under my tongue.

When we reached the Honeymoon, we entered through the cracked glass front door and went up the neglected stairway that led to Room #210. The place still had the disinfectant smell; tonight there was an added aroma of pot and a faint chemical odor. When we reached 210, on the second floor, the number 2 was still dangling loose on the door.

Tiny looked at me, tilted his head toward the door. I nodded. Tiny waved Janine forward. He and I moved to opposite sides of the door, our backs to the wall. We looked like a narc team about to make a raid. Janine looked nervously from me to Tiny, cleared her throat softly, and knocked lightly. I could hear someone scuffling around in the apartment. We waited. There was no response.

Tiny signaled Janine to try again. She did. This time footsteps approached the door. "Yeah, who is it." I recognized Shawn Fredette's voice immediately.

"Janine," she said.

"I dunno any Janine. Whattaya want?"

She lowered her voice. "I was hoping to get a little something."

"Who told ya to come here?"

"Calvin Baker." She used a name of another local junkie Tiny had come up with. It almost blew the whole thing.

"Baker? That shithead? That ain't no damn recommendation. He owes me dough. Now get the hell outta here before I call the cops."

That was a joke. Fredette was as likely to call the cops as a pot grower with a prowler on his property. It would've been funny except we weren't any closer to getting inside.

Tiny caught Janine's eye, silently mouthed something. She turned back to the door. "I used to dance over at the Silver Slipper," she said suggestively.

There was quiet for a long minute. "What name'd you use over there?"

"You wouldn't remember that. I used to wear roller skates during my act."

There was a longer silence. I held my breath.

"You alone?"

"Yes, I'm alone."

Again another minute, longer still. Finally I heard the deadbolt turn, followed by the doorknob. The door slowly opened halfway. Janine stared at who I knew must be standing there staring back at her. Tiny nodded, brushed by Janine, and bulled into the room. I came in right behind him. Fredette was already on the floor. Tiny had bowled him right over. He was staring up at us with panicky eyes. I noticed they were pinned. His left arm was in a dirty white cast and that was in an equally dirty white sling. The room was a mess, worse than the last time I'd been there. There was a sickening sweet smell of a chemical I recognized along with body odor, garbage, stale beer, and butts. The place stunk worse than a well-used Porta-a-John.

I could see Fredette wasn't going to make a move, not with Tiny standing over him, so I went back out to the hallway. I removed $200 from my wallet, almost all I had, and handed it to Janine. That was what we'd agreed on. Somehow she was able to jam the bills into her tight-fitting jeans.

She peered around me into the room. "Remember you guys said you weren't going to hurt him bad. I don't want to get mixed up in something like that."

"You got my word. I don't want trouble either."

"Okay, thanks." She headed down the short corridor in the direction of the stairs. Any other time I would have watched her go, but this time was different. I took a quick survey of the corridor. There was no sign of anyone. Apparently no one had heard us, or if they had, they were behind locked doors doing their own thing and couldn't have cared less.

Back inside, I closed the door and dead bolted it. Fredette was still on his back on the floor, up on his elbows. He looked around desperately.

"That no good bitch," he said as if he were trying to exude a little manliness from his humiliating position.

Tiny's huge motorcycle-booted foot shot out and caught him hard in the thigh. The man howled. That's going to leave a bad bruise, I thought. Fredette rubbed the area furiously with his right hand. He rocked back and forth as he murmured in pain.

"You got more important things to worry about than her," Tiny said. He reached over, grabbed the man by his good arm, and pulled him to his feet. "Now get your skinny ass over to that seat." He started to push Fredette toward the dirty love seat, than quickly pulled him back. Fredette shook like a rag doll." "You got a piece here, asshole?"

He shook his head furiously. "Naw, naw, naw. I got nothing."

"If you're lying, I'll break your other arm."

"I ain't lying, honest. The cops been here before. I can't keep no gun here."

"You don't have no trouble holding dope," Tiny said. "I can smell it."

"Yeah, but only a little. It's gone quick. For personal consumption."

"Yeah, sure," Tiny said. "Now get in that seat, scumbag." He gave Fredette a shove that caused him to stumble halfway across the room and fall face first into the love seat. The punk rearranged himself so he was sitting normally, facing us. Tiny and I both approached and stared down at him. The man was a freaking mess.

It was my turn now. "You know why we're here, Shawn, right?"

"I got no goddamn idea, Marlowe."

It was a ridiculous thing to say, but then again, what choice did he have?

"I'll tell you then. You splashed gasoline on the side of my house." As I talked I could feel my anger rising along with my voice. "You lit the whole fucking side of the building on fire. I could've been killed." Fredette's tongue danced around his lips like he'd lost control of it. His pupils were almost invisible but the rest of his eyes were wide as seashells. "And if my kids had been there, you could've killed them, you piece a shit."

I must've been really loud by then, because Tiny said, "Dan, come on. Keep it down."

"Yeah, yeah," I said. And I tried but I was agitated. "I said you could've killed my kids, Fredette."

Fredette looked like a man who'd been thrown into a lion's cage. He leaned forward, held his hand up in front of him, made it shimmy. "That wasn't me, man. I didn't do that. You got me mixed up with someone else."

Tiny was fast for a big man. Too fast for me to stop him and too fast for Fredette to get out of the way. He took two steps and shot a right fist the size of a softball in Fredette's direction. It landed dead center, covering Fredette's nose and mouth. And the fist was anything but soft. My stomach did a little flip-flop at the sound of the impact. Fredette's upper body bounced off the back of the couch. He had his one good hand up to his face, covering the damaged area. I was surprised he was still conscious. Little rivers of blood ran through his fingers and he whimpered like an animal. When he took his hand down for a moment, the sight wasn't pretty.

"Jeshus Chirsh, ya busted my nose," he wailed. He wasn't easy to understand. He spit blood and chips of teeth as he talked. Red flowed freely from both his nostrils and a gash down the center of his nose.

Tiny held up his right fist. Blood trickled from a cut on his middle knuckle. "I'll break your head if you lie to us again."

"I won't lie, I won't lie." Fredette's eyes were as wide and desperate as an escaped mental patient's.

I pulled a roll of paper towels off a wall holder, tossed them to Fredette. As he used them to sop up the blood on his face, I stepped over to a ratty little table at the end of the small couch. I could see a hypodermic, a burnt spoon, and a small square of paper. When I bent over to examine it, I was sure the grayish powder there was meth. Fredette must have just injected some before we knocked at the door. I turned to look at him and wondered what someone would feel like in this situation after doing that. He looked so jacked-up, I wondered why he didn't have a heart attack. I almost felt sorry for him. I'd felt what he was feeling. Well, maybe not quite as bad, but close. It's no fun. Then I remembered what he could've done to my kids and all sympathy disappeared.

"Why'd you do it?" I pointed toward his bad arm. "Because of that? Or the girl maybe?"

"I don't give a shit about no girl." Every so often he'd spit blood into a previously empty glass. Now it was half full of the red liquid. "I was only wastin' my time with her cause I had to."

He wasn't the brightest bulb on the tree and that, along with the meth and his fear, was keeping him talking.

"Your arm then?"

"No. I ain't stupid. I ain't never done nothin' like that before. 'Sides, I knew you'd know it was me."

He started bouncing around the couch so much I was getting dizzy watching him. "Then why'd you do it?" I said, anger in my voice.

"I had to."

"Why? Someone told you to? Who?"

When someone is as high on methedrine as this guy was their acting abilities are less than zero. He didn't speak but the jitterbugging tics that suddenly broke out all over his face left no doubt that he had been told to torch my cottage. Of course, I had a good idea by whom, but I had to know for sure.

I glanced at Tiny. He held up his right arm like a caveman's club. "Who the hell told you to do it? Tell us or I'm gonna break every fuckin' bone in your skinny ass body."

Fredette leaned back against the couch so hard I thought it would break. His head shook faster than a greyhound after the chute opens. "No, no, no, I can't, man. He'll kill me."

"He'll kill you when he finds out. I'll beat ya now." Tiny took a step toward him, his big fist shaking. A few drops of blood flew off.

The punk looked as terrified as I thought any human could, his head shaking like he had the palsy. I could see though that he was more afraid of talking than taking a beating from Tiny. And that meant Tiny's job was done. And because I was sure I could control my anger now and not use any more force than necessary, my job was just beginning.

I reached out, grabbed Tiny's arm. "I can handle it now."

He looked at me with a puzzled expression. "Go ahead then."

"No," I said. "You can leave."

He still had that uncertain look on his face. "I don't mind staying, Dan. Especially with this shit bird. The stuff he's pumping out around the beach." He nodded toward the table.

"No, you've done plenty. I've got to take it from here." I looked directly at Fredette. "I might have to do something I don't want you to be around for. I don't want you in trouble."

"I'm not afraid of trouble," Tiny said, puffing his chest out.

"I know that. Just no sense both of us being here for it."

"You're sure?"

"I am. And thanks."

"If you need me, you know where I am."

"Yeah."

Tiny took a step toward the love seat. His foot shot out and caught Fredette's shin, hard. The man howled and his good hand grabbed the spot.

Tiny smiled and went out the door, closing it behind him. I stepped over and secured the deadbolt. When I walked back close to the couch, Fredette was still rubbing his shin. His eyes were watering heavily and the tears mixed with the blood that was now drying on his face. The man looked like an extra in a zombie movie and the stench from his body made the small place smell like a locker room after a football game.

I crossed my arms in front of my chest, looked down at him. "Now tell me, who told you to burn my cottage?"

Fredette noisily blew out air. A little blood and spittle came with it. I took a step back. "Whattaya think I'm crazy?" he said. "I'm gonna tell you, when I didn't tell that biker asshole?"

"Yeah, I think you are," I said evenly. I reached back under my windbreaker with one hand. When my hand came back I had the .38 in it. I pointed the gun at him.

As jacked as he was, he could still smirk. And he did. "You ain't gonna use that, Marlowe. You ain't got the balls."

Maybe he was right. I'd never killed anyone. But could I take the chance that someday this punk would come back and torch my cottage again? And maybe the next time with my kids in it? I'd never get another good night's sleep if I didn't bring this to a head now. So maybe he was wrong. About me being able to kill someone. I wasn't sure. Figured it was a toss-up.

"I wouldn't bet on it," I said. "You could've killed my kids, Fredette." Even with all the tics dancing on his face, a few more stepped onto the dance floor. My statement had made him think. At least think as good as he could.

I walked to the sink, keeping the gun and my eyes on him. I didn't look for a clean glass. I didn't care and there weren't any, anyway. I filled a dirty tumbler halfway with tap water and walked to the end table. I set the glass down, kept the gun pointed at him. With my free hand, I gingerly lifted the small paper with the powder on it. There was quite a bit. A dirty grayish-white and ugly. I dumped it all into the glass and watched it sink into the water.

"Hey, what the fuck you doing?" He actually sounded pissed. Didn't surprise me. If anything can make a junkie forget a bad situation, it's losing his stash. What hadn't dawned on him yet, was that maybe he wasn't going to lose it.

I turned to look at him. "Now you're going to tell me who told you to set my cottage on fire."

"Bullshit. I'm telling you nothing. I ain't getting killed."

I'd taken the pill, but still I was surprised I felt so calm. In a minute I might have to decide whether to kill a man or not. "You have three choices," I said as easily as if I were discussing the best way to make a margarita. "You can tell me what I want to know. Or you can drink that glass of water. Or I can shoot you in the head."

Fredette sat up quickly. "Are you crazy? That's more than three grams of crank. Good stuff too. It'd kill me. I ain't drinking that." He shook his head. His greasy black hair flew back and forth, splattering blood on the couch.

"Then that leaves you only two choices."

"You ain't gonna shoot me, Marlowe. You ain't gonna do that." He smirked at me again. "You'll end up in prison."

"Wrong on both counts. You're probably right that I *usually* wouldn't have the balls to kill you. But you see, Shawn, I can't leave here wondering if you'd ever come back and do it again, maybe kill my kids the next time. You probably aren't a father. If you were, you'd know I have no choice."

I could practically see his mind working. He knew what I'd said meant something. "If you drink my little cocktail, the police'll just chalk it up to an overdose. You know that." By his face I could tell he did. "If I have to shoot you, by the time I leave it'll look like suicide." He looked at my gun; I knew what he was thinking. "It can't be traced to me," I lied. "Again, no one's going to bother investigating your blown-off head if it looks like you did it yourself. The cops'll be glad you're gone."

His Adam's apple slid up and down faster than I had known one was capable of doing. "Tell me what I want to know," I said.

He was breathing hard through his nose now, or what was left of it. Sounded like water gurgling through a clogged drain. "He'll kill me."

"No, he won't," I said. "Because you're leaving Hampton Beach for good and you're never coming back. That way I'll be sure you're not around to start another bonfire. I'll even give you twenty-four hours before I confront the man."

He stared at me. He looked so screwed up I couldn't even attempt to guess what he was thinking. If he was a normal man, and not mentally impaired, his silence would mean he was willing to go to the next level, see if he could bluff his way out of it. When he continued not to speak, I had no choice but to take the next step.

"Drink it," I said, glancing quickly at the glass of meth water, then back to him.

"I ain't drinking that." For a moment he looked straight. But I knew that was impossible. Crank isn't booze. There isn't a fear known to man that can snap you out of its effects. It would just make them worse.

I raised the gun, aimed it at his head, cocked it. The sound filled the little room. The gun shook in my hand. I hoped he didn't notice. "You could've killed my kids, Fredette. You'll try again. Last chance. Drink or talk."

For a minute he stared at the glass. Maybe he was wondering if he could actually survive that amount. When he turned to look at me, I could see he realized that, even with his big tolerance, he couldn't. His eyes went from my face to the gun and back again. I don't know what he saw in my eyes but it must have scared him. I know I was scared. If I didn't follow through, I'd never be able to close my eyes in bed again. And what about my kids?

No, if he called my bluff, I'd have no choice.

Luckily, he didn't. "All right," he said. "But you'll let me go? Get off the beach? They'll kill me if I don't leave."

"Don't worry about that. I want you off the beach, too. For good. I don't want you ever coming back."

"Don't worry, I won't be back."

"Talk. Who told you to light my place on fire?"

Fredette looked around the room like there were people hiding inside somewhere. I don't know if he saw them or not. In his condition, he might have. Anyway, he began to talk in a voice so low, I could hardly hear him.

"Speak up." I straightened my gun arm and his eyes widened.

"It was my uncle, Leo Karnack. He told me to do it."

That was no surprise, but at least now I had confirmation. "Why? Because of what happened to your arm?"

He looked at the sling. "He don't give a shit about that or me. He's a real prick."

I knew that. I'd met him. "Then why?"

He ran his hand through his stringy hair. "He said you was gonna mess things up."

"What things?"

"The thing with the piss-colored guy."

"Peenell?"

"Yeah."

I kept the gun on him. Occasionally he'd look at it. I was puzzled. "It seems like a pretty heavy thing to do. Killing somebody just because he's interfering with you trying to chase your competition out."

Fredette looked at me like I had two heads. "He ain't trying to chase him out, dude. He wants that building. Cheap."

Okay. So Karnack didn't just want to drive the competition out. He wanted to *buy* them out, and at a bargain-basement price. Made sense considering it was Karnack. Then Fredette added something that didn't make sense.

"Same with the chick's grandfather."

"Cliff Ingalls?"

"Yeah, that's him. The bitch you came here and tried to take away. Bambi? Her granddad. Leo wants his building, too."

"You were harassing him, too?"

"No. My uncle knew him, said he was a tough old nut. Said a better way to get at him was through his granddaughter. I'd mentioned that I sold her pot once in a while. Leo told me to get her strung out on crank. I did. It was easy."

I wanted to smash the smug look off his face with my gun. It wouldn't have done any good though. "Then what was supposed to happen?"

"Then we was gonna use the girl to get the old man to sell. For peanuts. Promise him I'd never see her again. Leo was sure it would work. If it didn't, he said he had other ideas."

Something still puzzled me. "Cliff doesn't have a hotel in his building. Just his gift shop and some knick-knack joints. He hasn't even been able to rent out the upstairs for a couple of years. What the hell did your uncle want that building for?"

"He wants the whole block."

Sure, that had to be it. Cliff's, Peenel's, and Karnack's buildings were all on the same block. There was only one other building on that block. And I remembered who owned it—Claddagh Realty Trust. I asked Fredette about it.

"Owns this place, too."

"And your uncle's listed as the manager. But he's the owner too, right?"

Fredette scratched at his pockmarked face. "Naw, it ain't him. I heard him takin' calls from someone who was telling *him* what to do. And I could tell my uncle was scared to death of whoever it was."

"That couldn't be the lawyer that's listed on the trust, could it?"

"Lawyer? You shittin' me? I never seen my uncle scared of anyone. Except whoever he was talking to on the phone those times. He sure ain't scared of no cheap shyster. I don't know who it was though. That's the truth."

I could believe that. Karnack would keep him in the dark. The less you told a junkie like this the better. "Why does your uncle want the whole block so bad?"

"I dunno. But not just the block. He told me we was going after others when we had this one wrapped up."

"Others? Other buildings? Other blocks? What for?"

"Dunno. I told you that."

"Anything else?"

"Nothing. Now can I get outta here?"

"Yeah, pack your bag."

"I ain't got no bag."

"Sure you do." I gestured with the gun at a small pile of brown grocery bags near the sink. "Use those."

He got up, and even with one arm, it didn't take him long to pack. He removed a roll of bills from a cabinet under the sink, jammed the money in his jeans pocket. When he was done, he held the bag in his one useful hand.

"You got a car?" I asked.

"A crate out back."

"Will it make it to Boston?"

"Yeah, it'll make it that far."

"Good. From there you can get anywhere. I suggest you go as far away as you can." I jiggled the gun. "And don't forget what I said."

He smirked again. "Don't worry. I ain't never comin' back here again. I got a lot more to worry about than you and that thing."

He looked from me to the cocktail I'd prepared, sitting on the end table. Back and forth. I nodded. Why not? The faster and farther he went the better.

He set the bag down, lifted the glass, studied the murky contents. He brought it up to his lips and sipped at it. I shuddered. When he set it down, it looked like almost half the liquid was gone.

He picked up the bag and left. I could hear him racing down the stairs, banging through the front door as he went. I put the gun in my rear waistband, pulled the windbreaker down over it. Looked at the glass on the table . . . dumped the contents into the sink and left.

Chapter 14

THE NEXT MORNING I walked to work. It wasn't a good beach day. The wind was blowing off the ocean and the sky was all black clouds, not a break between them. I didn't care. As long as it wasn't raining. Or oppressively muggy. That's no fun either. I knew some people who claimed they liked high humidity. Didn't believe them though.

On the other side of Ocean Boulevard, toward the ocean, a traffic enforcement officer was going from parking meter to parking meter, emptying the contents into a large round cylinder on wheels that he rolled along. Another meter man followed in a green state park truck. Be interesting to find out how much they collected during the summer. It had to be plenty.

A couple of the shops were already open. One worker at a T-shirt joint was rolling metal shirt displays out onto the sidewalk. I nodded; he nodded back. I thought about what had happened the previous evening at the Honeymoon and what I had accomplished. The main thing was that Shawn Fredette was gone from Hampton Beach and I doubted he'd ever be back.

I should have gotten a good night's sleep knowing that he wouldn't be around to toss a Molotov cocktail through my bedroom window as I slept. But I didn't sleep at all. Fredette was just a pawn. Leo Karnack was pulling the strings. If he still wanted my place torched, he'd just get some other beach low-life to do it. There were plenty of them and they came cheap.

But why would Karnack want to buy up the whole block so bad that he'd kill anyone who got in his way? Was he just a greedy beach businessman who wanted to build a real estate empire the crooked way? And didn't Fredette say something about his uncle wanting more than just that one block? What was that all about? If it was true, Karnack wouldn't find the going easy, I was sure of that. Maybe he could make a move on a scared immigrant like Peenell or somebody's grandfather like Cliff, but he wouldn't find it such smooth sailing with a lot of the other owners on the beach. Some had been around a long time and they were tough businesspeople. As a matter of fact, some were just tough people. It wouldn't be a cakewalk for Karnack if he tried to push some of them out.

Then I remembered it wasn't just Karnack trying to make the acquisitions. There was someone behind him. The someone Fredette had heard reading Karnack the riot act over the phone. The lawyer on the Claddagh Realty Trust papers? Maybe, but like Fredette had said, that was unlikely. I knew there were some tough lawyers. But tough enough to frighten Leo Karnack? I didn't think so.

By the time I reached the High Tide and entered through the back door, I had no idea what to do next, if anything. In the kitchen everything was as it was supposed to be. Guillermo over near the fryolators and stove doing whatever it was he did in the morning. Dianne had a huge bag of scallops she had sliced open and was dumping them in a blue plastic tub on the speed table. She glanced my way, then gave me what you could call a slight smile.

I went through the swinging kitchen doors into the restaurant. Ruthie and a couple of the other waitresses were getting their stations and the dining room ready for the lunch crowd. I passed the partition with the aquarium on top, rounded the corner, and walked into the bar area. The first thing I saw was Shamrock. He was down at the far end of the bar seated on Paulie's stool. As usual, he had the *Boston Herald* spread out in front on him on the bar. He had a scowl on his face. I knew why.

He saw me, pushed the paper away disgustedly. I walked up to him.

"I ain't never playing that damn thing again." He was shaking his head furiously. "You know what number came in?"

"Not yours," I said.

"Ha!" His Irish face looked both perplexed and angry. "That's just it, it *was* mine." I must've looked surprised because he added quickly, "But I didn't win one crummy pound. You want to know why, Danny?"

I knew he wouldn't speak until I answered, so I did. "Why, Shamrock?"

"Because the damn fix is in." He stretched his arm across the bar, thumped the newspaper with scarred knuckles. "That's my damn number."

"So why didn't you win?"

"Danny, I've played that number for years. You *know* that. Never won nothing. I got so pissed at it, I changed numbers last week. Now look what happened. It came in. My old number! If the Blarney Stone was as lucky as I am, it would've broken into a thousand pieces by now."

I chuckled a little.

Shamrock looked genuinely hurt.

"It ain't funny, Danny."

I wiped the smile off my face. "No, but in the long run you can't win at those things anyhow, Shamrock."

"You keep telling me that. I don't know why I don't listen." He grimaced and shook his head like he was trying to throw off his bad mood. He must have succeeded a bit, because his face brightened somewhat. "I found out something."

This was fast even for Shamrock. I slid onto the stool beside him.

"What?" I asked.

Shamrock slowly removed a pack of Marlboro's from the pocket of his white shirt, used a match to fire up. He took his time with the first couple of puffs, pulled an ashtray closer. It already had a few 'Boro stubs in it.

I couldn't hide my impatience. "Come on, Shamrock. What'd you find out?"

He held the cigarette between two fingers and took another drag. He blew smoke into the air. "Ole Shamrock's done it again."

"Knock it off, will you." I pointed up at the Clydesdale clock over the bar. "I got to get this place ready before I open."

"All right, I'll tell ya." Shamrock leaned closer. "It ain't good though. I'll tell you that." For an instant his voice shook.

"What?" I said again, lowering my voice.

Shamrock did the same. "That Irish thug up the knife shop?" He hesitated, glanced around the room.

"Yeah?"

"He's from South Boston."

I waited for more. It didn't come. Shamrock sometimes liked to drag things out.

"So?"

He leaned in closer. I could smell his cigarette breath. "He's got a buddy with him on the beach, and both of them work for Red Foley." He nodded solemnly and his eyes got wide. He took a deep pull on the cigarette, blew it out the side of his mouth so it didn't go directly into my face. Still I got enough of it that I could taste the smoke. I'd quit a two-pack a day habit many years ago. But the fumes didn't bother me. I was one of the lucky ones. Especially considering my profession.

But Red Foley? There was nothing lucky about that.

I pulled away from Shamrock, faced forward. Shamrock did the same. I knew Red Foley. Well, I knew *of* him at least. Everyone did. He was in the Boston newspapers occasionally and not for good things. He was the head of the largest Irish gang in Boston. Supposedly involved in everything from bookmaking to narcotics, loansharking to hijacking. And there were rumors that people who had crossed him through the years had disappeared. It was said even the Mafia stayed out of his way.

I thought about all this for a few minutes, then finally said to Shamrock, "What the hell would a couple of his goons be doing running a little shop in Hampton?"

"That I don't know, Danny. He's into everything though. Owns a liquor store, bars, dirty book stores. All sorts a shit."

"Yeah, but a rinky-dink head shop on Hampton Beach that's only open ten weeks a year? That wouldn't be worth his time, would it?"

"Beats me," Shamrock said, shrugging his shoulders. "There might be a lot of money in those knives and that dope stuff." He stubbed out his cigarette.

"Not that much." I was puzzled but I couldn't dwell on it. I looked up at the clock. I was under the gun. I pushed myself off the stool. "I got to get this goddamn place opened up."

"And I gotta get back to the salt mine, too," Shamrock said, rising from his stool and heading for the dining room.

Just before he rounded the partition, I called out to him. "Shamrock." He stopped, turned, and looked at me. "After my shift is over, you want to take a ride over to town?"

"Sure. Where we going?"

"The library."

"Library?" he said as if I'd spoken in Spanish. "I haven't been there since . . . I never been there."

"We'll get my car."

"Okay, see you later." He disappeared behind the partition.

I had a little idea. It wasn't much. But it was better than nothing.

Chapter 15

AFTER MY SHIFT, I walked to the cottage, grabbed the car, picked up Shamrock at his place, fought my way through beach traffic, and finally made it over to the library on Winnacunnet Road. On the way I'd filled Shamrock in on what I had in mind. I'd remembered reading that last year Red Foley had been indicted in regards to some big-time New England-wide gambling ring. Somewhere along the line the charges had been dropped. I didn't know why and I didn't care. What I did care about was who Foley's lawyer had been and if there had been any mention in the paper about him.

Inside the library we marched up to the front desk.

"Can I help you?" asked a young woman with an authoritative but pleasant air.

"Do you keep old issues of the *Boston Globe* and *Boston Herald*?" I was referring to the big city's two daily newspapers.

"Yes, we have them for the past week over at the magazine rack." She used a pencil to point in that direction.

"Ahh, no," I said. "We're looking for something from last summer."

She smiled. "Well, we do have those on microfiche. What dates were you looking for?"

I had attempted to narrow the timeframe down a bit earlier with Paulie, Eli, and a couple of the other bar regulars. I told her the best we'd come up with. "I think it was July or August maybe. Not sure exactly when."

She frowned. "Well, all right. Come this way." She walked around the big reception desk. Shamrock and I fell in behind her.

"What's this fish thing?" Shamrock whispered to me.

"Don't worry. She'll show us." And she did.

She led us to a long table with two contraptions that had TV-like screens on the front. She motioned us to each take a seat in front of the devices. We did. She walked away. Shamrock immediately started playing with the knobs.

"Do you know what the hell you're doing?" I asked.

"I don't even know what it is."

"Better leave it alone."

We sat there for a while, chatting. Every so often I'd have to remind Shamrock to lower his voice.

Eventually the librarian returned with two boxes.

She set them down on the table between us. Then she pulled up a chair beside me. She began her instructions.

"Okay, this one is the *Globe*," she said, pointing to the box marked "Globe." "This is the *Herald*. Now I'm going to show you how to load these." She removed a large spool of film from one box, put it on a cylinder on my machine, and then snaked it through the machine and out the other side, threading the film into an empty spool. She gave the cylinder a few turns to make sure the film was secure on the new spool before turning the machine on. She used a little handle on the side of the spool to thread the film through. As she did the newspaper popped up on the screen.

"Okay, so here we are. *Boston Globe*, July 1st, last year. Just turn this if you want to go forward. Opposite way to go back."

It looked easy. She went over to Shamrock's machine, repeated the procedure. "You get the *Herald*," she said.

"Good. That's my newspaper."

"Mmm," she said.

"Just for the number. I don't read the rest of it. They don't like immigrants, you know."

She looked at Shamrock to see if he was kidding. I could've told her he wasn't.

She explained how to remove the July spool when we were done and replace it with the August one. She told us to get her if we had any trouble and then left. We both started scrolling through the newspapers. Except for Shamrock becoming distracted occasionally by some trivial article, we moved right along. Every so often we'd find an article about Red Foley's gambling indictment. None of them contained what I was looking for.

I was done with July and just about to remove the spool and begin perusing the August *Globes* when Shamrock said loudly, "For the love a Jesus, look at this."

I shushed him, glanced around. A few people were looking at us in an annoyed way. I shrugged, silently mouthed sorry, then quickly leaned over to look at Shamrock's screen. And it was right there—what I'd been looking for. A front page photograph of a lawyer in front of a small bank of microphones. He was standing outside somewhere with what looked like a government building behind him. On his left, just behind him stood a beaming Red Foley. I knew what he looked like—almost everyone in New England did. His picture had been in the newspapers and on TV enough through the years. The caption underneath the black-and-white photo told me it was taken just minutes after Foley's indictment had been dismissed. It also told me something else—what I'd come here hoping to find out. The name of Red Foley's lawyer. Carlton Tremblay. The same name that was listed on Claddagh Realty Trust.

Shamrock and I struggled like Moe and Larry of the Three Stooges to remove the films from the machines in one piece. Finally we did. We returned them to the helpful librarian and said thank you and goodbye.

On the way back to the beach we tossed around what we'd found out in the library.

"So what do you think, Danny? Is Red Foley partners with Leo Karnack?"

I gave Shamrock a quick glance as I drove along. "Red Foley? Not a chance. If anything, I'd say Karnack's working *for* Foley. That'd fit with what his nephew told me about him taking phone calls from someone he was terrified of. Karnack certainly wouldn't be afraid of any lawyer."

"Aye. Not him. He's a mean one. But Red Foley? Sweet mother of God."

"What gets me is why a guy like Red Foley would want to buy buildings in Hampton Beach of all places? On the same block. And Karnack told his nephew they wanted other properties, too."

"Beats me, Danny. I heard gangsters like Foley like to own cash businesses like bars and restaurants and laundromats and vending machines and strip joints. Like that one in Salisbury."

I shot a look at Shamrock. "What strip joint in Salisbury?"

Shamrock pointed out the passenger window. "Look at that, Danny. I love seeing it every time I go by." It was the Emerald Isle, a motel painted in kelly-green and adorned with the requisite shamrocks. "Brings a tear to my eye."

"Yeah, I bet," I said. "What did you mean about the strip club in Salisbury?"

"The Silver Slipper. You know it." Shamrock gave me a slight smirk.

Sure, I knew it. The place Janine had worked at. It was a low-class joint down on Salisbury Beach. I'd been there more than once when I'd been out of control. At *least* one of those times had been with the man sitting beside me. "You do, too. I've got a vision of a drunken Irishman shoving dollar bills into dancers' G-strings."

Red crept into Shamrock's face. "I wasn't drunk," he said.

"Okay, whatever you say. Now what about the Slipper."

"Red Foley owns it. Has for a couple of years."

"How do you . . ." I started, then stopped. This was Shamrock after all and there wasn't much he didn't know.

"*Danny,*" he said, frowning and giving me a disappointed look.

I thought for a moment. "I guess that would be the kind of legitimate business a guy like Foley would want to get into. I didn't know he was up in this area, though." I gave Shamrock a quick look. "You know anything else?"

He surprised me when he said, "Well, I remember hearing that he owned some other businesses over that way, too."

I wondered if I was losing it. I was a bartender after all and we usually heard everything. I didn't remember hearing any of this in the past. I cut myself some slack. After all, this *was* Shamrock. Maybe I had heard the same thing but hadn't thought it important at the time and just forgot it like a thousand other useless pieces of local trivia I picked up working behind the bar. I had only a fair memory. Shamrock's memory was known to put a bookie's to shame.

"What businesses?" I asked.

"Nothing special that I remember. Just regular beach businesses. Doesn't matter now anyhow."

"Why?"

"I heard he sold them all just a little while after buying them. Kept the Slipper though. Probably likes the work staff." Shamrock let out a little snicker.

I chewed on that as we came out onto Ocean Boulevard and drove past Boar's Head. Why would Red Foley buy businesses in Salisbury Beach? Okay, I could see the strip joint. But the others? And if Shamrock's info was correct, why would he sell them so soon? And why was he buying up buildings on our beach? And using Karnack and his lawyer and Claddagh Realty Trust as fronts? To launder money or avoid the IRS, who I was sure would've loved to nail him? Probably both, I'd bet. Still, I didn't understand why he'd gotten out of Salisbury so fast and started buying up in Hampton. I had to find out why. How, I didn't know.

Chapter 16

I DROPPED SHAMROCK at his place down off Ashworth Avenue and returned to the cottage. I putzed around for a while before taking a walk up to the Crooked Shillelagh. I had a roast chicken dinner and returned home. I'd just cracked my first Heineken of the evening and was about to turn on the television when I heard someone stomp up the porch steps. I had the wooden door open, the screen door closed.

It was dark out now, but I could still see his shadow in the doorway. "Marlowe. I'm coming in."

My mind flashed on the .38 in my bedroom. Betsy, my double-barreled shotgun was in there, too, under my bed. I decided not to make a move for them. I was being melodramatic. He wouldn't dare try anything here. And I'd look like a fool and a coward going for a gun.

I didn't even have time to hope I was right because he didn't wait for an invitation. He just yanked open the screen door and barged right in. Leo Karnack. Of course.

He wore black cotton slacks and a knit red polo shirt that showed off his physique. His face was the same color as his shirt and he wasn't trying to hide his anger.

"You dirty punk, Marlowe. I told you to keep out of my business."

I sat there with the green beer bottle in one hand. I said stupidly, "You want one?"

He took a step toward me. "You chased my nephew out of town. I told you to stay away from him and my hotel."

"I don't know what you're talking about, Karnack."

"You're a fuckin' liar. There ain't nothing that goes on there that I don't know about. And someone saw you in his suite. And now he's gone."

The word *suite* distracted me for a moment. Was he kidding? Probably not. "How do you know it had anything to do with me?"

He leaned toward me, cords in his neck popped. "You're a troublemaker, that's how I know. You scared the kid. Chased him off the beach."

"Maybe he owed his connection money. You ever think of that?"

"Bullshit." Then his tone oddly softened. "You know where he is?"

I poured the beer in my glass, took a sip. "I have no idea."

Karnack just stood there, staring down at me. I wondered if he was going to make a move. If he did, I knew I'd have trouble. He was a big bastard and tough looking. I thought again of the guns only feet away. I wouldn't make it, and besides, I'd feel yellow if I went for them and he hadn't had violence on his mind. I didn't have to worry though. What he did next was nothing short of shocking.

He motioned toward the couch opposite me. "Mind if I sit?" he asked in a reasonable tone.

His anger and color seemed to have diminished. Apparently, he'd shifted gears. Why, I didn't know. But I was relieved. "Be my guest."

"I'll have that beer now."

"Want a glass?"

"No."

I got up, took my glass and bottle, and went into the kitchen. I drained the beer in my glass in a couple of big gulps and threw the bottle in the trash. I removed the scrip bottle from my jeans pocket, opened it, and tossed one of the pills under my tongue. While it dissolved, I got two beers from the fridge and returned to the main room. I handed one to Karnack, sat, and filled my glass.

Karnack spoke first. "This is a nice little place you got here, Marlowe." He looked around the room, checking out the nautical knickknacks and family pictures I had scattered about. "You been living here long?"

I didn't know what to make of his turn in attitude. "Yeah, a long time," I said vaguely. I had the feeling that any information I gave this man, no matter how insignificant, could come back to haunt me someday.

"This is a nice part of the beach, too. Quiet."

"Yes, it is." I wondered if he could hear the wariness in my voice.

He took a sip of beer, let out a sigh and set the bottle on an end table. "Maybe we got off on the wrong foot. I know my nephew can be a real pain sometimes. And that . . . well . . . it was no secret he had a problem. Still, Marlowe, you got to see my point of view. The boy's family, no father. I've always felt I had to look out for him."

I was almost waiting for the violinist to walk through the door. The man was actually looking at me in an almost affectionate way. My radar was going off like a baby crying in the dead of night.

"So when I heard what happened," he continued, "you know, pushin' . . . ahh . . . I mean him falling off the balcony, I naturally got protective."

Naturally, but of course I didn't believe a word of it. Maybe I'm a little naive, but stupid? No. I decided to keep my talk to a minimum, see where he was going with this. "Sure, I can see that."

He nodded, put both big hands on his knees. He wore more than one flashy ring on his fingers. "Good, good." Then as if he were asking me about tomorrow's weather, he said, "What did you and the kid talk about before he took off?"

So that explained the change in temperament. He wanted to find out what I knew. And he'd decided to use the good cop technique. For now.

"I just reminded him to stay away from the girl." That was something he might believe.

"Yeah, yeah, sure," he said hurriedly. "What else?"

I chose not to mention the fire. I wanted to see if he would. "Nothing else. After that, I left."

I could tell he was trying to control himself but it was a tough fight. It was against his nature. "You didn't talk about anything else?"

"Nothing. Why?" I had to tread carefully here. "What *could* we have talked about?"

"*You* tell me," he spit out.

"The weather?"

That must have broken his spell. His temperature began to soar. "Don't play smart with me, Marlowe. I just want to know what Shawn told you."

My mind was going over my options quickly. I figured the less I told him, the better off I'd be. "And I told you, he told me nothing."

The red was starting to seep back into his face. "How do I know you're not lying to me?"

I put on a shocked expression. "Lying. What would I lie about?"

Of course, he didn't answer the question directly. "You're playing games with me, Marlowe." His face darkened, his voice grew louder, and I could hear him breathing through his nose. "What did the kid tell you?"

"I said . . . nothing."

Karnack came up from his seat like he'd just bounced off a trampoline. He pulled something from behind his back on his way up. It was a silver automatic. The gun was pointed square at my chest.

"Last chance, Marlowe," he said, looking down at me. I could tell by his face he was going to use it. And by the way he held the gun, I didn't think it would be his first time.

My anxiety level was at a record high. The pill I took? What pill? If I told him what I'd learned from his nephew, that might be reason enough for him to kill me right then and there. But if I didn't tell him anything, I might end up in the same condition. So I decided to take a gamble.

My voice shook, but I got it out. "You better check with your boss before you do anything you'll regret, Karnack. I mentioned his name to the Hampton cops. You probably know I got a friend on the force—Inspector Moore."

I held my breath. It looked like Karnack was holding his, too. I didn't know what to expect. The worst was going through my mind. I could already see my brain matter splattered across the inexpensive seascape paintings I had on the wall. I could also see Karnack's mind going over his options. He looked like a monkey in an experimental laboratory. He wanted the banana, but he was worried that if he touched it, he'd get shocked.

Finally, he put the gun back into his waistband at the small of his back. Then he spoke through clenched teeth. "Stay out of my business, Marlowe. And if you do know anything, I'd advise you to fuckin' forget it." He glanced in the direction of an oak bookcase leaning against the wall. The shelves were lined with everything except books—framed photographs, seashells, sand dollars, a Bose radio, and beach memorabilia. His gaze rose to the top shelf, stopped on a picture of my children. "Nice looking kids. They're growing up in a dangerous time. Have to be careful. Anything could happen to them."

I got the message. I thought of making a dash for the bedroom, grabbing Betsy or the revolver. I could end his threat right here. The man had a gun on him. He'd threatened me and my children, then tried to shoot me. It was self-defense. I didn't think I could make it to the bedroom, though. He'd draw down on me with that thing before I could get to one of the guns. Then he'd probably have to get rid of me. I choked down my anger.

"You were lucky this time, Marlowe. Don't forget what I said." He turned, then stopped and looked back at me. "Stay away from my tenants, too." Had to be talking about the Irish thug in the head shop. He stormed out, banging the screen door behind him.

I reached for the beer on the table beside me and downed it. Then I just sat there like a dunce, thinking. How the hell had it come to this? I'd just been trying to help a beach shop owner with some teenage harassment and an old man whose granddaughter was hanging with an undesirable. Somehow that had all evolved into a very black situation. A situation that threatened my health. And worse now—my children's safety. I didn't doubt that Karnack was capable of violence. Not many people walk around the beach with a gun on them. But even if that was just a bluff, his boss, who I was sure was Red Foley, was no bluffer. Anyone old enough to read a newspaper knew that. If he gave Karnack the word, well . . .

I shuddered, went for another beer.

Chapter 17

THE NEXT MORNING I felt like shit. I debated whether or not to go for a run on the beach. I jog every other day and this was my day. If the way I felt wasn't a good reason to take a day off, there would never be one. Even so, I went for the run and I finished and I still felt bad, maybe worse.

For breakfast I had three Tylenol and one Xanax and a shower that didn't help. Before I left for work I made a call to Steve Moore. Things were getting heavy; I'd need his help or at least his advice. I asked him if we could get together, talk. We made arrangements to meet at Gerri's Sandwich Shop after my shift.

When I came through the back door of the Tide into the kitchen, Dianne took one look at me and wiggled her finger for me to follow her. I did. Right to her office. I closed the door behind me. She spun around.

"Dan, you look awful. What the hell happened?" She had the expression on her face that people get when they think you've fallen off the wagon. The *real* wagon. Everybody's got a different one. Mine was the cocaine wagon.

I felt my face get warm. "I just had too much to drink."

She looked relieved, but her tone turned cross. "You look like you drank half of the Shillelagh."

"I didn't go out last night." I made a dumb move by reaching for her shoulders and trying for a kiss, hoping to change the subject fast.

She turned her head, made a face like something smelled. "No thanks." She turned, walked behind her desk, and sat on the office chair. I plopped down on the sofa against the wall and hoped I could get back up.

She put her elbows on the desk, hands under her chin like she was praying. "Someone called here last night. For me." She waited.

"Who?"

"I don't know. By his brogue, I thought he was calling from Dublin."

One of the Irish thugs. "What did he want?" My throat felt like it was closing.

"He asked if I was your girlfriend." She studied me closely.

It would have been nice if that were the end of it. My anxiety started to climb. Alcohol was bad for anxiety, especially the day after. I made a mental note not to drink again.

"What did you say?" I asked stupidly.

She looked at me angrily. "I certainly didn't tell him I was your mother. This isn't funny, Dan."

"I'm sorry. I wasn't trying to make a joke. What'd he say?"

"To tell you to stop putting your big nose where it doesn't belong. And . . ." her voice cracked, "and if you don't, they'll bury you in the sand up to your neck at low tide."

She looked as worried as I'd ever seen her. And I'd seen her worried before. Still, I sensed she was holding something back. "What? What else?"

"I didn't want to tell you, but I want you out of this. And if you're stupid enough not to do it for yourself . . . well, they said if you keep it up, they'll slap me around and have some fun with me afterwards."

My stomach dropped lower than the receded tide. Now Dianne was in danger. Just like my kids. And me? I was sitting there like a loser who didn't have the balls to protect his loved ones. Worse, I was the reason they were all in jeopardy.

Dianne pointed at me, shook her finger. "Now you tell me what's really going on. This can't just be about Peenell being harassed or the Shawn Fredette incident. You've got me mixed up in it, too, whatever it is. I have a right to know."

She was right. She did have a right to know. So I told her the whole story. After I finished, I saw something on her face I didn't often see—fear. Her voice quivered. "Dan, you have to forget this whole thing. Now! This is crazy. That Karnack jerk is bad enough. But if he's mixed up with someone like Red Foley . . ." She shuddered and her eyes widened. "He's a murderer."

I tried to sound reasonable. "Dianne, they've threatened my children and you. I don't care about me. But I'm not sure if my dropping it would make any of you safer. They're up to something bad on the beach. Something that might affect everyone who lives or does business here. I can't just walk away and forget about it."

"You can and you will. This is a police problem. Let them handle it."

I chose my next words carefully. "I'm meeting Steve Moore later today. I'm going to tell him what's going on."

She furrowed her eyebrows. "Are you telling me the truth?"

"Yes." I hoped she wouldn't ask for any promises. Then I changed the subject quickly as I sprang from my seat. "I got to get out there. I'm running late as it is."

I made a move for the door, but she jumped up, too. "Wait a sec." She came around the desk, walked up to me, and put her arms around my waist. I could smell that wonderful Dianne smell. Not perfume, just a fresh smell, a nice smell. She looked up, raised herself, tried to kiss me. I turned away this time.

"I wouldn't if I were you. I drank a lot last night." I did pull her close. I could feel her breasts hard against my chest. Our jeans brushed together. Apparently that part of my body wasn't impaired by a colossal hangover. Dianne, and my feelings for her, could override even that. We held each other for a minute. Then the thought that she might still ask me for that promise caused me to pull away.

"I love you."

"I love you, too," I heard her say as I hurried out of the office, through the kitchen, through the restaurant, and into the bar.

Shamrock was there, plunked on a stool. He folded up the newspaper he'd been reading, pushed it aside, and surprised me by not badmouthing the lottery. "You're late again, Danny," he said in a joking tone.

I was going to walk behind the bar at the far end, away from Shamrock, and hope that he didn't pick up on my condition but that didn't work. He was the type of best friend who knew if your shoelaces weren't tied correctly. Even at a distance it didn't take him more than a minute to figure it out.

"You look like shit," he said. "You go out without your best drinking buddy last night?"

"I wish I had."

Shamrock picked up on that, too. "What happened, Danny boy?"

I told him about Leo Karnack's visit to my cottage and the threats he'd made against me and the kids. I also told him about the call Dianne received.

"Holy jumping Jesus. This Karnack's a crazy man. Maybe we ought to let this die, Danny."

"Too late for that now," I said. Shamrock lit a cigarette as I spoke and puffed like a steam train going up a hill. "After how Karnack responded to my *boss* gambit last night, I'm sure we've got more to worry about than just him."

"Red Foley?" Shamrock whispered. His cigarette puffing sped up.

I nodded. Then I asked Shamrock something that had been bouncing around my brain. "Do you know anyone who works over at the Silver Slipper?"

I could see his wheels spinning. He smiled and went into a dreamy state.

"Shamrock! Wake up, will you. You know anyone or not?"

"Well, not anymore." He looked disappointed and a touch of red came into his cheeks. Then he suddenly beamed. "I know someone who would, though. Two someones."

"Who?"

I almost groaned when he said, "Eddie and Derwood."

"How the hell would they know anyone at the Slipper?"

"For Chrissake, Danny, every time those two get a little something together, they cop some coke and go over there and blow it." He chuckled.

"That's not one of your best jokes, Shamrock."

"Yeah, you're right. But I got to try it out on someone before I use it on the general public. Might as well be my best friend."

"You sure you don't know anyone else?" I would have kissed his Irish face right then and there if he'd come up with another name. He didn't. Just shook his head.

Shamrock stubbed out his smoke, lit another. "You aren't thinking of getting involved with them, are you?" He looked at me like my nose had just fallen off.

"I don't want to. But I'd sure like to find out why Foley was buying beach property in Salisbury and then selling it shortly after. And even *more*, why is he buying buildings on our beach?"

Shamrock tapped the side of his head with an index finger. "That's all easy, Danny. Eddie told us why. Foley wants to take over the beach drug business."

"I don't know, Shamrock. Is there really enough going on here to interest a guy like Foley? After all, he's probably used to controlling markets the size of Boston."

"Hmm. You're right." Shamrock hesitated, then added, "Maybe that combination head shop/knife store is another reason. I bet there's big money in that shit."

"Probably. But again, enough to interest Foley?"

"Maybe he's using them to launder his ill-gotten gains."

"Through a head shop and a seasonal hotel? No, businesses that small could barely clean Eddie and Derwood's drug money." I thought of another possibility. "Maybe the real estate. Salisbury and here. That might be a way to wash a lot of his dough. That *might* be it."

"Could be."

"You got Eddie's phone number?"

"Me?" he said, as if I were asking him to pull down his pants on Ocean Boulevard.

"Come on, Shamrock. I know you still buy weed from him on occasion."

Shamrock looked resigned. "Yeah, on very few occasions. Only when I'm desperate." Then he scowled. "I still remember that time he sold my friend the oregano. Herb he sells now is only a wee bit better."

I held my palm out. "Can I have it?" He grabbed a cocktail napkin from a stack and a pencil from the pocket of his stained white shirt. The stain looked like gravy. When he was done, he handed the napkin to me. I shoved it in my jeans pocket.

"What've you got in mind, Danny?"

"I'll have to tell you later." I tilted my chin toward the big picture window that looked out on Ocean Boulevard.

Shamrock turned to look. Paulie and Eli were staring through the glass. Shamrock pointed at them and started to laugh. Eli's face darkened in anger. He left the window, pulling Paulie with him as he headed for the door.

"You didn't have to do that. Now I'll have to listen to Eli complain all day." Someone banged on the front door.

"Well, I don't." Shamrock jumped off his stool and made a beeline toward the kitchen. Over his shoulder he yelled, "Good luck," just before he disappeared around the partition.

For a few seconds I wondered if he meant with Eli and Paulie or Eddie and Derwood. Maybe both.

After I'd let the regulars in, I found out I'd been right about having to listen to them complain. They gave me the business most of my shift, complaining about the late opening. It had only been a minute or two. Unusual for me—until last week.

But no big deal. I didn't pay much attention to them, anyway. I had a lot more on my mind than what time I opened the Tide. I'd be happy if I was around to open it in the future, no matter the time.

Chapter 18

THE REST OF my shift was uneventful. After I turned over the bar to my relief, I left by the front door and started walking south on Ocean for my meeting with Steve Moore. It was a cloudy day, the temperature was about eighty-five degrees. There was no humidity. I walked the blocks, dodging other pedestrians. To get around people, I bounced out into the street and back onto the sidewalk like a Friday night drunk on his way home from the neighborhood watering hole. I was an expert at bobbing and weaving, and so even with the human traffic jam, I made good time.

Gerri's Sandwich Shop was in one of those beautiful old residential homes on Ocean Boulevard. There are very few actual homes left on this street. Most have been torn down or converted, like Gerri's, into commercial properties. To find them now you had to go to North Beach. There were plenty of nice homes there. And without the tables and chairs scattered around the open porch or the hundred-odd paper plates taped to the front facade of the building, advertising everything from steak bombs to lobster salad rolls.

I went up the few stairs to the patio. I saw Steve immediately. He was sitting on a far bench that was right up against the building. "Why are you sitting here?" I asked as I reached the table. I glanced back over my shoulder. "One's empty up front. You can see the traffic and people going by up there."

"Yeah and they can see you, too." He motioned toward a chair. "Sit down, will you?"

I could sense this wasn't starting out on a good foot. "What's the problem?"

"Problem?" He gave me a look like the one Shamrock had given me earlier. Like maybe my nose had fallen off. "Yeah, there's a problem. The problem is Gant's on the warpath and I don't want to be seen with you."

"What happened?"

"You want something to eat?"

"What've *you* got?" I asked, pointing toward his plate.

"Kielbasa," he answered.

My friend was either a very brave man or his stomach was wearing a bulletproof vest—on the inside. Neither one applied to me. I walked up to the little window, placed an order for a veggie sub with mustard and a coke. I paid and was handed a popsicle stick with a number on it. Back at the table we picked up where we left off.

"How can you eat that?" I asked.

"Never mind that. Have you lost your mind?" Steve was angry and was talking with his mouth full. My stomach did a little flip-flop.

"Not recently."

"Don't get smart. Were you up at the Honeymoon to see Karnack's nephew?"

I didn't like hearing that he knew about my little visit but I wasn't going to lie. It wouldn't have done any good. "I saw him for a few minutes. So what?"

Steve dropped his sandwich on the paper plate. "So what? I'll tell you so what. Gant wanted to question him some more. He thinks you hired him to burn down your cottage for the insurance money. He's convinced you told Fredette to get out of town. Cover your own ass. Maybe paid him some more to leave."

"That's insane. Gant said he thought *I* was behind the fire. What an asshole. He didn't even believe me when I told him about someone running away."

"He does now. A second guy from up on River Street came forward. Described the creep same as you and your neighbor." He shook his head. "Dan, how stupid can you be? If you'd just stayed out of this, Gant might have pinned it on that twerp. But now that someone saw you up at the Honeymoon *and* visiting Fredette's room *and* the fact that he disappeared just after your visit . . . well, Gant's more convinced than before that you hired the arsonist."

"Please don't use that word."

"What word?"

"Arsonist. I don't like it. Not concerning Hampton Beach at least. You know how fast this beach could go up."

"That's another reason Gant's apeshit. You could've burned down the whole Island."

"Whattaya mean *I* could've? Don't tell me you believe it, too?

"Of course not. But Gant sure as shit believes it."

"Gant'd believe anything about me. Anything bad, that is."

"That's for sure. He's got it in for you."

"There's nothing I can do about that."

Steve went back to his kielbasa. Just then the number on my popsicle stick was shouted from the pickup window.

When I returned with my sub, Steve wiped his mouth with a napkin. "So what was it that you wanted to tell me?"

I told him what really had happened with Shawn Fredette, keeping Tiny, Janine, and my gun out of it. How Fredette'd told me that his uncle was behind the arson. I mentioned Cliff, and I reminded him about Peenell. Also that Karnack was trying to get his mitts on other beach properties, all in the same area. *And* that I was apparently interfering so much, I'd received a threatening visit from Karnack.

Steve gave me a disapproving look. "If you're right about all this, you made a bad mistake chasing the kid out of town. We might've been able to get him to roll over on his uncle."

I finished the bit of veggie sub I was working on. "You already told me you wouldn't have had any luck with that. And from what the nephew told me, he was more afraid of his uncle than jail." I hesitated, wondering if what I was about to say was a mistake. Then I realized I had to tell him. I might need his help. "There's more."

He crunched up the paper that his sandwich had come in, took a sip of his soda, and rolled his eyes. "I was afraid of that. Don't tell me if it's going to cause me a headache."

I let out a deep sigh. "Steve, Karnack didn't just threaten me. The kids and Dianne, too."

He shook his head. "How the hell do you get yourself in the middle of these jams?"

"There's more."

For a short minute he looked like he was debating whether to listen to me or not. Finally, he shrugged. "Go ahead."

I cleared my throat. "Karnack isn't the owner of the Honeymoon or the one trying to buy up these other beach properties. It's a trust called Claddagh Realty Trust."

"That's nothing. Probably his trust. Or are you going to tell me something different?"

"The trust is fronted by a big Boston lawyer."

"And?" He leaned back in his chair and looked like I was about to throw a bomb at him.

"Red Foley's lawyer."

Steve tried to hide his surprise; he couldn't. "Red Foley? The hood?"

"Yes."

I could see him thinking. "That lawyer's probably got plenty of clients. Could be any one of them he's working for. Maybe it's even just him. He wouldn't be the first attorney to go into the real estate business."

"No. But there's still more."

"I figured that."

"The Irish tough running the knife shop? I've been told by a reliable source that he and a buddy are Foley's men."

He smirked. "Shamrock, huh?"

"His info's always good."

"Oh, I don't doubt it. He's always got his Irish ear to the ground. Still, that's pretty skimpy intel even for you, Dan."

"There's more."

He sighed in resignation. "Does it ever end?"

"Foley tried to do the same thing down in Salisbury a couple of years ago. Bought up a lot of properties, then dumped them shortly after. I don't know why."

"Look. Maybe Foley made a quick score on the real estate. In and out. People do it all the time. That's legit. Or maybe he was trying to clean some dough. That's not legit. But it's not my territory. That's for the Mass staties or the feds. I'm sure they watch a guy like Foley all the time."

I was getting a little frustrated with Steve. He was a good friend of mine, but as usual, he had to be convinced gold was under his feet before he'd start digging.

"Hampton Beach *is* your territory, though." I must have said it a little more angrily than I'd meant to because he gave me a nasty look, something that he rarely did. I tried to redeem myself. "And it's *my* home. We can't just let a guy like Red Foley come on the beach and start threatening people. And those thugs of Foley's have been trying to muscle in on beach drug dealers, too. You know what that means?"

"No, I don't—What?" Before I could answer, Steve blurted out, "You don't mean Eddie Hoar and his sidekick, do you?" He smiled. When I didn't answer, he burst out laughing. "Ha, you do. Good luck to Foley shaking down those two. They haven't got change for a quarter between them."

I had to get Steve serious before he forgot everything I had told him. "He doesn't want to shake them down. His people asked for way too much money. He wants them all off the beach. I figure so he can move his own dealers up here. Anyone who works for Red Foley won't be bumbling boobs like Eddie and Derwood. They'll be stone-cold drug dealers with hard drugs. And they'll push hard too. Instead of a few independent incompetents like Eddie dealing on the beach, you'll have a tough, experienced organized crime gang. And there's only one reason they'd want to take over the small beach drug businesses. To turn them into big drug businesses. *Very* big businesses. You know Red Foley's people wouldn't waste their time with anything less."

Steve's expression had turned serious. I watched as he mulled over what I'd told him. After a bit, he said, "Okay, you've raised some questions." He held up his hand. "I'm not buying it all though. It's still a lot of coincidences. I find it hard to believe a guy like Red Foley, who controls most of the rackets in Massachusetts, would be interested in Hampton Beach. Sure, there's drugs here. But not enough to interest someone like him. Even with his own people here, he could still only sell to as many customers as there are." He stopped for a moment. "But . . . I don't want to take a chance that you're right. So . . . I know this FBI agent. I don't want to say any names. I'll run it by him, see what he says. In the meantime you stay out of this. Otherwise, you'll have Gant all over you. And *worse*, he'll be all over me. Okay?"

I chose my words so as not to make any promises. I couldn't. If Steve didn't work fast enough or find out anything, I still had to protect myself and my loved ones. And if that meant pursuing this thing further . . . then that's what I'd have to do. "Sounds like a good idea, talking to your friend."

Steve wasn't fooled for a second. "What about you keeping out of it?"

There was no good way to choose my words now. I jumped up from my seat. "I'll do the best I can. Let me know what you find out."

Before he could react, I was striding across the patio and heading down the stairs. Behind me I could hear Steve shout something I couldn't make out. I didn't turn around. Just started walking quickly south on Ocean Boulevard.

I'd accomplished something by meeting with Steve. He knew almost everything I did now, so if anything happened to me, at least someone official would have enough information to follow up on it. And yes, I had to accept as a real possibility that something could happen to me. Something unpleasant.

I could only hope his FBI contact might come up with something helpful. They had to have plenty on Foley. Maybe he was under surveillance, too. That wouldn't be surprising. If the agent had any info on Foley concerning Hampton Beach, and if he'd tell Steve, I'd have to wait to find out.

In the meantime, I had a couple of other ideas that would keep me busy. As soon as I got home, I took out the number Shamrock had given me and made a call.

Chapter 19

IT WAS EARLY evening when I pulled up in front of where Eddie Hoar and Derwood Doller were staying. It was one of the roughest streets off Ashworth Avenue, bar none. Usually, the two small-time hustlers were so broke they had to move off the beach during the summer when the rents went up. They'd sell their dope on the beach but live elsewhere. When I heard they were living on the beach this summer, I first assumed they must have been holding onto a little of the money they were making from their business. When I saw where they were living, I changed my mind fast. It looked more to me like the landlord would have to pay someone to live there, not the other way around.

I got out of the car, stared at the place. It looked like it had been lifted out of the poorest pocket of the Appalachian Mountains in the 1930s and plunked down in the middle of Hampton Beach. It was a small, one-story wood structure. The building was covered with chipped asphalt shingles in a hodgepodge of colors. In front of the building were two large gray trash barrels. They were both overflowing with beer bottles and used pizza boxes.

I didn't get a chance to observe more, because just then I heard a loud growl from the corner of the building. A large pit bull was coming fast in my direction. I backed up quickly toward the car. I was ready to hop in when the animal reached the end of his chain. It was attached to a metal stake in the ground. I hoped it was secure because he was jumping up and down, trying to tear himself loose so he could tear me apart. His growls had turned into ferocious barking. Saliva flew from his mouth as he pull-jumped against the chain. I prayed it held.

I was in the process of trying to determine if I could make it around the dog safely and up the porch to the front door when the door suddenly banged open and Eddie Hoar stepped out. "Dan. Dan Marlowe. I hope you got good news." He motioned for me to join him. I didn't move. He saw me look at his pet and smiled. "Don't worry about Kilo. He doesn't bite."

I still didn't move. I rarely believed Eddie, certainly not now.

Eddie spoke like he was talking to a frightened child in their bedroom at night. "Just walk over this way." He motioned to the area of the dirt walkway on the opposite side from the dog. "He can't reach that far."

I did what he said. For some reason I felt embarrassed. The dog sprang against his restraint, trying to get at me like I was a juicy tenderloin, but he didn't break loose and I made it to the stairs. I had to be careful there, too. The stairs creaked under my feet and some boards were loose.

When I got up to the porch, Eddie put his arm around me. "Come on in, man. I'll get you a beer."

His breath wasn't any Christmas present. It was more a grab bag of beer, cigarettes, and poor dental hygiene. Inside the aroma of the house wasn't much different. I was in a little living room. The furniture was a bit better than the house itself, but not by much. There was a sofa that was either maroon or very discolored, I couldn't tell which, facing a television with rabbit ears. The television was sitting on a large decrepit lobster trap. The shades were drawn. There were no curtains. Light came from two mismatched lamps on small tables at both ends of the sofa. Beside each of the end tables was a barrel chair. Of course neither of those matched. Sitting on one side of the sofa with his eyes glued to the television was the big hulk, Derwood Doller. "Hey, Dan," he said without taking his eyes off what he was watching.

"Here, sit down." Eddie stepped over to one of the chairs, grabbed a pile of magazines from it, threw them on the floor. "I'll get you a beer."

I got myself uncomfortable in the chair, then took note of what Derwood was engrossed in. It seemed to be a rerun of the *Dallas* television series. I'd enjoyed it myself. Once. A long time ago.

When Eddie came back, he passed out beers and plunked down on the other end of the sofa, the end near me. "Sorry about the beer, Dan. Since the incident with the potato pickers, we been making ourselves kind of scarce. So our net profits are down a bit. We've had to cut our expenses."

I looked at him to see if he were kidding. Of course, he wasn't. Then I looked more closely at the beer in my hand. I'm a bartender so I know them all. Or so I thought. *Hickenpooper Ale*. For a moment I thought I might be on *Candid Camera*. Warily I tasted the beer. It was real and awful.

Eddie leaned forward and in an excited voice asked, "So you fixed everything, Dan? Squared it all with those Micks?"

Before I could answer, Eddie jumped up, went to the TV, turned it off the old-fashioned way.

"Hey, whattaya doing?" Derwood said, suddenly coming alive. "That's my favorite episode. Ray was just about to nail Lucy in the hay loft."

Again I had to look at someone to see if they were kidding. Again, they weren't.

"I don't care who nails who," Eddies said, sitting back down. "We got important business to attend to here. Right, Dan?"

"Ahh, yeah, right."

"See," Eddie said.

While the two boobs glared at each other, I faked a sip of the so-called beer and quickly set the bottle down on the end table.

When they were done with their staring contest, Eddie turned to me. "So tell us the good news. We can go back to work now, right?"

"Well, not just yet," I said. "It's a little more complicated than I thought."

Eddie looked indignant. "What's complicated about two punks trying to muscle in on me and my associate here?"

"There's a bit more to it than that, Eddie." I was on thin ice; I knew that. How much to tell a loose cannon like Eddie was a concern. On the one hand, I didn't want him running around the beach blabbing everything I told him. That could be dangerous for all involved. On the other hand, I honestly didn't want Eddie *or* Derwood to get hurt in any of this. No matter what they were, they were still Hampton Beach people, and I felt that bond even with them. So I had to pick my words carefully. Still, there were some things I was going to tell them, even though I wished I didn't have to.

"Have you heard of Red Foley?"

"Red Foley!" Derwood said, his voice sounding like he'd been castrated.

"The gangster?" Eddie asked. Then with his voice cracking, he added, "What's he got to do with this?"

I held up my hands in front of me. "Now I'm not sure, but those two Irish thugs might work for Foley."

"Where's our suitcases, Eddie?" Derwood whined.

Eddie was adjusting his shoulders and bouncing around like a sofa spring was pinching him in the butt. "Hold on a minute there. Let's hear what else he's got to say."

"Well, I want to find out if there's any truth to it. I heard that Foley owns the Silver Slipper over in Salisbury and I also heard that you guys might know some people over there." Derwood jumped up from his seat and Eddie's beady little eyes grew larger by three sizes. I quickly added, "But it's probably just one of a hundred businesses that Foley owns. I'm sure he's never at the place."

I'd been speaking to Derwood's back as he headed into another room. All Eddie said was, "This ain't good," over and over. When he was done, neither of us spoke. Eddie was thinking. If he was thinking rationally, I didn't know.

The silence was broken by Derwood lumbering back into the room. He was hyper. "I can't find those suitcases, Eddie. You must've sold them. We'll have to put our stuff in boxes and bags. Come on. Hurry up. Help me."

"Sit down, will ya?" Eddie said.

Derwood hesitated. Then before he sat he said, "Just for a minute, Eddie. We might not have much time."

This was getting out of hand. But that was my fault. I'd known that it easily could've gone south with these two oddities.

I wondered what would come out of Eddie's mouth next. I was about to be surprised.

"Where the hell can we go, Derwood?" Eddie adjusted his shoulders. "We're financially embarrassed right now."

Derwood furrowed his thick brows. "Hmm. Maybe over to your aunt's trailer, Eddie. We've hid out there before."

"You're kidding, right, Dumwood?"

Derwood looked like he'd just been insulted on the playground. "Don't call me that, Eddie. You know I don't like it."

"Yeah, yeah, yeah, whatever, *Derwood*. But I also know that my aunt's trailer is over in Seabrook, just a couple of miles away. If those Irish goons can find us here, they can find us there. Maybe we'd be safe in some other country, but we haven't got enough money to put gas in the car."

"And we don't have no passports either, Eddie," Derwood added. "We're stuck, ain't we?"

"Yeah, that's for sure." Eddie looked up at the water-stained ceiling, and I could almost see the dull lightbulb going off over his head. "Unless Dan's got an idea." They both looked at me like I might hold the secret to life itself. And then I realized, maybe I did. At least for them.

"Okay," I began, "I do have a few ideas. There's some other people being bothered by Foley and his boys. I don't want to mention their names right now." Eddie looked insulted, so I quickly added, "Just like I won't tell them about you." He seemed to like that, so I continued. "We might be able to get Foley's crew off our beach, but we're all going to have to do our part. The other people are pulling their weight. Will you help?"

Eddie looked at me warily. "What would you want us to do?"

"You're familiar with the Silver Slipper?"

Eddie straightened his skinny shoulders. "Of course, I'm familiar with it. Me and Derwood are regulars." He turned, looked at his partner. "Right, Derwood?"

"When we got money."

Eddie looked back at me. "We're like family over there."

I was skeptical but it was about the only shot I had at possibly finding out what Red Foley's big attraction with the beach was. I plowed on. "I'd like you two to go over there and see if you can pick up any scuttlebutt on why Foley bought into Salisbury and then dumped a lot of the property shortly thereafter. And now why he's buying in Hampton."

"Easy" said Eddie, a confident grin on his pockmarked face. "I'm on a first-name basis with every dancer and bartender over there."

"You have to be very discreet, Eddie," I said quickly.

"Whattaya mean, discreet? Careful?" Eddie looked at me like he thought I wasn't very bright. "Careful's my middle name. And I got the gift of gab, too. People like talkin' to me."

"I dunno, Eddie," Derwood said. The big man looked doubtful. "That sounds dangerous." I wondered if I made a mistake a long time ago pegging Eddie as the smarter of the two.

Eddie glared at his partner. "Don't you worry about it. Just keep your trap shut. Let me do my spiel. I'll sweet talk 'em for sure."

Derwood looked like he was trying to think of another way out. "We ain't got no money, Eddie. Drinks are expensive over there. And you know how you like to put those one-dollar bills in the girls' G-strings."

"Yeah, you got a point there." Eddie looked at me with a silly little grin.

This was getting to be an expensive inquiry, especially for a down-on-his-luck bartender. "All right," I said. "I can *lend* you a hundred bucks." I added quickly, "But I want it back."

Eddie threw up his hands. "Christ, Dan, that goes without saying."

Sure it does, I said to myself.

Derwood tried again. "What about the car, Eddie? You left it up on Q Street when it ran out of gas."

"Well . . ." Eddie gave me that silly little grin again.

I'd realized by this point that it was a crapshoot as to whether or not this was going to achieve anything positive. Still, like I said, I had no other avenue to pursue. I'd go along with these characters to protect my investment, but would stay in the background. If they said the wrong thing, which was quite possible, maybe I could somehow keep them from being killed. I didn't want their deaths on my conscience. I had enough guilt up there as it was. "I'll drive you. Matter of fact, I'll go in. Sit by myself though. Pretend I don't know you. Kind of like backup."

Eddie got indignant again. "We don't need no backup."

Derwood jumped right in. "That's right. Guess we might as well forget it."

I pulled out my wallet, removed a lone hundred-dollar bill. Held it up. Eddie's eyes lasered in on it. And again, that silly little grin.

"Ahh, I guess it's okay," he said. "Just don't interfere with my performance." Derwood let out a heavy sigh.

"Can you go now?" I asked.

"Sure."

I handed the bill to Eddie. His skinny arm shot out, snatched it. He was so quick, I didn't even see where he put it.

"You better get ready," I said, gesturing at the men's clothes. Eddie had on a wife beater and sweatpants. Derwood, dungarees and a blue T-shirt.

They both stood up. Eddie headed into what I assumed was a bedroom. Derwood tucked in his T-shirt. "I'm ready," he said.

Chapter 20

IT WAS A short ride from Eddie's over the Hampton Bridge, along 1A through Seabrook and into Salisbury Beach. It wasn't short enough though because I could barely breathe. And that was with all the car windows down. Eddie must have taken a quick bath in some cheap cologne before we left. The aroma was overpowering and for a couple of minutes, I actually found myself feeling nauseous.

"What the hell is that you're wearing?" I asked.

"Gent Toilet Water. Like it?"

"Like it? I might borrow some to keep the green heads from biting."

"Ha, ha. You're a funny guy, Dan."

I glanced up at the rearview, spoke to Derwood in the back. "That doesn't bother you?"

The big man sighed. "I'm used to it."

I looked at Eddie beside me. He had a big grin on his face. The man was decked out like he was going to a low-rent Studio 54. He wore a cream-colored polyester suit that could have used a good dry-cleaning. A thick gold chain around his neck, I assumed to be hot or a fake. And he'd slicked his thin black hair straight back so it was plastered to his skull. I wondered what product he'd used to do that? Whatever it was, the toilet water could overpower anything known to man. Including the cigarette he puffed as we drove.

I stopped the car and pulled over about a half block short of our destination.

"Hey, it's down there," Eddie said, flicking the stub of his cigarette out the window.

"I know that," I said patiently. "But I don't want us to be seen together. You guys walk from here. I'll park in their lot. Go in myself. Remember when I come in, you don't know me."

"Whatta we look like, ignoramuses?" Eddie said.

I didn't touch that one. I just kept quiet as they got out of the car and shut the door. Eddie gave me a little tip of an imaginary hat before they started walking toward the strip club. I shook my head as I watched them go. For a moment, I wondered about my own level of intelligence, getting involved with them. Too late for that now. Once I saw them go through the club's front door, I drove the short distance to the club's parking lot, parked, and waited.

I gave them a short while to get situated inside. When I felt enough time had passed, I got out of the car and headed for the front door. The building was probably as old as Salisbury Beach itself. It needed a face lift badly. The only thing fairly new about the structure was the large sign on the top of the facade. It was neon and the multi-colored lights blinked the words *Silver Slipper* over and over. Below that was a depiction of a woman's shapely naked leg from the thigh down to a stiletto-heeled shoe. The shoe had blinking white neon lights. What a high-heeled shoe had to do with a slipper, I had no idea. Maybe the management thought the high heel attracted more horny men than a slipper. Anyway, I went in.

The doorman, who looked like he'd just been released on parole, was dressed in a worn black tuxedo. He held his hand out. The cuffs of his white shirt were dirty. I gave him the five dollar cover charge. He didn't ask for an ID. I pushed through two swinging doors that, except for the peeling red paint, looked like the kitchen doors at the High Tide.

Inside, I let my eyes adjust a bit to the lesser light. There was thumping rock music coming from somewhere. But there was no band. Dead ahead was the stage with a semi-nude dancer doing her act. At this distance I couldn't rate either her talent or her looks. A scattering of men sat on captain's chairs at a thin countertop that ran along three sides of the stage. I expected to see Eddie and Derwood there. I didn't. I scanned the club until I located them. They were seated at the bar which was over near a far wall. They were together, sitting sideways on their stools, looking toward the dancer.

I walked in their direction and took a seat a few stools away. Two of the stools between us were occupied, the ones on either side of me were empty. If they saw me, they didn't react. I was surprised; they were doing good. Or maybe they were just mesmerized by the action on the stage. I noticed Eddie was drinking something in a brandy glass. Derwood had a domestic beer. A bartender came up to me. He looked like he could've been the ex-cellmate of the doorman.

"What'll you have, lad?"

His accent wasn't heavy like the thug's at the head shop and it was even less than Shamrock's, but still, it was unmistakable and it threw me. I wondered again if this visit was a mistake. "Heineken, please."

He brought the bottle and glass. I refused the glass. He glared. I tipped extra. His glare relaxed a point on the one-to-ten scale.

There was a mirror in front of me on the back bar and I could watch Eddie and Derwood in it. It wasn't long before Eddie was engaging the hard-looking bartender in conversation. I ground my teeth and hoped for the best.

I could only pick up bits and pieces from where I sat. I heard Eddie say, "So my good man, how long have you been pushing drinks here?" I saw the bartender's famous glare in response. I took a good-size chug of my beer. It was warm.

Someone took the empty seat on my left beside me. He was puffing on a Camel cigarette jammed into a sixty-something face. Gray stubble adorned his puss. He wore a tan trench coat. In summer. Buttoned. I glanced down to make sure he had pants on. Fortunately, he did. His cigarette smoke got caught in my throat; I coughed. He looked at me and smiled like a peep show patron. I tried to move my stool away. It was bolted to the floor.

That's when a male voice came over the loudspeakers. "Ladies and Gentlemen." He had to say it three more times before the whoops and hollers from the twenty-something-year-old males scattered around the premises finally subsided. "You are in for a real treat. Our next artist of the evening is the world famous *Honey Dew Melon*. In addition to being a gorgeous example of womanly femininity, she also exhibits a talent that is astounding. The Silver Slipper proudly presents, for your viewing enjoyment, the incomparable Honey Dew Melon." There was an explosion of catcalls and whistles.

This I had to see. I swiveled my captain's chair sideways so that I could observe Ms. Melon. I tried to ignore Trench Coat.

Donna Summer moaning *Love To Love You Baby* replaced the
announcer's voice on the loudspeakers. The lights over the
stage went on. Immediately the dancer appeared from behind
a curtain at the back of the stage. She wore a tight safari
suit like you'd see on the white *bwana's* girlfriend in an old
Tarzan movie. To say she was well-endowed would be pulling my punches. Plunked on her head was one of those
round metal safari hats. At this distance I couldn't tell if she was
attractive or not. I could see that she slithered across the stage
barefoot. She wasn't the only thing slithering on the stage
though. Hanging from Honey Dew's neck and extending to the
floor was one of the largest snakes I'd ever seen. I knew little
about snakes but assumed it to be a boa constrictor. From
my distance it looked as fat as a woman's thigh. Honey Dew
pranced seductively around the stage with the snake as her
partner.

I was stupidly mesmerized by the display and could have
easily missed who passed in front of me. But I didn't. First
came an oily little character who looked like he bought his
clothes the same place Eddie did. And wouldn't you know
it, trailing right behind the guy was Eddie himself. He gave
me his silly little grin as he passed. Neither of us spoke. I
watched as the two of them strutted to the men's room. I
had an uncomfortable feeling. I pushed it out of my mind.

I looked back at the stage in time to see Honey Dew
deftly maneuver out of the top of her safari suit and toss it
aside. She pulled the hat off and flipped it onto the stage and
it skidded toward the curtain behind her. I hadn't been mis-
taken about the immensity of her breasts—they were huge.
And bare now. They must have been some kind of implants
because as enormous as they were they defied gravity and

barely even jiggled as she and the snake gyrated around the dance floor.

"Hey. Another beer."

It was the bartender. He had both hands on the bar in front of me. It hadn't sounded like a question and I could see by his plug-ugly face he hadn't meant it to be. Considering what I was up to, I didn't want to get on anyone's bad side. Especially this guy. So I just nodded.

Just as he placed the beer down in front of me, I caught a glimpse of Eddie in the bar mirror passing behind me on his way back to his seat. I finished the old warm beer and sipped at the new warm beer, all the time watching Eddie in the mirror out of the corner of my eyes. I didn't like what I saw. He was bouncing around on his stool like there were tacks on it. He had a smoke going and was taking puffs before he even exhaled the last one. I could also see some type of peculiar eye tic doing a dance on his face. To top it off, I could actually hear him snort occasionally, even from this distance.

I didn't have to be of superior intelligence to know that Eddie had copped either speed or coke from the character he'd followed into the men's room. And probably with the money I'd given him. Instead of getting mad, I got worried. A guy like Eddie? A stimulant was all he needed. He could say the wrong thing without one. With one, I shuddered to think what words might slide out from between his thin lips.

I heard a roar from the crowd and spun around to face the stage again. Except for the skimpiest of G-strings, Honey Dew was completely naked. That wasn't what had caused the outburst from the customers, though. It was the huge snake and what she was doing with it. This woman didn't need a stripper's pole. She already had one between her legs. She was holding the head of the snake in front of her, moving her own face close to the reptile's and then away again, back and forth flicking her tongue as she did.

The body of the thick boa ran down between her abundant breasts, down her flat stomach and between her legs, all the way to the floor. She had her thighs against the snake and was gyrating to the music. I wondered for a moment if this violated any local ordinances. I glanced around and saw the bouncers, cocktail waitresses, and customers acting as if this happened every night. It probably did.

Just as I was considering what kind of people would be aroused by this type of activity, Eddie flashed by me, headed again for the men's room. My eyes went back and forth from the stage to the men's room. Eddie was inside only a minute before he came hurrying out. When he got near me, I tried to catch his eye. The one doing the weird cha-cha. I glowered at him as he passed. I think he tried for his silly little grin but it came out like he was chewing on his inner cheek. I was in trouble now.

When Trench Coat got up and headed for the exit, I quickly grabbed his seat. I was now one closer to Eddie. There were only two lone drinkers between us. Derwood was on Eddie's other side. I could hear Eddie's chatter and could make out most of what he was saying. I didn't like what I heard. I forgot completely about the obscene exhibition on the stage behind me.

Eddie was fully animated. Hands going, arms flailing about. "My good man, another Courvoisier," he said to the bartender loudly enough to be heard by the whole bar. Cognac. *And* cocaine. On my dime!

The bartender came over with a brandy glass that didn't look much larger than a deformed shot glass. It was barely half full. He put it down in front of Eddie. Eddie grabbed the glass off the bar, raised it to eye level, and studied the liquid as he swished it around in the small glass. I could see his eyes in the back mirror. I was sure he was glancing around to make sure everyone knew what he was drinking. With my money.

The bartender glared at Eddie in a way that made me fear for Eddie's safety. But Eddie seemed oblivious to the danger. The bartender had started to move away, and if Eddie had just shut up for half a second, maybe it wouldn't have gone the way it did. But he didn't shut up.

Instead, I heard him say to the bartender, "So Red Foley owns this place, huh?"

The bartender stopped, turned to look at Eddie. He didn't answer, but I could see a slight evil grin appear on his face as if he were glad Eddie had said what he had. I knew what the bartender was thinking as easily as if I had ESP. He was going to let Eddie hang himself. This was bad. And there was nothing I could do about it without exposing my own involvement. I tightened my grip on the beer bottle.

I almost broke it when I heard Eddie say, "I heard Red's bought and sold a lot of property down here. I wonder why he sells it so fast?" He craned his skinny neck across the bar toward the bartender. I wondered how the man could be so stupid as to put his head within range of those hairy knuckles.

Then leering at the bartender, Eddie said, "Whattaya think? Huh? How come he does that?"

I could see Derwood beside Eddie, and he looked as nervous as I'd ever seen a man his size look. He put his beer bottle up to his lips, tried to take a gulp, and looked shocked when he realized it was empty. The bartender's evil grin was anything but slight now and I watched with alarm as he signaled one of the bouncers near the main door. Eddie seemed oblivious to that, too. The bouncer headed our way. He was a walking mountain. He followed the bartender to the other end of the bar.

Eddie called after the bartender. "My good man. Where you going? You didn't answer my questions."

I gulped. I swear I could hear Derwood gulp, too. The bouncer and bartender both leaned over the bar so their heads were close. The bartender whispered. They both glanced occasionally in Eddie's direction. I tried to catch the dunce's eye in the mirror. Tell him to scram. Quickly. Once I did. He must have mistook my look of warning as one of admiration. He formed a circle with his thumb and forefinger, held it up.

The bouncer ended his conversation with the bartender, pushed his bulk away from the bar, and lumbered toward Eddie. "Sir, can you come with me?"

In the mirror I saw Eddie give the bouncer a look like he was riffraff. I didn't think the man would appreciate that. "Like hell I will."

To my surprise, the bouncer said, "Sir, please. Come with me."

"I have a cognac here that I'm working on."

Derwood's face looked like he was the one doing the stimulants as he slowly tilted his body away from his friend. I didn't think it would do any good; he was already leaning against the patron beside him.

Eddie reached for the little cognac glass in front him. He never made it. The bouncer's massive hands grabbed him by the shoulders and pulled him out of his seat. He shifted his grip so one hand held Eddie by the back of his jacket collar.

He lifted the jacket so high, it looked like he was about to hang Eddie with it.

The bouncer glanced at Derwood, nodded in the direction of the main door. "You too."

Derwood *was* smarter than Eddie. He was up and out of his seat as fast as if the place were on fire.

As the bouncer propelled Eddie toward the front door, Eddie blurted out in a strangled voice, "Don't you know who I am?"

"Yeah, the asshole that's gettin' thrown out on his ass. Now!"

Eddie's feet dragged across the floor as he was escorted out. Derwood followed along like an obedient school boy. Some people were watching but the music played and the dancer continued her act. I noticed most, especially those closest to the stage, still had their eyes glued to the reptile tamer. Either her act was shocking, even to the regulars, or so many people were tossed from this joint that Eddie's departure was of no particular interest.

When they had all disappeared out the front door, I turned back in my seat. The jailbird bartender had his butt plunked against the back bar with his arms folded across his chest. He had a smug expression on his face. I tried not make eye contact with him.

I couldn't leave just yet. I had to wait a decent amount of time so no one would know we were together, especially now that Eddie had handled the situation like the doofus he was.

It was definitely bad. But maybe not too bad. I was praying the bouncer, and the management if it went that far, would chalk Eddie's talk up to some coked-up disco duck being nosy and putting his beak in where it didn't belong. I was counting on them to be savvy enough to figure out that a clown like Eddie certainly wouldn't be any kind of undercover agent or a member of a competing criminal organization. Eddie's comical attire and absurd demeanor were so over the top that I was sure they would assume he couldn't be of any danger. That's what I was hoping anyway.

I began to get steamed at Eddie. But not for long. I couldn't avoid the fact that it was my own fault. The odds had been fifty-fifty that Eddie would at least keep out of trouble, less that he'd get any useful information. I shouldn't have rolled the dice. The odds were bad. And besides, maybe I was the only person on the planet that would have given Eddie even fifty-fifty. I'd been desperate, after all. And that's when mistakes are made.

After I was certain enough time had passed, I got up from my seat. I was relieved to see the bartender pay me no special attention. On my march to the door, I didn't see anyone watching me, although for some reason I thought that every eye in the place was glued to my back. I was all right, though. Even going through the small lobby to the outer door, the bouncer who'd tossed Eddie nodded in my direction, smiled, and said, "Good evening, sir. Please come again."

I smiled, nodded back, and hurried out the door.

When I got outside, I took a deep breath of the fresh salty air. Cars whizzed by on the street in front of me. The honky-tonk area of the beach was alive with lights and a racket of blaring music, excited voices, cars braking, and horns beeping. I was glad to be outside.

I headed around the side of the building where I'd left my car and hopped in behind the wheel. As soon as I got it started, Eddie and Derwood opened the doors and jumped in the seats they'd occupied on the way here.

"Where the hell did you two come from?" I asked, looking at Eddie.

"We was waiting around the corner for you. You took long enough."

I didn't feel I had to justify anything to him but I said, "I had to wait a bit so they wouldn't know I was with you. You really blew it in there, Eddie."

"Blew it? Me?" The tic on his face was jitterbugging and he chewed on his cheek as he talked. "I was minding my own business when that gorilla came over. I wish I'd had a piece."

That was a joke. Eddie was scared of a fistfight.

"Why?" I baited. "What would you have done?"

He gave me a cockeyed gaze. "You don't think I would've let him manhandle me like that if I'd been packing heat, do ya?"

I didn't know if that was just bluster or if the drugs had temporarily scrambled his brain more than they normally were. "Of course not," I said. "But forget that." I pulled the car out of the lot and headed on Route 1A back toward the safety of Hampton Beach.

"I can't forget it," Eddie said. "It was downright humiliating."

"It was your fault, Eddie," Derwood said from the back seat. "Dan told you to be descript."

"Discreet, Dumwood, discreet," Eddie said. "And I was. *Very.*"

Whack! Derwood slapped the back of Eddie's head. It was the first time I'd ever seen Derwood hit him. Eddie howled and turned around to look behind him. "Can't ya take a joke?

"It ain't no joke. You know I don't like that, Eddie. Call me Derwood or don't talk to me."

"Then you wouldn't have any one talking to you. If it wasn't for me, you'd—"

I cut Eddie off. "Be quiet. I'm not listening to you two go at it. I'd rather jump off the Hampton Bridge. And with a party boat underneath."

Eddie turned, faced front. They were both quiet.

But only for a minute. "What are we going to do now?" Eddie asked. "How're we going to get our business back? Me and Dum . . . er . . . Derwood need dough."

I glared at Eddie. "Speaking of dough. You were drinking Courvoisier, for chrissake. With my money! And what did you buy off that character you followed into the head?" Of course I knew, but I wanted to see what he'd say.

"Buy? Whattaya mean buy?" I glanced at him again and noticed his facial tic was dancing to an even faster beat.

"Eddie, you're wired. On my money. I didn't lend you money to blow on coke."

"Speed," Derwood offered from the back.

"Great," I said.

Resigned to the situation, I cooled down a bit. "Well, at least they don't know who we are."

"Well . . . ahh . . . ," Derwood said from the back.

"Ahh . . . what?" I said.

"*That* was humiliatin' too," Eddie said.

"What was humiliatin' . . . I mean humiliating?"

"Asking to see our IDs on the way out," Eddie answered. "I've heard of being asked on the way into a club, never on the way out."

Neither had I. But I knew what it meant. It meant someone wanted to know who'd been asking questions about Red

Foley. Whether they would follow up on it or whether it died there, only time would tell. I was happy to get Eddie and Derwood back to their rundown hovel and out of my car.

Before he slammed the door shut, Eddie said something that made him sound more like a beach real estate agent than a two-bit seaside hustler. "Don't forget to call if you need me. I'm always here to help."

Yeah, help me go from the frying pan into the fire.

On the short ride home, I wondered if I'd accomplished anything tonight. Anything useful that is. I came to the quick conclusion I hadn't. Now all I could hope for was that Eddie's idiocy hadn't started a chain reaction that could end up getting me, or someone close to me, hurt. No matter what happened, I couldn't blame Eddie. He was just being Eddie, after all.

The blame would have to fall on my shoulders.

Chapter 21

I'D BARELY STEPPED inside the cottage when the phone began to ring. It was Shamrock. "I might have a little trouble down here, Danny." I could hear the nervousness in his voice.

"What's wrong?"

"There's a car. Couple of guys in it and I think they're watching my house."

"Maybe it's your imagination, Shamrock," I said, although I didn't believe that for a second. "It's summer. Lots of people hanging around."

"I don't think so, Danny."

I didn't think so either, though I hoped I was wrong. "I'll be right down."

I grabbed the .38, took it to the car, tossed it in the glove box. It was around eleven and traffic was still heavy on Ocean. Inching along the street didn't help my anxiety. My symptoms flared like a bad case of hemorrhoids. I only had to drive a few blocks before cutting down a lettered street and coming out on Ashworth Avenue. But it took a while. I drove until I came to Shamrock's street. I took it, pulled up in front of his small place, and immediately saw what he'd been concerned about. Parked in front of the cottage two buildings down on the opposite side of the street was a large dark Lincoln Continental facing this way. It wasn't just the sight of a luxury car on this street that made me suspicious but also, as Shamrock had said, there were two male figures in the front seat. At this distance I couldn't make out who they were. I got out of the car, and making sure not to look toward the Lincoln, took the steps up to Shamrock's porch and rapped on the door. The deadbolt opened, followed by the door.

"For the love a Jesus," Shamrock whispered, "am I glad to see you." I brushed past him and he closed the door behind me. I heard the deadbolt slide home. We were in the main room of the tiny cottage. I only knew that because I'd been here many times before. The place was in total darkness. We talked as my eyes slowly adjusted to the lack of light.

"Did you see 'em, Danny boy? Did you see 'em?" Even in the dark, I could see Shamrock was in his work whites.

"I saw them. How long have they been there?"

"A couple of hours. Since just after I got home."

My eyes had almost adjusted to the light. Shamrock went to a front window shade and pulled back a corner. A sliver of light from a street lamp shone into the room. Shamrock peeked out.

"Still there?" I asked.

"Yes, they are."

I found my way to a couch, sat. "*They* could be anybody, Shamrock. It could be somebody watching a girlfriend's place. Or maybe kids just drinking."

"I don't think so," he said, still peering out the window. "I know everybody on this street. And kids don't use it for drinking. We chase them away. I got a bad feeling."

I did too but I didn't tell Shamrock that. I didn't know what he'd do if he got more shook up. "Why don't we just call the cops, say there's suspicious people in a car?" I asked. "Get them rousted?"

Shamrock came away from the window and stood in front of an ancient fireplace. I could tell he was just pretending to study the huge wall map of Ireland that hung above it.

When he didn't answer, I said, "What's the matter with that idea?"

"Well, Danny," he began, still looking at the map like it was a new planet he'd just discovered, "I don't really think it'd be wise to have the cops come here."

I knew instantly what he meant. Shamrock liked his herb. I could smell the sweet aroma that told me he'd recently indulged. "How much is here?"

He turned quickly to look at me. "Oh, less than an ounce. But still—if they smell it."

"I don't think they'd care about an amount like that for personal use."

"Maybe . . . maybe not. And what if those are cops in that car?"

"Watching you for not even an ounce?" My voice had gone up. "Come on, Shamrock. They're not going to be interested in a little thing like that."

"I dunno. It's funny times these days."

I was ninety-nine percent sure I was right. The Hampton cops, let alone county or state narcs, would never be interested in someone like Shamrock, who was known to be nothing but a consumer. Still, there was that one percent of doubt. And these were strange times, as he'd said.

"Would you like a bone, Danny?"

"No thanks. I'd be peeking out the window, too. Besides, I can get plenty anxious without it."

"Beer then?"

"One."

Shamrock hurried to the kitchen and returned with a Guinness for himself and a Heineken for me. He sometimes drank Heineken, too, and often used the Dutch beer to mix with the strong Irish beer, cut it down a bit if he was in the mood.

I took one small sip from the bottle. It was very cold. I sat there and thought. Shamrock stood back near the fireplace, apparently doing the same.

After a while, I said, "Let's take a ride."

"A ride?"

"Yeah. See if they follow us."

"What if they don't?"

"Well, you got anything valuable just in case it's some B&E guys?'

Shamrock shook his head quickly. "No, nothing." Then he added, "Except . . ."

"They aren't cops, Shamrock."

"Probably, but . . ."

"Well, you can't bring it with us. I don't want it in the car."

"I thought you said they aren't cops."

"I'm ninety-nine percent sure, not a hundred."

I could almost see the steam rise from Shamrock's head as he pondered his options. There were only two—hide it here as best he could or dump it. For him it was a tough decision.

Finally he walked slowly to his bedroom. I heard him rummaging around inside before he came out walking like a man on death row being taken to the electric chair. A few seconds after he disappeared into the bathroom, I heard the toilet flush. When he came out, I wondered if he'd really done it. Not only did Shamrock like his weed, I knew to him that was a lot of money to flush away. By the look on his face he'd actually done it. Either that or he was a very good actor.

"I bet Eddie Hoar'll be the only one on the beach with anything to sell." He genuinely looked sad.

"Don't worry. You got the luck o' the Irish, don't you?"

"Ha! You're kidding right? If I kissed the Blarney Stone now, it'd probably crumble into pebbles."

"Anyway, let's go. See what happens."

We left the cottage; Shamrock locked up. We both made certain not to look at the Lincoln as we went to my car and climbed in.

"Here goes," I said, starting the little Chevette and turning on the headlights. As I began to make a U-turn in the street, the headlights shone into the Lincoln. I didn't like what I saw. Both men inside quickly bent their head down.

Shamrock saw it too. "Oh, shit," he muttered.

I drove up to Ashworth Avenue, and just as I began to pull out, I glanced in my rearview mirror. The lights of the Lincoln flicked on. "Their lights just came on," I said.

"Oh, shit," Shamrock said again.

I drove a short distance along Ashworth.

"You see 'em, Danny?"

I looked in the rearview. They were just pulling out of Shamrock's street onto Ashworth. "Here they come."

"Sweet Jesus. Now we've done it."

I took the turnaround before the bridge at the first building on Ocean Boulevard. It was closer to midnight now and except for some twenty-somethings coming and going from a few watering holes, foot traffic was sparse. And vehicle traffic had eased. It was light, too. We'd only gone one block when I saw the headlights of the Lincoln round the corner onto Ocean and fall in behind us.

"Well, this ain't good," I said.

"What are we going to do, Danny?"

"I don't know."

"We could pull into the police parking lot out back."

"And say what? Two guys are following us? Even if the cops questioned them, they wouldn't find out anything. And they'd be back tomorrow. Better to see what they have in mind."

"I'm not sure I want to know what they have in mind."

"Let's keep going, see how far they stick with us."

"I hope you know what you're doing."

Of course I didn't.

It only took us minutes to pass the Casino, the Ashworth Hotel, and Boar's Head. As we drove by the sea wall at North Beach the Lincoln was still with us, although he was staying back at a respectable distance. I went through a set of lights and just as I passed Plaice Cove, I took a right along Ancient Highway to see if the Lincoln would come off the main road with us. It did. I drove along the oddly named short street and pulled back onto Route 1A, heading north again.

Shamrock turned to look at me. "I don't like this, Danny." He had a slight quiver in his voice.

"I don't either." My voice quiver was more than slight. "Buckle up, Shamrock. This might get hairy."

"They're right behind us." Shamrock twisted in his seat, looking over his shoulder.

I glanced in the rearview just as the driver flicked on the high beams. They were blinding but I didn't dare adjust the mirror. I wanted to make sure I could see where they were at all times. We were on a straightaway, so I gave the little car more gas. We flew past the parking lot for North Hampton State Beach and I floored it as we came to a slight upward grade in the road. The Lincoln was coming fast now and was so close to us its headlights lit up the inside of the Chevette like a searchlight.

As I took the car through a series of hairpin turns, I could see the moon shining off the ocean below us. There was a field of rocks that led to the water. Large boulders served as a guardrail in some locations.

We were in Rye now and I was struggling to keep the little car on the road and in its lane as we twisted through the oceanside turns. I could see Shamrock out of the corner of my eye. He was as white as his uniform and his hands gripped the dashboard so hard I thought he'd break it.

I was surprised he didn't when I glanced up in the mirror and shouted, "Jesus, hold on. They're going to hit us."

The lights of the car were so bright it might as well have been in the back seat. That's when the Lincoln slammed into the rear bumper and both Shamrock and I were bounced around. The little car swerved and I did everything I could to keep it on the road. We barely missed a car coming the other way. A horn blared.

When I had the car back under control, I gave it as much gas as I dared.

We were coming up on the Rye Beach parking lot. "Hang on," I shouted. "I'm going to try to turn here."

I don't know what I was thinking, except that maybe turning around and heading back toward Hampton might be a good idea. Even though I knew the roads ahead well, I didn't know them like the back of my hand as I did the ones on my own beach.

I braked slowly, even put on my blinker. The Lincoln gave us a love tap this time that wasn't as hard as the first. Still, the little car fishtailed and I barely avoided smacking into one of the two stone pillars that stood on either side of the entrance. There were only a few cars scattered about in the lot, all facing the ocean. Lovers maybe, getting it on and watching the moonlight shimmer on the water. I didn't have time to dwell on that because that's when I heard the shot and a loud thud from the trunk area.

"Sweet Baby Jesus, they're shooting at us, Danny." Shamrock hadn't moved an inch. He stared out the front windshield as if he were the captain of a boat during a nor'easter. His hands were still firmly attached to my dashboard. It'd probably have permanent fingerprints.

I whipped through the rest of the lot, came out the exit, again just missing a stone pillar. I banged a left and headed back on 1A the way we'd just come. Glancing over my left shoulder I could see that the big Lincoln had to slow down quite a bit to make it by the pillars and out onto the road. I floored the car again and flew back in the direction of Hampton. When I reached the treacherous hairpin turns above the rocks, I slowed even less than on my previous pass. I gripped the steering wheel so hard trying to keep the car on the road I was afraid I'd crack it.

"Sweet Mother of Mary," Shamrock shouted without looking at me. "You'll kill us before they do."

He might've been right, but this was the only chance we had to avoid being either shot or having the little car wrecked with us inside. So I didn't slow down at all. Once the Chevette got away from me and we crossed the center line. I was able to pull the car back inches from side swiping one of the huge boulders that acted as barriers. But not before a car coming the other way swerved to miss us and crashed into a similar boulder. I shot a look into my rearview; prayed no one was hurt.

We came out of the last curve and I accelerated as we flew down to a level grade. I took a slight turn at high speed and we had straight road in front of us. I floored the gas pedal. We zipped past the North Hampton Beach parking lot on the left. There was an ice cream stand on the other side. It was closed.

Halfway through the straightaway I saw the high beams of the Lincoln in my rearview. He'd just made the straightaway and I realized that the more powerful car could make up the lost distance. I had a green light in front of me near Plaice Cove, but I wouldn't have stopped even if there'd been ten red lights.

"Holy shit," Shamrock shouted. "Did you see that?"

"What?" Just as the word was out of my mouth I heard the siren and saw the flashing lights.

"Now you done it, Danny boy."

"Me?" I said, taking my foot off the gas, slowing the car down. "Remember they were watching you. You called *me* for help."

Shamrock peeled his hands off the dashboard. "Well, I didn't ask you to drive like an escaped lunatic. You're sure to get a ticket now."

I had to look at my friend as I pulled over to the shoulder of the road, see if he was kidding. He wasn't. His face was still pale white and I wondered if he was in shock. Maybe I was too, for that matter. The cruiser pulled in behind us. The gumball lights illuminating the inside of the car made Shamrock's face look like something out of a carnival sideshow.

"Would you like me to keep going with our little game of chase?"

"No."

A white spotlight joined the blue-and-red flashing lights. A voice shouted out something unintelligible but we both knew what it meant anyway. Shamrock and I both got out of the car with our hands up.

Two cops got out of the car with their guns drawn. I looked past them, hoping to see the Lincoln, try to get the cops to stop it. But it was gone. The cops came up to us fast. Threw us against my car none too gently. One held his gun on us while the other cuffed us both. He wasn't too gentle with that either. All the time, I tried to explain what had happened.

"We were being chased," I said, looking at them over my shoulder. The cops seemed to be two fairly young kids. Although lately everyone was starting to look young to me. I didn't recognize them. "They rammed us. Took a shot at us. Look at the rear."

The closest cop grabbed my handcuffs and spun me around to face him. He was so close I could smell the coffee and cigarettes on his breath.

"Bullshit," he said. "What the hell you think you got here, a fuckin' Corvette? We've been getting calls about you running cars off the road from here up to Rye. You could've killed someone, asshole."

"He's telling you the truth, officer," Shamrock said. "We—"

"Shut up," the same cop said. "Put them in the back," he said to his partner as he reached in my car and removed the keys. He slammed the door shut.

In the back of the police car, Shamrock and I moved around, trying to get comfortable with our hands cuffed behind us.

"Now we're in for it, Danny." As we were driven to the police station, Shamrock looked out the window as if he were seeing everything outside for the first time.

I was flustered. "We haven't done anything."

"We're still in for it. You driving like that."

Oh, boy. This should be interesting.

And it was, but not in the way I imagined. When we pulled into the Hampton Police lot on Ashworth Avenue, we had a reception committee. There were other cruisers with on-duty cops waiting to see the race car driver brought in. We were roughly dragged out of the back seat and marched toward the front door of the one-story cinderblock building.

If all this was a surprise to me, it was nothing compared to what awaited us inside.

Chapter 22

INSIDE THE STATION, Shamrock and I were led to a small interview room where there was a long butcher-block table with metal chairs scattered around it. A cuff was removed from one of our hands and we were told to sit beside each other. Our free cuffs were attached to the chairs' armrests. There wasn't much else to the room—some file cabinets; a large mirror, which I assumed was a see-through; a wall pay telephone; and a camera hanging from a corner of the ceiling. The camera was pointed directly at the table. The large school-like clock on the wall read ten past one. I noticed a map of the seacoast to the right of the telephone. The only door in the place had an exit sign over it. I hoped we'd use it soon. The room smelled of cigarettes. I had a déjà vu-type feeling that I'd been in this room before. If not this one, then one very much like it.

The two cops who arrested us stood over near the door. Except for a glance our way now and then and an occasional snicker, they ignored us. They chit-chatted about everything except police work. If their emotions showed anything, it was that they were bored.

"How long are we going to have to wait before we can explain what happened?" I asked the two cops.

"Why? You in a hurry?" said the original wise-guy. He followed it up with a phony laugh.

The other cop sighed. "It won't be long. I want to get out of here, too."

He'd barely gotten those words out of his mouth when the door opened and some uniformed cop who looked familiar, stuck his head in and motioned for them to step out. They did. The door closed and I could hear it lock.

"What do you think's going to happen, Danny?" Shamrock turned to look at me. His face had returned to its usual rosy red color.

"Nothing. We didn't do anything. Just tell them the truth. Then we get out of here." I wasn't sure it would be quite that easy, but I kept that thought to myself.

"Hey, look at this." Shamrock had both hands on his armrests and he was trying to rock back and forth. "They got these chairs nailed down."

I jiggled my chair just a bit. "Bolted to the floor," I said.

"Maybe they think we'd clobber 'em with it." Shamrock was leaning over, studying the chair legs where they met the floor. I figured he was trying to see how it was attached, Shamrock being a handyman and all.

"Some of the customers they get in here probably would."

"Hey, Danny," Shamrock said, still looking at the floor bolts. "This is a tile floor. If I could get something under the edge of this tile, I could—"

"Stop it, will you?" I interrupted.

"Just joking." Shamrock said, sitting up.

"Well, stop joking. This is serious."

As if I'd jinxed us, the door lock released and the door flew open. And what stepped in could only have been more serious if it was a pack of starving rabid hyenas. Gant. He had some papers in his hand. He closed the door, marched up to the table, and looked down at us. Again, it looked like he may have been called in from off-duty. His usually perfect iron-gray hair was unkempt and he had on a T-shirt tucked into black slacks. He looked like he'd just woken up. He stared down at us and we stared up at him. I could hear Shamrock breathing. Finally Gant spoke. "So here you are . . ." He stopped to clear his throat, then continued. "Do you know, shithead, that you almost killed a young couple up in Rye?" He was looking at me now. "You ran them into the rocks. And if the damn rocks weren't there, we'd be fishing them out of the ocean now."

"We didn't run anyone off the road," I lied, hoping to explain that later.

"Not on purpose anyway," Shamrock stupidly interjected. "We were—"

"Don't bother. I already know what you said." Gant was angry and he wasn't trying to hide it. "I got all your bullshit right here." He held the papers up, shook them like he was mixing a drink.

"It's the truth," I said. "Someone followed us from Shamrock's house, chased us up into Rye, hit us in the rear, and tried to run us off the road. They took a shot at us, too. You'll probably find the bullet hole in the back of my car somewhere."

"I don't think we'll find anything. I think what we'll find, as soon as we have you blow in the balloon, is that you're both drunk. You were probably both at the High Tide or the Irish gin mill, holding court with the other losers."

"We haven't been drinking," I said. I wasn't about to tell him about the two I'd had earlier at the Slipper.

"I wasn't driving and Dan wasn't drinking. Well, except for that one . . ."

I shot Shamrock a look. He shut up. I'd forgotten about the one at his cottage. Sometimes his tendency to be honest wasn't helpful.

Gant leaned over the table in my direction. He put both hands on the table, crunching the papers up in one hand. "Dope, then, knowing you, Marlowe. We'll have your blood drawn."

Now *I* was angry. "I haven't had any *dope.*"

"Since you got here maybe. Now do you want to hear the charges that are going to be filed against you or do you want to tell me some things I want to know first?"

I thought I caught the smell of alcohol on Gant's breath. That didn't help the situation any. "I told you—we were chased by another car, a big Lincoln. They tried to kill us. Shot at us and tried to run us off the road."

"Baloney. The officers who stopped your little joyride didn't see any other car. Quit trying to snow me. Tell me something I want to know."

I was puzzled. "Like what?"

"Did you chase that Fredette kid out of town?"

I said the only thing I could. "No."

"Did he torch your place?" He leaned in closer. I pushed back against the chair. It didn't budge.

"I wouldn't know."

"And did you pay him to do it?"

"I didn't pay him anything. Why would I want my own place burned down?"

Gant finally pulled back, stood straight. "Insurance money." He had a smug look on his face. "You're a goddamn bartender, Marlowe. A bartender who used to own the dump you work in until you got into the nose candy, ended up bankrupt." He snorted. "You're probably paying your poor wife and kids plenty, too." He gave me a disdainful glare. "Although I'll bet you're a deadbeat dad, too." His eyes narrowed. "And your drug business? Not as big-time as the old days, huh? With the big shipments of marijuana. Now you're stuck supplying lowlifes like Eddie Hoar and his type with hard stuff. And we got intelligence they can't even keep that together. That means you aren't making any money either. You're hurting, Marlowe. You're a desperate man."

I couldn't believe it. I felt like the main character in a bad noir movie. I looked at Shamrock. His mouth was slack and he was staring wide-eyed at Gant. I turned back to Gant. This was so far out, I didn't know where to begin.

"Why don't you try going after Fredette's uncle, Leo Karnack? He's behind a lot of things that are going on."

"Karnack, again," Gant shouted. "He's a legitimate beach businessman. Maybe you're trying to shake *him* down. And maybe it's you who's behind the problems other beach businesses are having." His voice grew louder and his face was as red as Shamrock's hair. "I wouldn't put it past you. Like I said—you're desperate for money. That's a good motive. And with your criminal experience you got the skill set to do it. *And* you got the opportunity. You're on this beach like seagull shit. You know it like the back of your hand. So it's easy for you to pull something and get away with it without being caught. Until now."

Now I was really mad. "You're crazy, Gant. I don't know what I ever did to you. But everything you said is wrong."

"People like you are ruining my beach. And you're the worst of them. I'm going to nail you if it's the last thing I do." He flashed a wicked grin. "And this time I think I can do it."

I was just ready to hit back, figured I had nothing to lose, when someone knocked at the door. Gant turned and I could see him trying to calm himself down. He took a few deep breaths before he said, "Come in."

The door opened and Steve Moore walked in. He shut the door behind him. He too held some papers in one hand. He was dressed as he almost always was—sport shirt and slacks. He was missing his sport coat, though. His gun was holstered on his hip. Unlike Gant, he looked presentable. I wondered if he was on duty. It seemed he always was.

Gant looked at Steve warily. "What?"

Steve stood near the door. "Got something."

Gant walked over, opened the door, they both stepped outside, closed it behind them.

Within seconds there were loud voices from the hallway.

"That doesn't sound good," I said.

"Aye," Shamrock said. "Danny, who do you think was in that car trying to kill us? Karnack or maybe that thug from the head shop?"

"I don't know, but they're at the top of the list." Shamrock and I didn't look at each other. We were both distracted by the loud voices outside the door.

It was only another minute before there was a last flurry of the voices in the hallway, then silence. A few seconds passed before the door opened and Steve stepped in. He closed the door behind him. He looked about as dejected as a man could look. He went directly to Shamrock, released him from the handcuff on his wrist. Then he looked at me. It wasn't a friendly look.

"I think I'll leave you like you are."

I smiled uncomfortably. There was a short period of awkward silence before Steve scowled and removed my cuff.

"I told you to keep out of this," he said.

I didn't want to alienate Steve, so I didn't argue. Besides he was my friend. "What happened with Gant?" I asked.

"Oh, not much," he answered sarcastically. "He just stormed out of the building and almost broke the glass door on his way out."

"He's a very angry man," Shamrock offered.

"Yeah," Steve said. "And now he's angry at me, too. I know you guys could give a shit less, but he is my boss. And now you got me in the dog house."

Neither Shamrock nor I got up. We just sat there, took a bit more of a tongue lashing from Steve.

When I thought he'd gotten most of it out of his system I said, "So what did happen?"

"What happened?" Steve shook his head slowly in resignation. "We found the bullet hole in the trunk of your heap. Some kids who were driving around also came in to say they saw the car you described slamming into your rear. When I told Gant, I thought he was going to break down and cry."

"Ha, ha," Shamrock began, "I would've loved to see that."

I glanced at him and Steve glowered in his direction. Shamrock turned away, face reddened. "Sorry."

Steve pulled out the chair across from us. I could tell he didn't like saying it, but he did. "Tell me the whole story." He took out his pocket notebook and pen. We told him.

"Any idea who?"

"Maybe Karnack," I said. "Maybe the Irish thug from the head shop."

"Can either of you identify them?"

We both shook our heads.

"You're pestering a lot of people on the beach, Dan. So it could've been anybody."

"What about the Lincoln?" I asked. "It must have front end damage."

"I'll look into that. For now, I'd advise you two to stay out of trouble. That means other people's business. Let us handle it." Steve stood up. "And Dan, Gant still thinks you're behind the cottage fire and more. He'd give his left nut to hang something on you. I wouldn't make it easy for him if I were you. Now go."

Shamrock and I stood. He led the way to the door, opened it, and stepped outside into the hallway. I stopped short and told Shamrock I'd be right with him. He looked puzzled, didn't speak, then walked away. I turned back to Steve.

"Thanks for the help with Gant, Steve."

"Don't mention it. I just hope I still have a job tomorrow." He studied me for a second. "You could have said that in front of Kelly. What else do you want to say?"

I knew I was pushing my luck, but it was too important not to risk angering Steve further. "Did you talk to your FBI friend?"

"Man, you got big balls tonight, huh? I got in a shouting match with my boss over you and you still want to push the envelope."

Not much I could say to that, so I put on what I hoped was a contrite expression. Steve blew air out of his mouth. "What's the use? Yeah, I talked to him. And absolutely no intelligence about Red Foley having anything to do with Hampton Beach. He was sure of that."

That was disappointing.

"He *did* say though, for me to tell my friend not to mention Foley's name to anyone and to stop nosing around on him. He says Foley's been known to disappear people who get too inquisitive about his activities. He told me that a couple of times. I believed him the first time. *You* better too, Dan."

I did, of course. But after tonight, the advice might've already come too late.

I said goodbye to Steve. He grumbled something. Outside the police station Shamrock and I walked along Ashworth Ave, headed for Dave's Garage. My car would be there. There was nowhere else it could be. Dave's was the only garage on the beach. Shamrock talked. I listened half-heartedly. I was thinking about what Steve's FBI buddy had said about Foley. That should've been enough right there for me to turn and run the other way. But I couldn't now even if I'd wanted to. Why not? Simple. Because my kids, Shamrock, Dianne, Peenell, and Cliff were all in danger. And maybe all of Hampton Beach, for that matter. That was more than enough. Wasn't it?

Chapter 23

AFTER THE CHEVETTE was finally released from Dave's Garage, Shamrock and I went to my cottage. He wasn't comfortable returning to his place after what had happened. I didn't blame him. I did blame him for my lousy night's sleep. I could hear him snoring right through the wall in my daughter's bedroom.

Fortunately, he only had a couple of hours before he was up and off to the High Tide. I lay there, listened to him moving around until he left. Blessedly, I was able to get four more hours of sleep before I woke again. I went for a run. The sky was a mass of billowy gray clouds and it looked like it could rain any second. It didn't, but I wouldn't have cared anyway. I was lost in thoughts about what I was going to do.

I was still lost in thought later that morning when, after setting up the bar, I opened the front door of the High Tide. In trooped Paulie and Eli, of course, but right along with them came someone I hadn't expected—Bud Phillips. He was a bigwig with the Chamber of Commerce and a beach icon, with his styled white hair and a belly that led the way when he walked. He had on a sport coat and tie. Same thing he always wore. How anyone could wear a tie every day in the summer on the beach, I didn't know. He waited until Eli and Paulie had taken their stools and then went directly to the opposite end of the bar as far away from my two regulars as he could get. The man had never been here in the morning before. Something was up.

First I waited on Paulie. Over his shoulder, I saw a man with a black beard peering in the big picture window. He stared, then turned and hurried away. I headed for Eli. When I placed the draft down on the bar in front of Eli, he finally spoke up. "Did ya hear about the big gunfight and car chase up on North Beach?" he said loud enough for everyone to hear. "And I heard somebody got shot, too. Maybe a few somebodies. Yep."

He had some of it wrong, but I didn't want to get into it with him, so I quickly turned and headed for the Chamber guy. When I reached him, he beamed like I was a big lottery winner and he was my best friend. "Dan, how have you been? I haven't talked to you in quite a while."

The truth was we'd never spoken. A "Hi" in passing was the extent of it. "Good to see you, Bud," I said. "What would you like?"

His round red face beamed. "Oh, a little too early for me, Dan, my boy. How about a ginger ale. Can I buy you one?"

"No thanks."

I took a few steps to the tonic gun. I could feel his eyes boring into me. I wondered what was coming as I returned with his drink. I put it down in front of him, leaned my butt against the back bar, and crossed my arms in the traditional bartender defensive stance. Bud was directly across from me.

"We're looking at a crackerjack summer this year, don't you think?" He didn't give me a chance to answer. "You been following the Red Sox? I think they're going to take the pennant this year. I do. I'd love to go to a game or two but I can't get away during the summer. Businesses are counting on my presence. Short season. You know all about that, of course. We all have to pull our weight. Don't we? Help each other make the most of every possible advantage for our Hampton Beach business people. You're all for that, right?"

This time I could tell he wanted an answer. I didn't give him one. Didn't have time. Something thumped on the bar and I turned to see Eli rapping his empty glass against the hard wood. I pushed away from the back bar, went to refill his glass.

"You know about the big shootout, Dan?" Eli asked, head cocked. Again, I felt I was being asked a question I wasn't expected to answer.

"Not much," I answered anyway, semi-truthfully. It was irritating that Eli already knew about it. But I wasn't surprised. Hampton Beach is like a little village—word gets around fast. And now that Eli knew, the story was sure to make the rounds even faster.

"Ha," he spit out. I headed toward the front end of the bar with a fresh beer for Paulie.

"You'll never guess in a million years who was in one of the cars, mailman." Eli shouted behind me.

"Who?" Paulie said.

Eli didn't answer.

I scowled as I marched back past Eli towards Bud Phillips. I tried to tune them out, but I could still hear Paulie throwing out names and Eli responding each time with a loud, "Noooo."

I barely made it back to Bud when the front door opened. A couple more customers came in, took seats at the bar. Bud didn't look happy when I hurried over to wait on them. Drinks and lunch orders. It took me five minutes to get them squared away. Eli was playing the shootout guessing game with them, too. If he'd already told Paulie the answer, I hadn't heard it.

I was still anxious to see what Bud was driving at, so I returned to him as soon as I could and took my old position leaning against the back bar. His lips were pursed and he was playing with the straw in his ginger ale. I knew he wasn't the nervous type, not with his job. So I pegged it as irritation. He glanced up at the Clydesdale clock over the bar.

"Looks like you're going to get very busy any minute," he said

"Yeah, they'll all be parading in soon."

"Well, I'm not going to beat around the bush then." He took a deep breath, let it out his nose. "As I was saying, we all have to help each other out on the beach, Dan. Sometimes we're fortunate enough to have businessmen from other areas who see the potential on the beach and they want to come in and be a part of it." He stopped for a moment, studied my face. I had an idea where this was going. "And we all want to make these people feel welcome. Don't we?"

"I guess so."

"Sure we do," he said cheerily. "We want to make it easy and pleasurable for these people to invest in the beach. There's nothing but profit in it for the businesses already here."

I wondered what businesses he meant.

He must have read my mind. "And not just the big businesses either, Dan, my boy. Even places like the High Tide would get a shot in the arm if big money came here. That would help you *and* Ms. Dennison, too, wouldn't it?" He was referring to Dianne, of course, and I could tell by the gleam in his eye he knew our relationship was more than employer and employee.

I was distracted momentarily when Eli said loudly to a new customer, "And guess who was in one of the cars?"

I struggled to block the rest out, concentrate on Bud. This might lead somewhere. Besides, it was way too late to do anything about Eli's yapping.

"It might help business," I said.

He sat back on his stool, beamed. "Good then. So I'm sure you wouldn't do *anything* to disrupt an investor's plans on the beach."

I shrugged, told him the truth. "Depends who the investor is."

The silly look on his face disappeared instantly. "An investor is an investor. All money is green. You should know that. You're a . . . well, you used to be a businessman."

I decided to go a little out on a limb, see if I could find out more. "We don't want certain kinds of people getting a foothold on the beach, though."

He looked shocked. "I'm surprised at you, Dan. We don't discourage any race or nationality from doing business on our beach."

He was a good bullshitter. I guess in his line of work you had to be. I wasn't in his league; I knew that. So I gave it to him straight. "I meant dirty money, Bud. Those people get in somewhere and they slowly absorb a place, then run it their way. They bring a boatload of problems with them, too. A place like Hampton could go from a nice family vacation spot to a dump like Revere Beach used to be." I decided to keep going. "And the only people who'll make out are the criminals and a few crooked businessmen and politicians."

His face darkened. "I think you're exaggerating quite a bit." He looked slowly around the room. My heart thudded in my ears. Finally, he looked at me, his color back to normal. "You used to own this place, didn't you, Dan? How would you like to own it again? Maybe not this exact place, but another one, a better one, right here on Hampton Beach? Your own bar and restaurant. You'd be a big man again." He lowered his voice, leaned toward me. "I've heard a little about your financial situation. If half of what I've heard is true, you'll be on Social Security before you get together enough money to own your own place. So what do you think?" He sat back, a satisfied look on his puss.

I didn't give myself time to be tempted. "I'd love to own my own business again someday and I will. But I'm not going to do it by helping Hampton Beach turn into a Revere Beach. I couldn't stay here after that, whether I owned my own place or not."

"You're being foolish and pigheaded." I could almost hear his teeth grinding. "You've got kids. Don't you want to be successful enough to take good care of them? You surely can't do that on a bartender's wages?" He looked at me disdainfully.

My anxiety had been replaced with anger. My arms tightened across my chest. "I have to look at myself in the mirror every morning, Bud. Don't you?" I had nothing to lose now. "And I get the feeling you're more worried about your own bank account than the beach."

I must have raised my voice because Bud blushed and quickly looked around the bar. I realized there was complete silence in the room. Out of the corner of my eye I could see the rest of the bar patrons looking my way. Eli was almost falling off his stool, leaning in my direction. Paulie was watching too, smoke rings coming out of his mouth and heading toward the ceiling faster than a cartoon train going up a hill.

Bud got off his stool awkwardly. "How much?"

"Nothing. Forget it." I said. I stepped over, cleared his glass, and used a rag on the bar like there was some type of permanent stain.

Bud lumbered off toward the front door. His big ass jiggled as he walked. It took me more than a few minutes to calm down after he left. Mercifully, Eli didn't pump me about what had just happened. Not yet anyway.

I went through the motions for the rest of my shift. It seemed that I'd been doing that more and more lately. I wasn't quite sure what to make of the visit from Bud Phillips. He had tried to bribe me, no doubt about that. But why? Did he just want investment money flowing into the beach, no matter who it came from? I assumed he'd been referring to Red Foley, even though the name had never been mentioned.

Maybe I was naive. Was the man just doing his job? Or did he have a financial stake in Foley's infiltration of Hampton Beach?

With Phillips' position at the Chamber, he could certainly grease the wheels for a Foley takeover. Unless he didn't realize Foley was involved. Or maybe he didn't want to know? He might have dealt only with Foley's lawyer.

I'd made a mistake there. I should have thrown Foley's name into the conversation. If I had, I'd probably know now whether or not he was aware that Red Foley, Irish gangster, wanted a piece of our beach and not some slick Boston lawyer representing unknown investors.

Something else was bothering me—the bribe. There was only one thing I wanted more in this world than having my own business again. That was getting my family back. Not Sandy, we were divorced, that was over. But my children, so at least I could have as normal a relationship with them as a divorced dad could. A new business would help prove to my ex-wife—and the courts—that I'd turned my life around and should have full visitation rights with my kids. Maybe even joint custody.

So it hadn't been as easy a choice as it might have seemed. If I took Phillips' offer, not only would I be out of the horrible financial situation I was in, I'd have a good shot at a normal relationship with my kids again. So the two things I wanted more than anything in the world, that might take me years and years to obtain if ever, had been offered to me on a silver plate. I don't think Phillips realized how much it really meant to me. I did though. And I still couldn't take the bribe.

And it wasn't just that stupid code of mine again. The one I'd boxed myself in with by promising to never back down from something just because of fear. I had to keep that promise. It was my handle. Sometimes it was all that kept me hanging on.

So that explained why I couldn't allow myself to be frightened off by threats of violence. It didn't explain why I couldn't accept the offer to help me acquire my own restaurant. That was something else.

The way I looked at it, the *damn* way I looked at it, was that—except for my kids and the people who stuck by me in my most down times—Dianne, Shamrock, Steve Moore and maybe a couple of others—I only had one other thing left in this world that meant anything to me.

Hampton Beach.

And what kind of a place would it be if a gangster like Red Foley was running it? Certainly not the beach it was now, the beach that I'd spent my entire childhood roaming. And still roamed. The beach my kids had grown up on and the one I hoped they'd spend lots more time on. The place where I planned to finish out living my life, no matter which way everything went.

And what about the new business I'd own if I accepted Phillip's offer? I'd always know where the money came from. And that knowledge would gnaw at my insides. What would I be getting into anyway? Would I really be the owner, or would I be just another front for Red Foley? With the beach deterioration that I was sure would follow a Foley takeover, the days of Hampton as a family vacation spot would grind to a halt. I could see it all as clear as the Isle of Shoals on a picture-perfect day. Hampton Beach would end up a dump and I'd end up right back down in that little hovel off Ashworth Avenue with a rolled-up bill up my nose, or worse. Like I said, I know myself. Very well.

So that was that. What I was going to do, I didn't know. I only knew what I wasn't going to do—sell out my kids, my friends, myself, or Hampton Beach.

Chapter 24

EARLY THE NEXT morning I got a call from Peenell asking me to see him at his hotel. So I hurried up Ocean Boulevard to the Waterview before work. I entered his neat and clean establishment and found him standing behind the registration desk. The instant he saw me his dark skin turned darker. He called to a young girl vacuuming the far section of the lobby. She turned off the vacuum and took Peenell's place behind the desk. Then he escorted me down a short hallway into a small room marked *Office*. It wasn't fancy, but it too was neat as a pin. He sat behind the desk. I sat facing him in a folding chair.

"I have something to tell you," he said. "I hope you won't be mad. You have been a very good friend and you have tried to help Peenell. I know this."

The man was squirming in his chair. I wondered what was coming. "I am selling the hotel." He lowered his head, looking up at me like he'd done something shameful. "I am sorry, Dan."

I shrugged. "There's nothing to be sorry about, Peenell. It's your business. You have to do what you think is right."

Peenell frowned. "I feel like I have no courage. I know what has happened to you since I asked you to help me. I got you involved in this bad thing. I am to blame. Now I run away." He glanced at the ceiling, then looked right back at me. "But they threaten my family, Dan. I believe them. You see what they do."

Yes, I'd seen what they could do. And I couldn't blame Peenell one bit. He was worried about his family just like I was. And just like me he was doing what he thought was best for them. I couldn't fault a man for that.

There was only one thing I wanted to know. I was pretty sure what his answer would be, but I needed verification. "Who are you selling to, Peenell, if you don't mind me asking?"

"Oh no, Dan. I tell you anything. It is a real estate trust. Cla . . . Clad . . ." He gave up, rustled through the papers on his desk. He picked one up, handed it to me. "Very hard for me to say."

I took it. It was a copy of a Purchase & Sale Agreement. There was only one item I was looking for and it was right there in the first paragraph. Claddagh Realty Trust. I didn't read anymore. There wasn't any reason to. I handed the paper back to Peenell.

So now Foley had another piece of Hampton Beach. A specific part he wanted for some unknown reason.

I smiled, tried to make Peenell feel more comfortable. "So what are you going to do now?"

He sat up in his chair, smiled back. He seemed relieved that I wasn't disappointed. I guess I was a good actor. "I not sure. Open another hotel, I think. It is the only business I know."

"Are you looking at something on the beach?" I asked stupidly.

His face darkened again. "No. I think we will go somewhere else." Then he quickly added, "It is my wife, Dan, she is frightened."

So it had started already. Good people were being driven off Hampton Beach and the bad were rolling in. "I don't blame her, Peenell. She has to think of your children."

He nodded rapidly. "Yes. Yes. I hate to leave like this though. You have done so much to help. And . . . and . . . ahh . . ."

"What, Peenell?"

He looked at me with black eyes wider than they usually were. "I am worried that you will be hurt. You must be careful. Maybe you leave beach for a while, too?"

"*That's* not going to happen." I must've said it more harshly than I intended because I could see the shame on his face again. I tried to make him feel better. "I have to stay. I've got a house, a job, and besides, I don't have enough money to leave." It was all true but it didn't seem to ease his guilt.

I stood. He jumped up. We shook hands. "Good luck, Peenell. I hate to see you go."

He wouldn't let go of my hand, just kept his arm pumping away. "*Please* be careful, Dan. And I thank you for everything." His black eyes glistened. I pulled my hand away. Turned and left the office and the hotel.

The only good thing that had come from my stop at Peenell's was an idea. A little idea. And I didn't know if it was crazy or not. I did know that it was a dangerous idea. Still, I decided to make one stop and see if I could put that little idea in motion right now, before I returned to the Tide.

Chapter 25

IT WAS SHORTLY before the lunch hour when I got another one of those bad feelings. I'd left Peenell's hotel, made a short stop after that, then went to the Tide. I'd set the bar up and opened the door. Paulie and Eli were at their usual stools now, sharing the bar with a few other regulars. Eli was holding court.

"And that's how it was," he said for the umpteenth time. "Dan outraced their car and their bullets too. Hey, Dan?"

For the umpteenth time I didn't answer him. I didn't want to get into it. Not here, not with these people, not now. I wasn't angry with Eli. It was just his way, after all. And if it wasn't him, it would have been someone else spreading the story. Even still, I hoped it wouldn't be in the next issue of the *Union*. *Then* my wife might hear about it. *That* wouldn't help convince her that I was the trustworthy and reliable father I was trying to prove to her I was.

Just then a newcomer came in. He looked like he'd stepped out of a hard-boiled paperback novel. He had a lopsided nose planted near the middle of a face you might see on a wanted poster. A cheap brown imitation leather coat that looked plastic was stretched over his wide shoulders. He glanced around the bar. A couple of people seated at the bar who'd turned their heads at the sound of the opening door, quickly looked away. He sauntered in the direction of the L-shaped end of the bar, lifted himself onto the stool beside Paulie.

I headed that way, greeted the newcomer. "Schlitz," he said. Out of the corner of my eye I could see Paulie grimace for my benefit.

I was back with his beer in seconds. I put the bottle and a frosted beer mug down on the bar in front of him.

"I don't need no glass," he said.

"Menu?" I asked.

"Just gimme a rare cheeseburger and some fries. Make them well done, pal."

I had my order book on the bar and scribbled into it. As I got the new customer's setup ready—utensils, condiments, and such—Paulie lit up another cigarette even though one was still burning in his ashtray. He puffed out smoke rings one right after the other, like there was a prize if he did enough of them fast enough. I left, put the order through the slide window. I tried to keep an eye on the newcomer but I was busy. The lunch crowd filtered into the restaurant area and it was filling quickly. Ruthie and the other waitresses were coming up to the service bar at the far end and placing drink orders for the dining room. It was that hour-and-a-half to two-hour period every day where I was as busy as a one-armed paper hanger. That's probably why I didn't notice the other stranger until he was seated.

He'd hijacked a stool from a customer who'd already been sitting there and pushed his almost empty pilsner glass aside. The original stool-warmer had just gone to the men's room.

He was standing over near the partition now, checking out the aquarium. I got the impression he was faking it though. Because I hadn't actually seen how the newcomer had gotten possession of the stool, and no one complained, I didn't have the incentive or the time to do anything about it.

Even though a couple of other patrons should have been served first, I went directly to the new guy. I was hoping that he'd have a quick drink and scram. I didn't like his looks. He was a good size, not muscular like Plastic Coat at the end of the bar, but very tall, six-six maybe, very thin though. And the pores on his face were so big you could've stuck your fingers in them. His skin was the color of a dirty picket fence. Sunbathing on the beach would've done him a lot of good, but the last time this guy had done that was probably in another life. One customer, a young nerd wearing a tie, was seated between him and Eli.

"What can I get you?" I asked in a hurried voice.

"Bud. Very, very cold. Don't bring no warm shit."

Oh, this was going to be a fun day. When I returned with the beer and the glass, I noticed Eli, Camel hanging out of his mouth, looking around the nerd seated beside him, peering in the direction of Big Pores. I prayed that he'd keep his mouth shut. Of course, he didn't. In retrospect, I guess he made it easy for them. It didn't take long for the trouble to start. I don't know if I was slow or naive or both but when it did, I assumed Eli had instigated it.

The first hint that something was about to happen was the departure of the nerd seated between Eli and Big Pores. Pores quickly took the vacated seat and started talking to Eli. It didn't take long for the conversation to turn contentious.

"I'm tellin' you the Red Sox are going to win the pennant."

"You're fulla shit, old man."

I couldn't catch much, I was straight out busy. Waitresses at the service bar yelling out drinks, the kitchen slide door banging open every couple of minutes with another meal being shoved through it, not to mention my own bar customers' drink orders.

I glanced warily in Eli's direction every chance I got, praying I wouldn't see happen what I thought I might. That's why I was surprised when I heard the first shout come from the L-shape end of the bar. I would've bet my last dollar if there was going to be trouble with these newcomers, it would've started with Eli. He was known for stirring the pot. Paulie was easygoing and much less confrontational.

"You blow that smoke in my face once more, hippie, I'll break your fuckin' head," Plastic Coat shouted.

I hurried to that end of the bar. Paulie had his hands up. "Sorry, man, I'm sorry." His cigarette smoldered in the ashtray.

My heart jacked up as I said, "Keep it down and watch your language here."

Plastic Coat turned toward me. "This long-haired asshole been blowin' smoke in my face. I told him to knock it off. He keeps doin' it."

I didn't believe for a second that Paulie would blow smoke in a gorilla like Plastic Coat's face. Still, I had to deal with it. Situations like this were the most unpleasant part of a bartender's job. I looked at Paulie, glanced at the butt in the ashtray. His eyes were wide and he'd lost two shades of color, but he snapped out of it and rapidly stubbed the cigarette out like he was beating an egg. The level of noise at the bar behind me had dropped more than a few decibels. I pictured all the other barflies straining to hear what was going on.

"Okay, no harm done," I said. And even though I would have bet my last pair of underwear that Paulie was about to make a hasty retreat out the door, I said, "Can I get either of you gentlemen another beer?"

Before either could answer there was a new commotion behind me. I spun around. What I'd expected to see happening first was happening now. Pores had the front of Eli's white shirt scrunched up in his fist. And the fist was jammed up under Eli's chin, stretching the older man's head back on his thin wrinkled neck. Eli squawked unintelligibly, like a seagull who'd just lost a choice piece of bread to a competitor.

I dashed down the bar, but I was too late. Big Pores rose off his stool, taking Eli with him. In one fluid motion he shoved Eli with enough force to topple a much bigger man. Eli stumbled backwards across the small space between the bar and the bar tables. He crashed dead center into the middle of one table, scattering glasses and dishes in every direction. The three men sitting there, local plumbers, pushed their chairs back, and jumped away.

Pores wasn't stopping there though. He yanked chairs out of his way, trying to get at Eli. Eli didn't seem badly hurt, but he looked like he thought he soon would be.

"Hold it, hold it," I shouted, leaning across the bar.

Eli was squirming around on the floor, trying to avoid the tall man's grasp. "Dan, Dan," he screamed. "Help me. Jesus Christ."

I was about to come around the bar when there were shouts from down Paulie's way. I looked just in time to see Paulie take a punch from Plastic Coat that knocked him off his stool. Plastic Coat got off his seat but instead of going after Paulie on the floor, he turned and sucker-punched an electrician who'd been seated on the other side of him. I think the guy was out cold before he hit the deck.

The room was a madhouse of shouts and yells and screams and that's when I went for the Georgia toothpick under the bar. As I came up with the baseball bat, one I'd never used, I was stunned to see Big Pores pick up a chair and hurl it at the aquarium. The damn thing shattered in a loud explosion of water and glass. The water drenched people close to it. I had no idea what it might have done to the customers seated underneath it in the restaurant section. There were a half-dozen booths over there that were situated directly below the aquarium. The commotion coming from the dining room told me it wasn't good.

People were running, scrambling for the door. Pores had forgotten about Eli who was cowering beneath a table and had turned his wrath on a slow-moving man who he grabbed from behind, spun him partially around, and gave him a brutal punch in the side of the head. The sound was sickening; the man went down like dead weight.

I had the bat in one hand and was coming around the far end of the bar when up at the other end I saw Plastic Coat heave a chair through the front picture window. Then he started to throw anything he could get his hands on—dishes, bottles, glasses, ashtrays. There was no sign of Paulie.

I wasn't a hero, so when I got within ten feet of Big Pores, I shouted, "Get the hell outta here. Now!"

"Fuck you," he yelled. He lifted a small two-customer table over his head and before I could do anything, it sailed over the bar and crashed into the mirror. Dozens of liquor bottles shattered. The place suddenly smelled like a Chinese Scorpion Bowl.

I held the baseball bat in two hands over my shoulder, lunged toward Pores.

He stepped back. "I'm gonna take that fuckin' thing away from you and shove it up your ass," he growled. From his jacket pocket he removed something metal, a dull gray color. He slid his fingers through the holes in it. I couldn't remember seeing one before outside of an old movie, but I knew instantly what I was looking at—brass knuckles.

"You'll love the taste of these," he said as if he couldn't wait to do me damage.

I knew I was in trouble. Even if I got in one swing with the bat, I was unlikely to get him in the head. He was too tall. A blow to the arm wouldn't even slow down this animal. Then he'd be on me. And I had a good idea what kind of damage those metal knuckles could do to flesh and bone. My flesh and bone!

He took a quick look at me and the bat, snorted, and started to move forward.

"Get out of here," a voice yelled. Diane. "Both of you. Right now. Get out of my restaurant." Her voice bordered on hysterical. I didn't look; I was afraid to take my eyes off Big Pores. I could see him looking over my shoulder at Dianne who was just to my right and a bit behind me. His eyes went up and down.

"You ain't gonna use that little toy, sweetie," he said. There was a mocking tone in his voice.

When he said that, I glanced quickly toward Dianne. I was shocked to see she was holding what looked like a small semi-automatic in her hand and it was pointed right at Pores. The gun was shaking badly.

I let go of the bat with one hand, reached over for the gun. Dianne gave it up. It was tiny, with a pink grip. I turned it on Big Pores. I wasn't confident it could stop him.

"You ain't got the balls either, pussy." He had an ugly smirk on his face.

I lowered the gun so it was pointing just below his abdomen. He lost the smirk fast but I could see he was still debating whether I'd use the gun and if he should make a move on me or not.

Just then sirens sounded outside on the street. This whole episode had taken only a few minutes but it'd felt like hours.

"Cops coming," Plastic Coat shouted as he headed for the front door. "Let's go, man."

Big Pores took one last look at me with the little pink gun, snickered, turned, and started to leave. As he pushed through debris and stepped over a body or two, it crossed my mind to shoot. But in the back? I couldn't have done that. But I *can* tell you if he and his brass knuckles had taken one more step toward Dianne and me, he would have been singing soprano for the rest of his life.

As soon as they ran out the door, I dropped the bat, tossed the gun on the bar, and turned to Dianne. She came into my arms; I held her tight. She was trembling.

"It's alright, honey," I said inanely. "They're gone." I squeezed her harder.

There was a loud groan from somewhere. That snapped both of us out of it.

"Jesus, someone's hurt, Dan," she said. I let her go. She took a few steps forward, turned back to me. "Oh my God, it's Eli." I brushed past her, threw a couple of overturned chairs aside and pushed away the two tilted tables he was cowering under. When he saw us, his hands went to his back and he moaned. "Jesus, I think my back's broken. Is he gone?" His eyes looked like a frightened animal's.

I didn't dare move him. Eli was known to exaggerate everything, but with the way he'd been thrown, I didn't want to take a chance. "Just sit there. Wait for the ambulance." Dianne knelt down in the clutter beside him.

I moved toward the front of the bar. On my way, I passed one of the plumbers holding a bunch of blood-soaked napkins against his face. "Are you all right?" I asked.

"Oh great," he answered. There was a pool of blood on the floor near his feet.

When I reached the front of the bar, I could see beyond the partition into the dining room. Children were crying. Ruthie was trying to comfort a couple of them. The rest of the waitstaff seemed to be running around like chickens with their heads chopped off, doing what, I didn't know.

When I looked around the L-shaped end of the bar, there was Paulie and the electrician, both of them stretched out on the floor, flat on their backs, out cold. There were glass shards all over them. I bent quickly, saw they were both breathing. I didn't try to move them either, just picked the chunks of glass off and tossed them aside.

Just then I heard two cars screech to a halt out front and within seconds Hampton's finest barreled through the front door.

Chapter 26

THAT WASN'T ALL the bad luck Dianne and I had that day. Almost as bad was when Lieutenant Gant showed up to take over the scene. And he hadn't taken a happy pill that morning either. He had Dianne and I in the dining room seated at the farthest booth from the door. The room was a mess. Water, broken glass, dead fish, dishes, and food scattered everywhere. The only good thing was that Steve Moore was there, too, seated in the booth beside Gant. Gant was on the outside; I was opposite him with Dianne beside me. She was shaken and didn't look good. I had no idea how I looked, but I was shaken too.

"Tell us what happened," Gant said. Even though he had a sour look on his face he sounded reasonable for a change. I hoped that would last.

"I came in, set up the bar like I do every morning," I began. I noticed Gant was looking at me like he was waiting for me to slip up. I shook off the observation and continued. "Couple of regulars came in and then around noon, a man came in and sat down at the end of the bar. He was kinda tough looking and had a—"

Gant interrupted. "Forget that. We'll get to it later. What happened?"

"He wanted a beer and a hamburger. Then the lunch crowd came in. I got busy and forgot about him. Until he got loud and accused another customer of blowing cigarette smoke in his face. I was just getting that cooled down when there was an uproar with some other rough-looking character I didn't know. He started a fight with Eli halfway down the bar."

"Eli who?" Gant said.

I realized I didn't know Eli's last name. "I don't know his last name. He's an old guy. Small. A painter. This punk picked him up off his stool and threw him over a table. Could've broken his back. That's when the first guy sucker-punched Paulie. Paulie's the customer he said was blowing smoke in his face, though I'm sure that's bullshit. Then the other one threw a chair into the aquarium. Then another chair went flying through the front window and one of them even heaved a table across the bar, smashing the mirror."

Gant smirked. "And what the hell were you doing all this time while your customers were being assaulted? Hiding behind the bar?"

I didn't like the dig at all. "I was trying to calm everybody down. When I couldn't, I grabbed the baseball bat we keep under the bar."

"What the hell were you going to do with that?" Gant asked.

"Nothing probably. Just scare them out of the place."

"And this?" He pointed at the pink-gripped gun on the table.

I stared at the gun, didn't answer.

"Must match your underwear, huh, Marlowe?" Gant snickered.

"It's mine," Dianne said

"What do *you* need a gun for?" He spoke to her in a way he wouldn't have to a male business owner.

Dianne wasn't intimidated. "Because I usually close up *my* business and it's late at night and I usually have a good amount of cash. *That's* why."

"When they heard the sirens, they took off," I said.

Gant shrugged. "Looks like a case of over-serving customers to me."

Dianne and I looked at each other, then back at Gant. Steve was looking out the window as intently as if a parade of bikini-clad beauties were strolling by.

"You're kidding, right?" I said.

He leaned halfway across the table. "Do I look like I'm kidding?"

Unfortunately, he didn't.

"The two that caused the trouble had one beer each," I said.

Gant smirked. "They must've been big beers."

"That's very funny, Lieutenant," Dianne said. She was fuming.

Gant ignored her. "So what—were they loaded when they came in?"

I spoke slowly. "They . . . were . . . stone . . . cold . . . sober."

"I bet." Then he looked around the room. "I hate to think what they would've done if they'd been drunk."

I took a deep breath. Dianne touched my arm.

"Look," I said, trying to stay calm, "this wasn't just some drunken bar fight. First off, those two knew each other. They came in separately, started trouble with other customers, but they took off together when they heard the sirens. The whole thing was planned." I was sure of that.

Gant looked at me disgustedly. "All right, Marlowe. Let's hear it. Why would two men want to come into your . . . ahh . . . I mean Ms. Dennison's bar and start trouble?"

"Maybe because of what's been happening to some of the beach business owners? Maybe a warning from Leo Karnack?"

Gant shook his head. "None of those people have any proof that Leo Karnack's behind their troubles. We haven't found any evidence of his involvement either."

Just then I noticed a man walking by on the sidewalk outside. Our eyes locked. He had a bushy black beard. I'd seen him before. I watched him go.

"Wake up, Marlowe," Gant said. "Or are the drugs kicking in?"

I ignored what he'd said. "Karnack thinks I'm interfering with his plans. Whatever they are. The two goons were here to trash the place because of that."

"How the hell would you know?"

"I was already threatened by Karnack once."

"Your word against his. And besides, you threw his nephew off the hotel balcony. *If* he threatened you, I don't really blame him.

"I didn't throw anybody off of anything." I was getting angry now and I knew he could see it. Dianne squeezed my arm. "And you know that. You also know someone tried to burn my cottage down."

"And that's another thing." Gant's face turned dark. "That Fredette kid conveniently disappeared before I could interview him again. *And* he pulled his Houdini right after he got a visit from you."

I didn't touch that. Instead, I headed down another path. "What about my friend and I getting shot and almost run off the road up in Rye?"

"Kelly?" Gant let out a laugh. "You two have probably antagonized more people on this beach than the parking meter enforcers. Could have been anybody. I wouldn't be surprised if you two had been drinking here or at that damn Shillelagh. Probably taking something else, too, and you gave the bird to the wrong car. Road rage, maybe."

"Look here," Dianne said. Red had crept into her cheeks. I wasn't sure if it was anger or embarrassment. "My restaurant has been completely vandalized. You have the nerve to accuse my employee of being responsible for it somehow. Those thugs were *not* over-served here. Dan wouldn't do that and I don't allow it anyway. Those men came here looking for trouble. I was threatened over the phone the other night. I—"

Gant interrupted. "Did you make a police report?"

"A police report?" Dianne said incredulously. "What the hell good would that have done? By the way you're handling everything today, you probably would have arrested me for making a false report."

Two cords in Gant's neck popped and his voice rose. "I don't have to take that kind of sarcasm from you. Your hands aren't clean, either."

Dianne removed her hand from my arm, grabbed the edge of the table. "What the hell do you mean by that?"

"You're tied up with him, aren't you?" Gant nodded toward me. "Your *bartender?* Hah, he's as much the bartender here as I'm—"

Steve grabbed Gant's arm and finally spoke. "Lieutenant, we're getting off track here, aren't we?"

Gant looked down at the hand on his arm like he'd never seen one there before. He looked at it for a few seconds and then seemed to cool down a bit. "*We're* getting off track here, Inspector? *I'm* on track. It's these two friends of yours who are off track and apparently they've succeeded in bringing you along with them. I told you before—you're too close to these people."

Steve removed his hand. "My personal relationships don't influence my work."

"Sometimes I wonder," Gant said. "Anyway, I've had it. You wrap this up. Over-serving and a fight broke out. That was it. I don't see any evidence it was anything else." Gant looked back and forth from Dianne to me. "I'll be getting in touch with the Liquor Commission and letting them know this establishment is serving drunks."

Dianne came halfway over the table at Gant. His eyes popped open and his hands went instinctively to his face. When he realized she wasn't going to slug him, he brought his hands down quickly. His face was bright red. I loved it.

She was in his face now. "Listen, you sorry excuse for a cop, I've got friends on this beach and I'm *sure* you've got enemies. You tell lies about this business and I'll go to the chief and tell him my own stories. And if that doesn't get you disciplined, I'll bring it up with the selectman. I won't stop there. You hurt my business—I'll hurt your job *and* your pension."

I saw a little flicker of fear in Gant's eyes. Dianne had struck his Achilles heel. My girl was a tiger. But I had already known that.

Dianne leaned back in her seat. She seemed as calm as a flat ocean now. Gant glared at her with slitted eyes. I could almost see the steam coming from his ears and hear his teeth grinding. He was an obsessed man, but apparently he wasn't a stupid one. He said to Steve without looking at him. "Finish this up." With that he slid out of the booth and marched out of the restaurant.

"Well, that was fun," I said, hoping to break the tension. All it did was lower it a notch.

"You shouldn't insult him," Steve said to no one in particular.

"Insult him?" Dianne said. "He accused me . . . or Dan . . . of over-serving those two bums. You know I don't allow that. We told him what happened, anyhow."

Steve nodded. "I know. I know. It's just that Dan . . . and I guess you now . . . aren't Gant's favorite people."

"That goes both ways." Dianne said. "When he threatened to report us to the liquor people, that did it. My business gets completely trashed, not to mention some customers were injured, and it's my fault? Baloney."

"I think you scared him with the magic word, though. Pension," I said.

Steve slid over to the outer edge of the booth. "Maybe. But that doesn't mean you're still not on his shit list."

"You don't think it was just a random thing, do you, Steve?" Dianne asked.

"No, I don't. But if I tell him that, he'll have me walking up and down the boulevard every tourist season with the summer cops." He shuddered. It didn't look like he was kidding.

"But you can still help us?" I asked. "Right?"

"Help you? How? What do you have?"

"Well, you know most of it: Karnack trying to buy up the rest of his block. Using his nephew to scare people into selling. Karnack warning me, trying to get me to back off helping Peenell and Cliff. Fredette torching my cottage. The threatening call Dianne got. Me and Shamrock getting shot at and almost run off the road. And what about the Irish tough running the head shop in Karnack's building? The Boston lawyer that Karnack's fronting for? The one on the Claddagh Realty Trust. He's Red Foley's lawyer, too." I had to think for a few seconds before I started again. "Oh yeah, and Foley buying up Salisbury Beach property and then turning around and dumping it." I waved my hand around the dining room. "Now this."

"It's plenty, that's for sure," Steve said. "But I'm not sure it's all tied together. Anyway, I'm just a local detective, Dan. Considering Gant and everything else, what the hell can I do?"

"You could have our backs," I said. "Maybe make some inquiries that I can't. Something big's definitely going on, Steve. I'm sure of it. And I got a feeling if it comes together, Hampton Beach'll never be the same." I didn't like saying what I had to say next. "We want this beach to be just as good a place for Kelsey and everyone else who lives or vacations here as it has been for us."

He looked at me disapprovingly. I didn't blame him. I'd thrown in the name of his adopted son. Kind of low, but what I'd said was true and I believed it.

Steve thought about it for a minute. "All right. I'll see what I can find out. Try and run interference for you with Gant. But I warn you, Dan, be careful. You're riling up some dangerous people and I don't mean just Gant. Although you'd better watch out for him, too."

He turned toward Dianne, gave her a concerned half-smile. "You should be careful too, Dianne. I don't know what's going on here but it isn't good. You two are in a very dangerous spot. And probably from a few different directions. You better give Shamrock a heads-up, too. I don't want him stuffed into an ice machine again."

I chuckled nervously. A misadventure Shamrock and I had been involved in a while back had ended up with him getting put on ice. Literally.

Steve slid out of the booth, stood up, looked down at Dianne and me. "Take care, you two. I'll keep in touch." We both watched him walk out the door.

"Look at this mess," Dianne said. She slid across the bench and banged into me. "Get up. I've got to fix this place. What a nightmare."

It was that for sure. The waitresses puttered around, straightening chairs and tables, picking up what they could, but there wasn't a lot for them to do. Dianne would have to get professional help to get the place back together. She'd done it before. And it had been my fault that time too. I pushed that memory right out of my mind.

I stood up, let her out. "Do you want me to call someone about the window?" I asked.

"No. I'll take care of that." She seemed a little angry.

"What can I do?"

"Nothing. We're closed for today. *Obviously.* Why don't you just leave? Maybe you can do something to make sure this doesn't happen again. Before someone really gets hurt."

"Dianne." I reached for her hand; she pulled it away.

"Just be careful whatever you do. And don't do anything to make things worse. I'll talk to you later."

She hurried toward the kitchen and probably to her office to make calls to repairmen. I headed for the front door. Broken glass crunched under my feet. Outside there was a milling crowd of gawkers. I pushed my way through them. Police cars and a rescue truck lined the curb. Some emergency vehicles had already left for Exeter Hospital. I knew Eli and Paulie had been two of their passengers. I'd been assured by rescue personnel before they'd left that neither man was seriously hurt.

It was hot as hell out now. As I walked south on Ocean Boulevard I could feel sweat coming from every pore in my body but it wasn't just from the oppressive heat. What had just happened back at the High Tide had been the final straw. Things were escalating rapidly. And almost as bad, Dianne was more than mad at me now. Before I reached the cottage, I made a decision—to have my .38 close at hand from now on.

Chapter 27

NOTHING OF IMPORTANCE happened the rest of that day or the next three for that matter. Something did happen four days after the donnybrook at the High Tide. Shamrock and I had closed the Shillelagh the night before. I had the day off and was sleeping in. That's why I wasn't a happy camper when the phone started ringing exactly at nine a.m. I dragged myself out of bed, banged my toe on the bedroom door, and stumbled into the front room to answer it.

It was a woman's voice on the other end, a professional-sounding woman. "Mr. Marlowe?" After I mumbled an answer, she said, "Hold the line please for Attorney Tremblay."

I did. He came on quickly. "Mr. Marlowe," he said in a syrupy tone. "This is Carlton Tremblay. How are you today?"

Of course, I wasn't going to answer that truthfully. "Fine." The fog of my brain was dissipating just a bit and it was dawning on me now who this was.

"Good, Mr. Marlowe. I'm wondering if you would be able to meet with me for a business discussion. It won't take much time." When I didn't respond immediately, he added, "It might be very lucrative for you."

I couldn't say no, and not just because of the "lucrative" comment. This was *the* lawyer, yes, but I still had to be careful what I was getting into. It could be a trap. "All right. I can do that."

"Would you be willing to come to my office?"

I hesitated. His office? Would they try anything there? I doubted it. The last thing a hotshot Boston lawyer would want was any rough stuff at his place of business. To ask him to come to the beach was out of the question—too many prying eyes. And any neutral place he mentioned might really not be so neutral. So his office wasn't a bad bet.

"Okay," I said. "When?"

"Would you be available this afternoon? Say three o'clock?"

"I guess that's okay."

"All right. I'll see you then. Hold for my secretary."

Before I could respond, the pompous ass switched me over to his secretary. She gave me the address. I thanked her and hung up.

When I pulled the Chevette out of my driveway for the trip to Boston around one thirty, I felt semi-human. The hangover had receded and I'd sworn, again, never to drink. I knew that *might* last two or three days. Then again, it might not. Depending on what happened today, I might be hoisting an ice-cold Heineken by eight o'clock tonight. I was confident I'd make it until the sun went down.

I took Route 95 straight into Boston. I was lucky, traffic was light. I knew it wouldn't be on the way back. It would be rush hour. I'd made a mistake there. Should have made the appointment earlier.

On the way in, I wondered what Lawyer Tremblay wanted to discuss. I had a pretty good idea. I didn't have a good idea about what my response would be. I was distracted trying to come up with something and didn't really see any of the landmarks on the way in. Before I knew it, I'd driven fifty miles and was paying the toll to get over the Tobin Bridge into Boston. The address Tremblay's secretary had given me was in the financial district, a prominent address. It was a big building for Boston, almost forty stories high and had so many windows it seemed to be made of glass. It also had the requisite underground parking garage. Just before I got out of the car, I gave some thought to bringing the gun I'd placed in the glove box. I decided against it.

I took the elevator up to the thirty-second floor and got out in a long corridor with plush plum-colored carpeting. I followed the hallway until I came to the door I was looking for. It was easy to find. It was the only business on this floor. Carlton Tremblay's name was the first of five names in the corporate title stenciled in gold lettering on the exotic-wood door. I walked in.

The reception room looked like what I would expect a high-priced plastic surgeon's in Beverly Hills would resemble. The first things that caught my eye were the diplomas hanging on the walls. Tremblay and his associates had more degrees than Albert Einstein. As far as furnishings, there were coffee tables, two very long leather couches, and three matching barrel chairs—all very expensive looking. A few clients sat in the waiting room. There were a series of doors, all marked *Private* in a half-moon semicircle against the far wall. Centered directly in the middle and in front of the doors was a desk. I hate to call it an office desk because it was something that an oil baron would have killed for, it was that ostentatious. Seated behind the massive piece of furniture was the receptionist. She also looked like something an oil baron would have killed for.

"May I help you?" she asked. She had honey-blonde hair pulled up in a kind of aristocratic hairdo. She wore the customary glasses but they didn't disguise the fact that she was a knockout. I fantasized for a moment about what she'd look like in something more casual than expensive business attire. I gave myself a mental shake, remembered why I was there. "I have an appointment with Mr. Tremblay."

"You're Mr. Marlowe?" she asked in a businesslike tone, flashing her blue eyes at me. I was momentarily distracted. Again.

"Ahh, yes."

"Right this way. Attorney Tremblay will see you immediately." I heard a groan from one of the waiting clients.

The secretary set the papers she'd been perusing on the desk, stood, and walked the few feet to the closest *Private* door. Even her conservative dress couldn't hide what was underneath. I tore my eyes away just as she turned and opened the door for me. She motioned me in and when I walked past her, Calvin Klein's *Obsession* hit my nostrils. I only knew this because Dianne used it sometimes too.

The room I stepped into was massive and so was everything in it, including the portraits on the wall—previous partners in the firm—the furnishings, and even the man who stood behind a desk that made the secretary's look like one in a first grade class. He was thin, but it was his height that was unusual. He looked to be about six and a half feet tall. He had on a dark suit that even someone with my lack of fashion knowledge could tell was extremely expensive, a light blue shirt, and a tie that seemed to blend into it all. He had styled white hair, a sharp nose, and an old Yankee air about him. When he spoke I was sure he had *Mayflower* relatives in his bloodline.

"Mr. Marlowe, it's good to meet you." He stretched his arm across the wide desk. I took his hand. He had a limp grip; I didn't like it. "Take a seat, please."

The chair I sat in was an antique, I believe, but it was unexpectedly comfortable. He sat back down and studied me over steepled fingers as I imagined he might study a new client when he was trying to determine how much of a fee he could charge.

"May I get you something to drink? Coffee? Soda? Something stronger perhaps?"

"No, thank you. I'm fine." I glanced around. There were other paintings on the walls besides the portraits of old men. I know nothing about art but I assumed they were all expensive originals.

"Well, then—how is Hampton Beach? Anything new going on up there?"

"New? Nothing new. Same old, same old." I wasn't going to enter into a hackneyed conversation with this guy. I wanted to know what he wanted. And fast. *He* apparently wanted to feel me out. I wasn't going to help him with that.

He leaned back in his chair, smiled broadly. "It's a wonderful resort area. Hampton." He quickly frowned. "A little rundown though." Then quickly smiled again. "It could use some investment. A shot in the arm, as they say. It has quite the potential. Don't you agree?"

"I like it the way it is."

The smile dimmed. "Ahh, yes. Certainly I can see how some of the natives have a soft spot for the way it is. But progress is a wonderful thing *and* it can't be stopped anyhow. Most people would like to be abreast of change, Mr. Marlowe. Otherwise it might run them over."

From anyone else that would have been a threat, but this character was so smooth he could have said he was going to toss me down the elevator shaft and I might've wondered if that would be good for me.

"I guess I'm just an old school guy," I said. "It's a great beach. *Just the way it is.*"

Tremblay didn't like what I was saying. His face didn't really give him away; he was too good for that. But his wild unclipped white eyebrows did. They jumped up and down every time I'd finish speaking. I don't think he realized it.

I guess he'd decided he wasn't going to become my best friend, so he turned more serious. He sighed before he said, "Mr. Marlowe, I know you are aware that I'm involved with a corporation that is purchasing some property on the beach." He stopped, stared at me.

"Yes," was all I offered.

"And," he continued, "one property . . ." He stopped, fumbled with some papers on his desk with one hand as he placed glasses low on his nose with the other. When he had the document he wanted, he read an Ocean Boulevard address. He looked up at me over the glasses.

I let a slight grin creep onto my face. He knew I'd had Cliff's property transferred to me. I liked that. And I wasn't worried. I was safe here. "Yes?"

He let go of the papers, tossed his glasses on the desk. "All right, Mr. Marlowe. Let's stop fencing here. You've gained ownership of that property. The corporation I represent wants to purchase it. We want—"

I interrupted. "What do you want it for?"

Even as slippery as he was, for some reason that threw him. He hesitated before saying, "That's confidential client information."

"So it's not just you in this *corporation*? You're fronting for someone else?" I didn't really mean to be insulting. It was just that I didn't know any other way to say it. Still, I was glad I had.

Tremblay's face was redder than a lobster thrown into a boiling pot. "I don't like that term, *Mr.* Marlowe. Real estate business is often handled this way."

I was sure it often was, just not by the type of people I was convinced Tremblay was representing.

"Maybe in Boston," I said. "Not so much on Hampton Beach."

He was silent for a short minute, studying me again. "All right, Mr. Marlowe. Let's cut to the chase here. I've heard that you're an experienced businessman on the beach. And I've already explained I have a client—"

"Claddagh Realty Trust," I interrupted.

There was no look of surprise on his face. He just continued. "As I was saying, I have a client interested in that property. Would you entertain an offer?"

No, I wouldn't. But I wasn't going to tell him that. "Sure."

He beamed. "Excellent." His smile immediately turned to a frown. A frown I knew he must have used in thousands of negotiations. "Now you realize it's a very small property and the building itself needs extensive work. It might even be a teardown. But my client would like to purchase it anyway. As you know, the corporation owns the adjacent properties." Then he added quickly, "But of course it isn't necessary for them to purchase it. They just thought it might be a good idea, controlling adjacent property." Smiling again, he asked, "What figure did you have in mind?"

"One million dollars." Now I was smiling and Attorney Tremblay wasn't.

His voice was flat when he finally said, "You're joking?"

"No. I'm as serious as a fishhook in an eye."

He fooled around with the papers on his desk. He didn't look at them. I knew he was gathering his thoughts. When he was finished with the housekeeping, he stopped and said, "That property isn't worth a third of that figure."

"It is if someone will pay it." I tried to keep the smirk off my face. I don't think I succeeded.

"No one will ever pay that!"

"Then I guess I won't sell it then."

"Now, Mr. Marlowe, let's be reasonable here. I am prepared to make you a very nice offer. But *not* one million dollars."

"Like I said, that's my price. Nothing less."

Tremblay's facade began to crumble right before my eyes. His prominent Adam's apple moved up and down like a bouncing ball and he tugged at his tie. This from a man who ate people like me for lunch. So I knew it was someone else who had him acting like he was the comic relief in a haunted house movie. And I also knew that to make this old Brahmin sweat bullets, it had to be someone very big. *And* very dangerous. "Please, Mr. Marlowe. Can't you reconsider? A more reasonable price? You'll still be making out quite nicely."

Tremblay moved around in his chair like his hemorrhoids were flaring. I almost felt sorry for the man. I knew there was no way Red Foley would pay a million bucks for Cliff's building. And it looked like Tremblay knew it too. I didn't envy him having to go back to Foley to tell him that he couldn't get what he wanted. Foley wouldn't like that.

"No," I said. "That's my price."

The old Yankee looked like he hadn't expected this and hadn't prepared for it. "All right. I'll . . . I'll take it up with my client. But I don't think it will do any good."

I stood up. He stood too, but he rose like he'd aged ten years in the past few minutes. We shook hands. It was even limper than before, like a string of over-cooked spaghetti.

Before I turned for the door, Tremblay looked at me with desperate eyes that actually seemed to be watering. Old age? An eye condition? I wasn't sure. "If you have a change of mind, Mr. Marlowe, please call me immediately. My secretary will put you right through to me." He glanced down at his desk. "In fact, take this." He removed a business card from a holder on his desk. He wrote something on the back, then handed it to me.

I examined the card. He'd written a telephone number there. I could feel the raised lettering on the front.

"That's my . . ." he cleared his throat before he finished. "My home telephone number. Call me at any time of the day or night if you wish to moderate your price."

I wondered how often he handed out his home phone number. Not much, I was sure.

We said our goodbyes. My last impression of Carlton Tremblay was that he looked as uncomfortable as someone about to make their first parachute jump.

On the drive out of Boston, I had lots of time to think. I'd stupidly agreed to a time that assured I'd be heading home during the rush hour. The traffic was horrendous. If it was any slower, it would have been going backwards. Anyway it gave me time to mull over my consultation with Attorney Tremblay.

I'd known that Cliff was going to tell Tremblay he'd sold his property to me. Temporarily, of course. Although Tremblay wouldn't know that. That's how we'd planned it. I had only recently approached Cliff with the idea. I had a plan, and for it to work it would be better to have Cliff's building in my name. At first, he had resisted. He knew the whole story about Fredette getting his granddaughter all strung out to put pressure on him to sell his property. About Karnack being behind Fredette. And Red Foley behind Karnack. He wanted to fight Foley and his gang head on. And he had good reason too. His granddaughter hadn't even made it to rehab. She was in a hospital with both severe physical and mental problems caused by mainlining the meth. Cliff wasn't sure she'd ever be normal again and he wanted those responsible for his granddaughter's condition to pay. But he was old and his health wasn't good. I'd convinced him I would have a better shot at pulling my plan off and resisting whatever blowback was to come. Finally, he'd agreed.

So now I was the owner of property that Tremblay, or more correctly Red Foley, wanted badly. I still didn't know why. It certainly wasn't just because of what the lawyer had said about it being adjacent to their other property. It had to be more. A lot more.

I also knew that Red Foley would never pay a million dollars for Cliff's little place. That was an outrageous figure, as I'd intended. Not only would a man like Foley not allow himself to be taken advantage of, I also felt that that price was so high it might very well throw a monkey wrench into whatever he had planned.

By the time I finally broke free of city traffic and reached Route 95, I'd come to the conclusion that I had to be on high alert now. Foley knew I was the only thing standing between him and his plans, whatever the hell they were. And the minute he spoke to Tremblay he'd also learn I couldn't be bought off. I knew in Foley's world that would leave him only one option.

I glanced at the glove compartment and felt a bit better knowing the .38 was in there. By the time I crossed the Hampton Bridge that feeling had worn off. I was having second thoughts. Like anyone in my shoes would have. And I had no one to blame but myself. I'd put myself in this position. And now I had to see it through to the end. I'd left myself no other choice.

Chapter 28

IT WAS SUPPER time when I returned to the cottage. I ate and then called Shamrock. I had to touch base with him, let him know what was going on and find out if he'd picked up on anything new. I agreed to take the five-minute walk to his house later that evening. I took my gun along for company. When I reached his house, it was just beginning to turn dark. I could still see the shamrock hanging above the door of the small weathered clapboard home as I walked up the rickety steps. My shoulder grazed the green, white, and orange flag of Ireland on a pole protruding from the edge of the porch roof.

Inside, the first thing Shamrock asked was, "Shall we head up to the Shillelagh?"

"Later, maybe. I've got to talk to you privately. Besides, it's too damn noisy up there to talk anyway."

"All right, then. Grab a seat. I'll get the adult beverages."

I plopped myself down on the worn sofa. Shamrock's place was a standard bachelor pad. A bachelor pad where the bachelor didn't have much money. Kind of like me, I guess. He kept it clean, though. As clean as he could. But he could have used some decorating advice. Everything was mismatched, old and dark. And if it wasn't for Shamrock's jovial presence, it would have been downright depressing. The television sat in a corner on what was once an end table. The box was on, the sound off. Some old movie I couldn't identify was on the screen. There was the smell of old ashes and burnt wood from the fireplace Shamrock would use during the colder seasons.

It only took him a minute to return with the beer. He handed me a Heineken and a chilled mug. He must have poured his in the kitchen because his mug was already filled with the dark Guinness beer he loved. He sat in his customary chair off to my side. It was well used and probably had more farts in it than those in a nursing home's day room.

I explained to him what had happened earlier with the lawyer.

"Ahh, Danny, I don't like this." He took a quick gulp from his mug. "Now you're the only thing standing in the way of them getting their dirty hands on a building they want."

"It's better me than Cliff, Shamrock. He's a nice guy but an old man. He wouldn't stand a chance. At least I know what I'm dealing with and can take precautions."

"Aye, but I'm not sure that'll do any good." Shamrock furrowed his red brows. "A million dollars, Danny? That's a lot of money. Would Cliff want to sell if that barrister changes his mind?"

I frowned. "He wouldn't sell it to Foley for ten million. He wants him to pay for what happened to his granddaughter. And Cliff's like us—he doesn't want to see Hampton turned into a cesspool which is what will happen if Foley and his gang get their way."

Shamrock took a swig of beer, sighed, and set the mug down on a table beside him. "So what will happen now? What do we do?"

I shook my head. "There's nothing left to do. Hopefully the lawyer'll tell Foley there's no way I'll sell and he'll lose interest in Hampton Beach."

Shamrock reached for his beer. A bit of it sloshed over the mug's side as he hastily brought it up to his lips. "Ain't that a wee bit of wishful thinking, Danny boy?"

Of course he was right. A man like Red Foley more'n likely wouldn't give up so easy. On the other hand, and that's the hand I was betting on, there just didn't seem to be enough money to hold Foley's interest, especially if it was too much of a hassle to acquire the property.

The only reasons I could come up with that would attract Foley to the beach just didn't seem worth it. There was Eddie Hoar's puny drug business, along with those of maybe a couple other small-time dealers. The head/knife shop couldn't have been making enough in ten weeks to interest him more than a little. And I remembered now that beach real estate was in a slump. It would take years, if not decades, before he could sell the buildings at a profit. And the beach businesses like Peenell's hotel and Cliff's gift shop? There was no big money there. I knew for a fact they had to work twelve-hour days, seven days a week in-season just for a moderate income. Those certainly weren't the types of businesses Red Foley would be attracted to.

No, I just didn't see how he could make much money on the beach. Certainly nothing compared to a place like the Silver Slipper in Salisbury, the kind of business that wasn't allowed in Hampton anyway. I could only imagine how lucrative his Boston businesses were.

I shook my head again. "It's just not worth it to him. It can't be." I drained my beer in one gulp.

Shamrock did the same, jiggled the empty mug in his hand. "Another? Or you want to head for the Shillelagh now?"

I was just about to answer when I heard a fast shuffling on the front porch steps and the door was thrown open. The Irish thug from the head shop stormed into the room. He still wore his scally cap. He also had a wicked-looking magnum in his right hand, pointed directly at me. Behind him was another man. He was short, thin, and his face looked like a potato. A real runt. The Runt closed the door behind him and locked it.

Shamrock sat up with a start. "Hey, what the fuck . . . ?"

"Stay put, mate," said the Runt. He had a high feminine voice.

The two of them stood there and stared at us. I never realized that magnums had such big barrels. I felt my breath going shallow and I wished I could pop one of the Xanax tablets in the scrip bottle in my jeans pocket. I took a couple of deep breaths. It didn't help.

"What do you want?" I managed to say.

"You know what we want, asshole," Scally Cap said. "You been making yourself a real pain in the ass around here. And you've had enough chances."

My heart started to gallop. I had the unpleasant thought that they were going to kill us right then and there.

I must have showed my fear because Scally Cap said in his thick brogue, "Don't crap your pants, Marlowe. We ain't here for you. We didn't even know you was here. Did we?"

He glanced at the shorter man beside him who shook his head. Scally Cap continued. "I guess someone wants you in one piece for some reason. We're here to show you what's gonna happen to your girlfriend and your kids if you don't play ball."

He stopped for a moment, smirked. "We're gonna demonstrate on him." He waved the magnum at Shamrock whose eyes were as wide as a full moon. "And seeing you're here, you can see now—instead of visiting him in the hospital tomorrow—what's in store for your slut and your brats." He let out a sick little chuckle before nodding to his partner.

The Runt pulled something from his back pocket. I'd only seen them before in old B movies, never in real life, but I knew right away what it was—a sap, a blackjack, a persuader. Whatever you wanted to call it, it was bad news. Like a little night stick on steroids. The thing was made of soft black leather and had a flexible strap handle. The business end bulged about the size of a small fist. I figured that part was stuffed with lead weight. It was a mean-looking thing. I could imagine the damage it was capable of doing to flesh and bone. If he used it on Shamrock, he'd be hurt bad. Maybe not even survive. I had to think fast.

The Runt held the blackjack by the handle and slapped the fat end against the palm of his other hand. I could tell this wasn't the first time he'd handled one. He turned his gaze from me to Shamrock. The Runt grinned. Easy enough to see he was going to enjoy this.

Shamrock shoved deeper into his chair. "Now hold on there, lad," he said, his voice shaking.

When I spoke, my voice was shaking too. "Wait a minute, wait a minute. What if I tell you that you can have whatever you want? I mean it. I'll sign over that property." Then stupidly I added, "Cheap, too."

They both laughed. "We already know that, Marlowe. We're just gonna make sure you still feel that way in the morning." Scally Cap tipped his head at the Runt who took a couple of steps closer to Shamrock. Shamrock threw his arms up to protect his face.

I could feel the .38 in the small of my back like it was an asylum patient tapping at me for a cigarette. Yes, I had it, but I didn't know what good it was going to do. Scally Cap had his eyes glued on me, the magnum pointed dead center at my chest.

The Runt grinned like an insane person, thumping the sap against his palm. Shamrock had one of his legs up now. I didn't know if that was a good move. Better a broken arm than a leg.

The Runt moved so fast I could barely see it. His arm shot forward and his wrist seemed to move like he was handling a lasso. The sap whipped back and forth once like it was made of elastic and then connected with the back of Shamrock's forearm in a sickening noise. I could hear bone shatter and Shamrock howled like I'd never heard anyone howl before, let alone my friend. He doubled over his arm, cradling it into his stomach. The moans were awful. All I could see was the top of his head. Then he was silent, just holding his arm. It took a little while before I realized he was out cold. Scally Cap let out a laugh. "You look worse than him," he said to me. "Have a drink of your beer. There's more to come."

I reached for the mug, had it up to my lips before I realized it was empty.

I watched as the Runt lifted Shamrock's head and pushed him back in his chair. Shamrock's head lolled from side to side, loose as a Times Square streetwalker on Friday night.

The Runt walked to the kitchen and came back with a glass of water. He threw the liquid into Shamrock's face.

Shamrock shook, started to come around.

"Wake up, ya fuckin' fire crotch," the Runt said. Then quickly glancing at Scally Cap, he added, "No offense." Scally Cap glowered.

Shamrock was conscious now, but his eyes were rolling and he wasn't focused. He reached with his right hand, touched the arm that took the blow. "Ohhh, sweet Jesus," he moaned.

I snuck a peek at Scally Cap. He still held the magnum on me, but he kept glancing at Shamrock and smiling. He was enjoying this too. Even though his eyes strayed every so often, I didn't think there was any way I could get the gun out in time. He'd be able to empty his before I got mine free.

The Runt stepped closer to Shamrock and started his little warmup again, slapping the heavy leather sap against his other palm.

I didn't need Scally Cap to say it, but he did anyway. "Here comes the big finale, Marlowe. We'll make it a good one just for you. Kinda like the end of the Wednesday night fireworks."

The Runt smiled like a rabid weasel. "Ya ever hear a jawbone crack?"

No, I never had. And I didn't plan to now. Just the thought of that sap smashing Shamrock's jaw sent a wave of nausea through my body. Shamrock was awake but his eyes were glassy. He was holding his injured arm and moaning. I couldn't tell if he was aware of what was about to happen.

The Runt rhythmically slapped his palm with the sap. I didn't know when it would snap out and shatter my friend's jaw. The last time it had happened so fast I'd barely seen it. I had to move.

Scally Cap looked toward the Runt. "Stop fuckin' around. Take care a bus . . ."

He never finished his sentence. I still had hold of the heavy beer mug on the table beside me. I threw it as hard and as fast as I could. Thank god, my aim was good. It struck Scally Cap on the side of his head. He fired the magnum, but the shot went high. The roar was deafening, but I was glad to hear it. The slug crashed into something behind me.

I jumped off the couch and barreled into Scally Cap, struggling to get my .38 out. I was surprised how easy he went down with me on top of him. His gun slipped from his hand. I had my left forearm against his throat, pushing as hard as I could. He bucked underneath me. Out of the corner of my eye, I'd seen Shamrock somehow raise himself from the couch. He had the Runt's sap arm locked up with his good one. The Runt was trying to throw him off, but even in his condition, Shamrock was still strong enough to hang on.

Blood streamed from a cut on the side of Scally Cap's head. I had my .38 out now and he was trying to grab my gun hand. He was a big guy and I knew I'd be no match for him. I pushed myself backward. Landed on my ass facing him. He saw his gun a few feet away from him, jumped to his feet.

I leveled the .38 at him. "Don't try it."

He stood there, blood running down the side of his face, dripping off his jaw. He looked at me, then at the gun on the floor, than back at me. I could almost hear him weighing the odds, wondering what I would, what I *could* do. My gun hand was rock solid. Everything was happening too fast to be frightened. I would have shot him in a heartbeat. He must've seen it in my eyes. Even still, his next move surprised me. He turned, ran for the door.

I almost did it—pulled the trigger, shot him in the back. But Scally Cap must've been a good judge of men. I didn't shoot.

I stumbled to my feet just as Runt freed himself. Shamrock collapsed to the couch. Runt turned toward me. His rat-like eyes swiveled around, looking for his partner. Both of us turned toward the door as the engine of a car roared to life outside.

Runt's eyes widened. He looked back at me, glanced at the gun pointed directly at him. I was too far away for him to use the sap. I wasn't going to let that change.

Runt spoke. "All right, mate," he said hurriedly. "You win. We won't bother you no more." The tires of the car outside squealed.

Runt glanced frantically at the door. "I'm going now." He stepped sideways in front of me, then backed quickly toward the door.

Maybe I should have just let him go but just then I heard a godawful moan from Shamrock. I aimed for a specific spot and fired until I hit it. The first two shots missed him completely. The third caught Runt where I'd hoped it would—in the meaty part of his bicep. He screamed and the sap went flying. He grabbed his arm, turned, and almost tumbled over as he banged against the door frame on his way out. I heard him fall as he went down the stairs. Then he shouted, "Don't leave me!"

I could hear the car jam on the brakes, a door open and slam shut. The car sped to the end of the street and peeled out onto Ashworth Avenue. I heard the brakes of another car, waited for the crash. It didn't come.

I dropped my gun on the floor, went to Shamrock. He cradled his arm. My friend was hurting bad. His eyes watered heavily. Not crying really, just tears of pain. I would've grabbed the keys to his car and taken him to Exeter Hospital myself, but it was too late for that.

Footsteps thudded on the porch stairs and then faces appeared in the doorway. The looks I saw were half fear, half concern. Neighbors. They'd heard the commotion. The gunshots, especially from the magnum, would have woken a hibernating bear.

The first person to step into the room was a woman who definitely wasn't a tourist. She was seventy if she was a day, with gray hair in a bun. The robe she held tightly around her was like something my mother used to wear.

Her bony hand flew up to her mouth. "Oh, my god. It's Shamrock. He's been shot." She turned toward the door. "Call an ambulance, quick."

A long-haired man hurried in next. "We already called the cops." The words had barely left his lips when I heard the sirens in the distance.

Chapter 29

BY THE TIME the ambulance, Shamrock on board, pulled away, the inside of his cottage was a madhouse. Shamrock was a popular man on Hampton Beach. Even more so down here where he lived. The neighbors were pumped by police for information before they were herded out. They all talked a lot, but none really said anything. A few had seen the car, no one had thought to get the plate number. The police had an eyewitness to everything though—me. But with what was going on now, you'd think I was a suspect and not a witness and victim myself.

I was using my tongue to try and get the taste of gunpowder out of my mouth when I heard, "Marlowe, get your ass in that chair and don't get out of it."

That line was spoken by Lieutenant Gant, of course. He stared at me with fire in his eyes. I sat myself down in the chair he was pointing to. Besides Gant the only ones left in the room were four uniformed Hampton Police, another detective from the Hampton force, a couple of uniformed state police troopers who were among those assigned to Hampton on summer nights, and two gloved crime scene inspectors. The crime scene people were examining the blood Runt had left behind on the floor after I'd shot him. One of them stepped over to Gant, whispered in his ear.

Gant listened, then brushed the techie away and glared at me. "Tell me what happened."

I told him everything. Exactly as it went down. The look on his face told me he didn't believe a word of it.

Gant stepped closer, looked down at me. "So now you think *Red Foley* is Leo Karnack's boss? And one of them sent the owner of the head shop and another guy down here, for no good reason, and assaulted your . . . ahh . . . *friend* and you shot one of them. Is that it?"

I didn't like his tone. He spoke as if I'd just recited a fairy tale. "No, that's not right. They did have a reason."

Gant blew air through his lips. "I'm sure they did. You've probably been harassing them too. You seem to enjoy doing that to people on the beach. It's kind of like a hobby with you, isn't it? I don't know how you've lived this long."

"I haven't *harassed* anybody. I told you they're Red Foley's men. That he's trying to take over parts of the beach. Why, I don't know, but I've been trying to help some business people he's forcing out. Obviously, he doesn't like it."

"Nothing's obvious with you, Marlowe. I don't believe those men work for Red Foley. Why the hell would a gangster like Foley be interested in a place like Hampton Beach? A ten-week season, then it folds up like a card table. Even if your visitors were tied into Foley, it's more likely they're after your drug business than any legitimate beach business."

"My *drug* business? What the hell are you talking about, Gant?"

"It's *Lieutenant* Gant and what I'm talking about is your association with Eddie Hoar and his dumb sidekick. We keep a close eye on those two sleaze bags and you've been observed with them." Gant looked at me smugly, then said, "They're not too bright, to put it mildly. Someone's supplying them and pulling their strings. They wouldn't know what to do otherwise. Christ, they couldn't operate a hot dog stand. We've been looking for their supplier for a while. I think it might be you."

"You've lost your mind, Gant."

Gant's face came down close to mine. It was beet red. "Look, you little weasel. Somebody's been shot here. On Hampton Beach. *My* beach. And *you* shot them." Spittle came flying out of his mouth. A couple of drops hit me in the face. "Everywhere you are, there's trouble. You're a cancer on this beach, Marlowe. And I plan to cut you out."

More drops of spittle hit me in the face. I stood up but Gant was crowding me so much, I bumped into him. He took a step back. His face was purple now.

"You just assaulted a police officer," he shouted. Every head in the place turned to look except one. And I was damn lucky that person had already been watching us. Steve Moore. He was standing in the doorway, dressed in a T-shirt and jeans. His gun was on his hip.

Gant reached for me. "Turn around."

Steve came over, held up his hand. "Lieutenant, you aren't going to arrest him for that, are you?"

Gant looked at Steve like he was me. "You bet your ass I am and it's none of your goddamn business."

Thankfully, Steve wasn't intimidated. "Lieutenant, he bumped you. That was all. It was an accident."

"Bumped?" Gant said it like he had no idea what the word meant.

Steve lowered his voice. "Yes, I saw it from the doorway."

Gant stared at Steve like he was debating whether to arrest him instead of me. He looked back and forth between us. Then he glanced around the room at the other personnel watching the scene. They all looked quickly away. Gant's color slowly went from purple to red to close to normal again.

He glared at me like I was dirt. "Inspector McSweeney's going to handle the rest of your interview, Marlowe. I'm not wasting any more time on you." He turned toward Steve. "You're not on duty now. Go home. I'll talk to you later." He walked away in the direction of the other detective who was examining one of the pistols.

When Gant was out of ear shot, Steve said softly, "Now you've done it."

Steve and I were standing, facing each other. "Done what? For Chrissake, Steve, they broke Shamrock's arm with a black-jack and were just about to use it on his face when I made a move."

"So you shot him?"

"I shot one of them. The little one with the blackjack. But that was after the big guy took a shot at me with a magnum." I rubbed my ears with my hands. "My ears are still ringing."

"I bet." He pointed behind me. I turned to see one of the techies working on a large hole in the back wall. "If that had hit you, you'd be missing something now. Either that or dead."

Dead. A slight wave of nausea rolled through me. "Steve, I saw the lawyer I told you about. He tried to buy me off. Something big is going on. I have to find out what. Not just for me. For my friends, my family, and the whole damn beach.

"Now you're sounding hysterical."

He was probably right. I fought to calm myself down. I wasn't going to get anywhere if I didn't have Steve on my side. When I felt a little calmer, I said, "I know something very bad and very big is going on here, Steve."

"Maybe, but—"

He was interrupted by a shout from Gant. "Break it up over there, Moore. Out!"

Inspector McSweeney stepped up to us, looked at Steve, made a face, and shrugged. "Sorry, Steve. Gant wants me to handle it."

"I know. I'm going," Steve said.

"Steve, you believe . . ." I started, before he waved me off.

"I'll talk to you later." He turned and headed across the room and out the door.

"He's a nice guy," McSweeney said.

"Yeah, he is," I answered. "A real nice guy."

Chapter 30

THE NEXT MORNING I walked slowly to the High Tide for my shift. I stared at the low black clouds hanging over the Atlantic and the white caps being churned up by a strong wind and thought about what had happened the previous night. How close Shamrock had come to being permanently injured. I tried to shake that terrifying thought out of my mind. Think more about why it had almost happened and what it all meant. About how I could resolve the entire mess without my family or any of my friends being hurt in the process, any more than they had been. But I was baffled by the whole thing and had to admit I had no idea what to do.

I'd called the hospital first thing that morning. I'd been told Shamrock had been treated and released. I didn't call his house. I assumed he might be sleeping in, recuperating. So I was surprised when I came in the back door of the Tide and heard him call my name from Dianne's office. I stepped inside. Dianne sat behind her desk, looking worried. The few light laugh lines she had on her face were deeper than I'd ever seen them. On the couch to my right was Shamrock in his restaurant whites. The only difference was that the left arm of the long-sleeved white work shirt had been chopped off at the shoulder. His arm was in a cast. The cast was in a white sling.

He looked up at me glumly. "Hello, Danny."

"Jesus, Shamrock, are you okay?"

He waved his free hand. "I'm fine, fine. A clean break, that's all. Doc said it'll heal proper."

"How long do you have to wear that?"

"Too long."

"Hurt much?"

"A wee bit." Then he brightened, chuckled. "But they gave me some very pleasant pain pills. Want any, Danny?"

"No, he doesn't," Dianne said angrily.

"Only kidding," Shamrock said sheepishly. Then he added, "About Danny wanting any, I mean."

"Sit down," Dianne said.

I sat in a folding chair in front of the desk and scooted a bit closer to Shamrock.

I knew what was coming and Dianne didn't prove me wrong. "This is just lovely," she said. She pointed an index finger in Shamrock's direction.

"I'll still be able to work," Shamrock said, holding his right arm, fist closed, up in the air and shaking it. "I've still got my strong right arm."

"I don't mean that," she said irritably. "I mean what's going to happen next?" She looked at me. "Shamrock's told me the whole story. We've got to forget this crusade you're on, Dan. Otherwise someone else is going to get hurt. Or worse."

I let out a sigh like I was letting out my last breath. "Dianne, I'm sorry about what happened to Shamrock but . . ."

"It's not just what they did to him." She said it as if Shamrock wasn't there. "It's everything. I don't have to say it all. Too much has happened. You can't stop them from getting what they want. And . . ." Her green eyes narrowed. "And I'm worried about your children, Davy and Jess. These people have threatened them. They mean it, Dan. Look at Shamrock. You're going to have to stop this now while there's still time."

"There might not be time," I said.

"You can't know that for sure. You can't make that bet. You don't have the right. Even if you don't care about your own life, you have to think of your kids."

She was right, of course. I couldn't deny that. "These people are trying to take over the beach, Dianne. I don't know why but I'm sure of it." It sounded lame even to me.

Two angry little furrow lines formed between her brows. "They own a couple of properties on the beach. So what? Is that worth your kids' lives?"

She wasn't going to give up that tack. I didn't blame her; it was working. "You didn't think that before. You agreed with me that if they got control, they'd ruin Hampton."

She picked up a pen off the desk, then set it down heavily. "Well, now I think we were being melodramatic. No one wants control of this beach, Dan. Why the heck would they? I have one business and that's enough of a pain in the butt. No one's getting rich either. *You* know that."

She knew all the buttons to push. Even still, I could tell it was more than my kids that she was worried about. I knew Dianne as well as I knew this beach. She was worried about me, too. Maybe even more than my children. She knew if she said it, though, it wouldn't stop me. And she was right. It wouldn't have.

Shamrock hadn't said a word. I looked at him sitting there with his busted arm in a sling. His lips were thin and tight. He didn't look happy. I thought about what might have happened if Runt had gone further with the sap. "What do you think?" I asked him.

He moved his butt around on the sofa. "Well, Danny," he began very slowly, "Dianne might be right. Maybe Foley just wants those properties because he's got nothing else to do with his money. You weren't positive he was trying to take over the beach. You were just speculating. I guess I got carried away with that idea. There's nothing here for him. Sometimes I wonder if there's anything here for me."

Oddly, that last sentence stunned me. Shamrock was Mr. Hampton Beach. He loved the place. I'd never heard him say anything like that before. Dianne cleared her throat.

"Oh, yeah," Shamrock continued. "And what about Davy and Jess? It's not worth anything happening to them." He stopped. I could see he wanted to say something else. He glanced at Dianne, then back at me. "But I'll help you anyway, Danny. Whatever you decide. You're my best friend."

Dianne glared at him.

"I hear you both," I said.

"Then you'll stop this crusade you're on?" Her face wasn't angry now. It wasn't happy either. More hopeful, I guess.

"Let me think about it a little bit."

"Oh my god, are you thick!" Dianne was angry again. "Well, think fast. Please!" Then she turned to Shamrock. "And don't you help him to think the wrong way either!" She got up from her chair. "I've got work to do."

She stormed out of the office, slamming the door behind her.

I looked at Shamrock. He shrugged. "She's probably right, Danny. Maybe it's for the best."

"Maybe."

We both got to our feet like we'd aged twenty years in the past twenty minutes. Before we left the office, Shamrock said, "You know if you still have trouble, Danny, I'll help you. I'll always be there." He straightened up, a little Irish fire coming into his eyes. "You know Michael Kelly's not afraid of anyone. Especially when they might be hurting Hampton Beach."

That made me smile. A little anyway. As much as I could under the circumstances.

Then, as an afterthought, he added, "Don't tell Dianne I said any of that though. She'll have my red scalp on a pole."

My smile grew a bit bigger. We both trudged out of the office and into the kitchen. Shamrock stopped there, joined Dianne and Guillermo who were busy prepping. Dianne's gaze followed me as I walked into the dining room and toward the bar.

I reached the front door just in time to hear someone pounding on it. Glancing up at the Clydesdale clock over the bar, I saw that it was 11:05. I hurried to the register, got the key out, went back and opened the door. Eli trooped in with Paulie right behind him. Evidently their injuries hadn't been too serious. Still, I hadn't seen them since the brawl.

"You're late again," Eli said. He had a large square bandage covering one side of his face. "Don't do it no more. You're lucky we're here as it is." He brushed past me and marched to his center stool.

Paulie scooted in behind him. "Dan," he said as he walked past me. I wasn't happy to see him sporting one of the worst black eyes I'd ever seen.

I hurried around to the business side of the bar to get them their beers, pleased to see they'd returned. While I was grabbing Paulie's beer, he called out, "Gimme a shot of brandy, too, will you please, Dan?"

"Sure," was all I said even though it was very unusual for Paulie to have anything except beer. In all the years I'd been serving him, I'd never seen him drink liquor here.

Then I got another surprise. Eli chimed in with, "Well, you might as well set me up with one of those things, too. I never drink hard stuff no more. Used to make me mean." Then he glanced from side to side, like there were other people seated at the bar. "But this is a tough place now. Any damn thing could happen. So I need it to calm my nerves."

Unfortunately, it didn't sound like he was joking, so I didn't say anything. Before I could grab the bar brandy bottle, Eli said, "Seeing this is for medicinal reasons, you might as well make it that Corvarsseo stuff."

The same top-shelf brandy Eddie Hoar liked to spend my money on. At least Eddie could pronounce it correctly. I pulled the bottle down from the back bar. They both shouted in unison, "Rocks."

I poured them their drinks over ice, a lot more than a shot. Then I placed the drinks and the beers down in front of them.

Eli pulled out the short sipping straw I'd stuck in his rocks glass and tossed it onto the bar. "No damn straw," he said disgustedly. He raised the glass to his thin, dry lips and took a sip. He made a face like I'd given him a glass of lemon juice. "You sure that's the Corvarsseo?" he asked as his whole body shuddered.

I nodded, looked down the bar. Paulie was using his straw like a vacuum. After he'd swallowed the big pull, he looked at the glass in his hand like it held 300-year-old cognac. "Very good," he said.

While I ran around the bar like a whirlwind, trying to get everything ready, I chatted with my two customers, my friends. "I'm glad you guys both came back. I've missed you."

"We almost didn't," Eli shouted as I dashed by him, tossing ashtrays on the bar. "This damn place is like a war zone."

Paulie was coming alive now, too. The brandy had loosened him up already. "Yeah, and we should get combat pay for coming. Or at least the drinks should be free."

Eli jumped on that like he'd spotted a saw buck on the floor. "That's a damn good idea. And after what happened to us?" He pointed at the bandaid on his cheek.

Paulie laughed. "He got two damn stitches, Dan. He's been playing it up like he got hit with shrapnel."

Eli glowered in Paulie's direction. "Like I was sayin' . . . a drink or two on the house wouldn't hurt none."

I knew Dianne had already spoken to Eli and Paulie and that the Tide's insurance was going to take care of their medical bills. None of the bartenders were supposed to give out free drinks, as opposed to when I'd almost ran the place into the ground. Some days I'd been so out of it, I'd given away more booze than I'd sold. Still, if these guys didn't deserve a free drink after what had happened to them, I didn't know who did.

"The brandies are on me," I said, looking from one man to the other. "And keep it under your hats, please."

"Oh, that goes without saying, Dan," Paulie said, tipping his glass in my direction. "And thanks."

"Don't you get any perks for being the owner's boyfriend?" Eli muttered. "Goddamn world's gone crazy." He saw me frown and added, "Thanks."

Just then Shamrock came around from the dining room, walked to the service end of the bar, and got himself a soda out of the tonic gun.

Eli was the first to speak. "What the hell happened to you?"

"I got my arm caught in the dishwasher," Shamrock answered, not looking up.

"Jesus Murphy," Eli said. "This place is going to hell in a handbasket."

"You ought to get combat pay working here, too," Paulie added.

"Aye," was all Shamrock said before disappearing back around the partition.

"Busted?" Eli asked.

"Yeah," I answered. "It'll be all right though."

"He's lucky the damn machine didn't chop his arm right off," Eli said, nodding.

Paulie chuckled. "He was just pulling your chain."

"Naw, he wasn't," Eli responded. "Those big dishwashers can be damn treacherous."

"Oh, bullshit," Paulie said before blowing a series of smoke rings toward the ceiling.

"Is that how he did it or not, Dan?" Eli looked at me with his white eyebrows arched.

I was saved from answering by bar customers coming through the door. I wouldn't have told Eli what happened anyhow. This was their first day back since the brawl and I didn't want to listen to Eli go on and on about it. Of course, the story might be in the *Union* next week, but I'd worry about that then.

What I did want to do was work. Work and try to make a decision about what Dianne, Shamrock, and I had just discussed in her office.

Dianne was right, I knew that. It *had* gone too far. *I* had gone too far. Someone I loved was going to be hurt or killed. I'd been a fool to think I could somehow take on Leo Karnack, not to mention Red Foley. I must've been out of my mind. I was in way over my head.

I threw myself on automatic pilot again, so I had the entire shift to think. There was only one idea I could come up with. A way I might be able to get myself and my loved ones out of the situation I'd gotten us all into. It was a dangerous option. As dangerous as something could be. But it was the only option I had.

When my shift ended, I went to the pay phone near the front. I wanted more privacy than I might have gotten from the bar phone, with its three extensions. I took the business card out of my wallet. I dropped some coins in the slot, dialed the number. It rang twice.

"Law office," the clipped female voice said.

"I'd like to speak to Attorney Tremblay, please."

"Attorney Tremblay is out of the office right now. May I take a message?"

I took a shot that this was a run-of-the-mill response from a busy lawyer's secretary. "This is Dan Marlowe. He said I should call him at any time."

By the change in her tone you'd think I'd just told her I was the mayor of Boston. "Yes, Mr. Marlowe. Certainly, Mr. Marlowe. As a matter of fact, he's just returned to his office. I'll put you right through."

I barely had time to compose my words before Tremblay came on the line.

"Mr. Marlowe. I'm glad to hear from you. How have you been?"

I knew he didn't really want to know, so I didn't answer. Instead, I said, "I've decided to possibly take your advice."

"Splendid," he said. "When would you like to come in and discuss a reasonable price?"

"I want to talk to Red Foley face to face first."

He gasped like I'd just asked him to sell me a kilo of heroin. "I don't think that is possible." His voice actually shook a bit. I didn't think that happened often, if ever. He cleared his throat, continued in his normal rock-steady tone. "And I *never* discuss other clients."

"That's the only way it'll happen," I said. "If I can have a meeting with him."

"*That* won't happen," Tremblay said forcefully.

"Then *it* won't happen."

"Mr. Marlowe, please. Be reasona—" I hung up.

There was one thing I was sure of. Only one person could guarantee that if I dropped my probing into what was going on around Hampton Beach, my friends and family would be safe. And that person wasn't Leo Karnanck, Lawyer Tremblay, the Runt or Scally Cap or anyone else for that matter. The only one who had that power was the top man himself—Red Foley.

Chapter 31

MY ANSWER CAME a lot sooner than I thought it would. That night. Just after nine thirty. I'd finished my first beer when the phone rang. It was Leo Karnack.

"You know the place Eddie Hoar got bounced out of?" he asked.

I knew he meant the Silver Slipper. I also knew enough to do as he did and not mention it over the phone. "Yes," was all I said.

"Be there at two o'clock this morning." He said it like a command.

"I've got no interest in meeting with you, Karnack."

"Look you . . ." Then I could hear him take a deep breath before he continued, a bit less hostile this time. "You're meeting with someone else."

"Who?"

"What, I gotta spell it out for you?"

He didn't have to. I knew who I'd be meeting and I didn't like the sound of it. I don't know what I expected. Maybe to meet Foley in a tea room or something. But the Slipper *did* make sense. I just didn't like being told so late at night and with no time to think it over. But on the other hand, it was better than not hearing anything. I couldn't back out now. I had to take the chance.

"I'll be there."

"Park out back," he said. "Come in that way."

I hung up, and looked back and forth between the television and the clock on the wall for the next few hours. Before I left, I popped a Xanax. That was the least I could do for myself.

It was 1:59 when I parked the Chevette against the back wall of the Silver Slipper. There was one security light that illuminated the parking lot. I could see a half-dozen cars scattered about. I got out, marched up to the back door of the one-floor cinder block building. There was a light over the door. I tried the knob. The door was locked. I knocked, my mouth dry as sand on the beach in July.

It didn't take long for the door to open. I was shocked to see Scally Cap, the tall Irish thug who'd almost shot my head off in Shamrock's living room, staring back at me. For a second I thought he might slug me. But he didn't show any emotion. Just held the door wide, motioned with his head for me to step in. I could smell booze on him as I squeezed past.

I found myself in a corridor, brightly lit with a series of doors on either side. I'd never been in the back of a strip joint before, so I had no idea what to expect. Scally Cap closed the door and came around me. I followed him for a few yards. When we came to the second door on the right, he opened it, stepped inside. I took a deep breath, noticed the Xanax wasn't working, and followed him in. I half expected to get a blackjack in the face.

I didn't. Instead, I was in an office that could have been the office of any legitimate business on the beach. Except for the pictures on the wall, that is. All the walls were covered with framed photographs of exotic dancers who I assumed were, or had been, employees. I tore my eyes away from the pictures and checked out the rest of the room. File cabinets lined the walls on either side. On the left was a long couch with two men sitting on it, stiff as boards. They looked like they both were members-in-good-standing of the mob enforcers union. Tight black leather jackets stretched across pumped-up frames. Jet black hair on both, combed straight back. They didn't look Irish. They did look like they might be brothers. They both stared at me with dead eyes. One chewed gum, snapped it loudly every so often.

On my right, sitting in a fire engine-red barrel chair facing a desk, I was surprised to see my old friend—Runt. He didn't look happy to see me. I wasn't happy to see him either. I did smile inside though when I saw that his right arm was in a sling like half the people on the beach it seemed. Maybe I let my smile slip out a bit, because he glared at me and leaned forward in his seat.

"Relax!" commanded the man seated behind the desk. Runt sank back into his chair.

I didn't have to be introduced to the man who'd spoken. I'd seen his face enough in the newspapers through the years. It was Red Foley and his hair wasn't red. It was white and thin and combed back on his head. The designer track suit he wore *was* red, a maroon shade of red. What I could see of him showed that he was well built and in good shape.

"Sit down," he said to me. It was a command. I sat in a stiff-backed chair in front of the desk. He stared at me, hands folded under his chin. No one spoke.

Finally, Foley lowered his hands. "So you're ready to sell that little shack you bought, Marlowe? I was wondering if you were going to play it smart. You were giving some friends of mine a lot of trouble." He smiled. His already thin lips disappeared. "You got balls though. I got to give you that. You want a drink?"

I shook my head.

Foley had a trace of a South Boston accent in his speech. He expressed himself well. I assumed he was self-educated. "All right, how much?" He gazed at me with a look that said if the number was too high, I might not get out the door.

"Nothing. *Now*," I began. I noticed my voice shaking. I hoped Foley hadn't.

He put his hands down on the desk. His forearms bulged in the sleeves of his warmup jacket. He leaned toward me, looking as suspicious as a man could. "Don't play games with me, Marlowe. Put it out there."

I swallowed hard. "I want to be a part of what you've got planned for Hampton."

The Runt snickered. Foley gave him a look that shut him up. Foley turned to me, pointed a finger at my face. "Don't you say another fuckin' thing." He raised his right hand up in the air. "The rest of you go out front. Have a drink. I want to talk to Mr. Marlowe alone." The three men rose, and along with Scally Cap, headed for the door. I could hear one of the lookalike enforcers snapping his gum as they left.

When they were gone Foley leaned back in his seat, looked at me. "What makes you think I have anything planned for Hampton Beach, Marlowe?"

"Intuition." He could have taken it as a wisecrack but he didn't.

Instead, he lifted a pack of smokes from the table and offered me one. When I refused, he tapped one out and took his time lighting it with a silver lighter. He savored the first puff, blowing the smoke up toward the ceiling. I had the feeling this was a stall, that he was planning what he was going to say next.

Finally, he set the cigarette in an ashtray with *Salisbury Beach* stenciled on it in fancy script. "What do you think I got planned for your precious beach, Marlowe? *You* tell me."

I didn't know for sure but I'd had a crazy idea bugging me lately. I had to word it just right though. If I didn't, and Foley sensed I was bluffing, he'd have no use for me. "A beautiful place for it, right on the seacoast. You could—"

"Shut up." He said it like he said it all the time.

"But I just meant it's a great location. I—"

He raised himself in his chair. "Shut up. I won't say it again." He looked around the room. "I'm *never* sure I'm alone. Get it?"

I got it. And I breathed a little easier. I'd hit a nerve.

Foley must've thought his office might be bugged. And now that he thought I knew his plans, he didn't want anyone who might be listening to know too. I didn't dare speak.

Foley lifted a clicker from the desk and pointed it in the direction of a wall-mounted television. As soon as it came on, he increased the volume to a high level. It was an old gangster movie. Fitting.

Foley put the clicker down, stared at me. He was thinking hard. I could almost smell his brain cells burning. Finally he motioned for me to lean forward and meet him head to head near the center of his desk. I could smell cold cuts and cigarette smoke as he spoke.

"You think I'm going to cut you in because you own a little shithole?"

I wondered if I ought to pull back out of range of his fists before I said anything, then decided against it. "I can offer you more than that. I know a lot of people on the beach. If there are other properties you want, I can make it happen. If someone has skeletons in their closet, I know about them. You can use that information to get you other places you might want. Probably cheap too."

Foley stared at me like he was debating whether to accept my offer—or kill me. I had no idea which one would win. In a moment of desperation and fear, I tossed in another incentive for him to forget about the killing part.

"I told someone I was meeting you," I said. Yes, it was an old gimmick. Still, I was gambling that Foley couldn't be sure if I actually had told someone where I was going or not.

Foley smiled. "Yeah, I bet."

Looking at his slitted eyes studying me, I suddenly had the sick feeling I'd gambled wrong. I quickly raised the pot. "You'll be paying for me to keep my mouth shut, too. Like I said, I know a lot of people on the beach. Some of them very savvy businesspeople, and if they knew what I know, it would be *very* expensive, if not impossible, for you to get what you want."

Foley didn't speak for a while. My heart thumped like an oversexed rabbit's. I imagined all the ways I might leave this office and none of them were good. I didn't know if he was actually mulling over my proposition or if he just enjoyed watching me squirm. I was doing a lot of that. Inside at least.

When Foley spoke, I was glad to hear I was going to get out of there alive. "Like I said, you got big balls, Marlowe." He smiled then. I liked most smiles; I didn't like his. "I'll give you a piece of what I've got planned . . . a *small* piece—*if* you come through for me *and* keep your mouth shut."

"You won't have any trouble with me, Mr. Foley."

"I'll have my lawyer work something out. He'll let you know what."

I didn't like saying it but I had to. Foley might smell a rat if I didn't. "No lawyer. Cash. I don't want any paper trail that connects me to the deal. I have to live on that beach. I don't want people knowing I sold them out. I deal with you, or it's no deal."

Foley smiled. "I figured you'd say that, Marlowe. I know all about your background."

Inside, I breathed a huge sigh of relief.

He looked at me for another minute, then said, "All right. That can be done. But remember, keep your trap shut, even with my people. There's things even they don't know."

I wanted to act nonchalant when I got up, but as I stood, I was so nervous, I stumbled. After I recovered my balance, I sheepishly said, "I'll wait to hear from you then?"

"Yeah, that's right. Wait till you hear from me. Then we'll work out the details. Don't worry—I'll make you happy."

I left the office and walked back along the short corridor the way I'd come. It seemed as long as I imagined the walk from a prison cell to the death chamber might seem. When I reached the rear door, opened it, and stepped out into the night, I still wasn't sure I wouldn't get a blackjack to the back of my head. I made it to my car and pulled out onto the roadway, feeling a sense of relief that actually made my hands shake. The ride back to the beach was the nicest ride I'd ever taken. Just a short while ago, I'd wondered if I'd ever see Hampton again. Now I could see the lights of the beach ahead. And they looked real good. I sailed over the bridge and returned to my cottage.

Inside, I grabbed a beer, chugged it down. The second bottle I took to my chair. I wasn't that concerned about the time. That was the least of my worries. I was more worried about what the hell I had gotten myself involved in now and what I was going to do about it. I didn't know then that it had all been decided for me. That I had more trouble coming than I could've imagined. A lot more.

Chapter 32

THE NEXT DAY at the Tide was uneventful. I could see Dianne watching me warily. I was sure she was wondering if I'd taken her advice. I avoided her like the plague. I didn't want to have to lie if she asked me. So I didn't give her a chance to ask. When I had to go through the kitchen past her, I was faster than a seagull behind an inbound fishing boat.

The day went fast. The only thing I accomplished was setting up an appointment with the only person who might still be able to help me—Steve Moore. I had no idea if he could or even if he would. He did agree to meet me at the White Cap the next day after work.

Things started going downhill late that night when I heard someone jimmying my front door. It wasn't very loud, but I'm a light sleeper. With what had been going on recently, a spider walking on the wall would've sounded like a 200-pound gymnast doing flips in the next room. I knew what it was right away. I could hear them coming through the front door. The police still had my .38 from the incident at Shamrock's, so I rolled off the bed and stuck my hand under it to grab Betsy, my double-barreled shotgun. Nothing. I moved my hand around frantically, searching for it. My bedroom door flew open. It almost banged against my head.

A voice growled, "Don't bother, Marlowe. It's not there."

I could see the big shadow filling the doorway. I couldn't make the face out, but I didn't have to. I recognized the voice. Scally Cap again. I could see the pistol in his hand and it was pointed directly at me.

"Get up," he said. "And don't try anything stupid."

I got up off the floor and took the few steps with him as he walked backward into the front room. It was dark. Lights suddenly came on and I threw up my hand, shading my eyes. When I lowered my hand, I saw someone else standing there—Runt. He was near the light switch, looking at me with that sick grin of his. I glanced at his arm in the sling. His grin turned to a snarl.

"Get in that chair." Scally Cap motioned with the pistol, indicating where I would've sat anyway—*my* chair. I sat, looked around. I'd drawn the shades earlier. Which meant no one outside could see what was going on in here. If anyone in the neighborhood was even awake. I looked at the ship's clock on the wall. Four thirty.

The only damage I could see to the door was a thin strip of wood pulled away from the jam. I didn't think that could have made much noise. So the odds of anyone hearing or seeing anything going on were zero to none. I was in trouble. Big trouble.

Runt sat at the far end of the couch. He picked up the telephone, listened. He set it back in its cradle. The sick grin again. "Works good," he said.

I looked up at Scally Cap. The big man glared down at me, gun pointed directly at my chest. "We're gonna wait here for a while, Marlowe. Until we get a telephone call. And you're gonna be a good boy while we do."

"Then what?" I said.

"Then you're gonna get what's comin' to ya, cocksucker." Runt sprang forward in his seat, yellow teeth bared. "You didn't think you was gonna get away with this, did you?" He patted his injured arm, the one I'd shot.

I didn't answer. Just considered my options. They weren't many. The only good thing was that I didn't have to ask again about what they had planned. Runt couldn't resist filling me in. "I bet you were surprised not to find your greeter under the bed, huh?"

Again I didn't answer.

"While you were over at the Slipper someone came over, took their time on the door and came in nice and quiet like. Took your little toy. You didn't even know they'd been here, you dumb shit. Did you really think Red'd invite you over for a drink and you'd get whatever the hell you wanted?"

"Shut up," Scally Cap said, glancing at his partner.

"Why? He ain't gonna be around to tell anyone." The sick grin got bigger.

"We ain't supposed to say anything. Just do our job."

"Yeah, but I owe this guy. I want him to sweat." Runt removed a plastic eyeglass case from his jacket pocket. With his one good hand, he flipped it open, tipped it just a bit so I could see what was in there. I didn't like what I saw. It was a hypodermic needle and syringe. It looked old but frightening. "Pretty, huh," Runt said before letting out an evil little cackle.

"Shut up," Scally Cap said again.

Runt ignored him. "You know what's in this, Marlowe?"

For the third time, I didn't answer.

"Cocaine. Lots of it, too. I would've used smack but the boss is a smart guy. He done his homework on you. You wouldn't use heroin. You'd use coke. So coke it is. Enough in here to stop almost anybody's heart except maybe someone with a big tolerance. We know you ain't got that no more. Right?" He cackled again, closed the cover of the case, and placed it beside him on the couch. "When that phone rings—"

"Will you shut the fuck up!" Scally Cap sounded more nervous than a man his size with a gun in his hand should.

Runt glanced at him, then continued right on. "You see we got somebody with your red-headed leprechaun friend right now." He studied my face. I must've reacted. "Yeah, that's right. Up at the High Tide. They're just waiting for your girl-friend to come in."

I must have given myself away again, because he said, "That scares ya, huh Marlowe? It should. See when your slut comes in, they're both going to be taken care of. Probably in the walk-in refrigerator. That way no one'll hear the shotgun blasts. The blast from *your* shotgun. Like it?"

I was stunned. Every anxiety symptom in my body went off like the Seabrook Nuclear Power Plant just exploded. My head spun and I thought for a moment I'd pass out. But I didn't. I couldn't. Not now.

"That's right. You're going to be blamed for killing them both. With *your* shotgun." He glanced at the phone, smiled, then looked back at me. "And when that rings, we'll know it's done. You killed them, stole money from the place, got some coke somewhere, and shot it up. You made one mis-take though. You took too much dope. Sad. You died."

"You talk too much," Scally Cap said.

With that, an idea slid into my mind. Maybe it was what the big man just said. Or maybe it had been in one of those old paperbacks I liked to read. Or maybe it was just that old saw about "Necessity being the Mother of Invention." It didn't matter. I was as desperate as I'd ever been in my life. "You're right, he does," I said, staring at the big man. "To more people than you think."

"Whattaya mean by that?" Scally Cap looked at me suspiciously.

"Your friend's a police informer," I said, not taking my eyes off Scally Cap. Runt let out a belly laugh. I continued to speak as fast as I could. "My best friend's a Hampton detective. He told me." I didn't know if Runt had ever been picked up on federal charges, but someone in his line of work probably had been in his home state if nowhere else. "He's working for the Massachusetts State Police."

Now Runt wasn't laughing. "Shut the fuck up, you lyin' sack a shit." He looked at the big man. "He's lying. Trying to get outta this jam. It's bullshit. You know that."

I could see something in Scally Cap's face that told me he wasn't a hundred percent sure. I plowed on. "Your buddy here took a fall and made a deal with the staties a while back. They cut him loose."

"Fall? On what?" Scally Cap asked me.

I could've been vague, but that would've been obvious. I decided to take the biggest gamble of my life and go all in. I was betting on the times we were in and where the illegal money today, at least most of it, was being made. I looked at the Runt, pointed at the hypo beside him. "That," I said. "It was a drug arrest."

I heard the big guy grunt. When I looked back at him, his eyes were wide and he was looking back and forth between the two of us.

Runt's eyes were wide, too. "You ain't believin' him, are you? He's a fuckin' liar."

Scally Cap spoke in a low voice. "What *about* that bust you took with the smack?"

I'd hit a triple. I still didn't know if I'd make it home.

Now Runt was talking fast. "You know all about that. It was tossed 'cause of an illegal search."

"That's what *you* said." The big guy moved the gun so it was pointed halfway between Runt and me. "I didn't like the sound of it back then."

"Don't you see? He's trying to get us fightin'." Runt sounded one step short of hysterical. "Don't listen to him. It's crazy talk."

"Crazy talk?" I said, looking at the big man. He glanced from me to Runt. I could see that he didn't trust anyone in the room except himself. That was good. "Can you risk it? If anything goes wrong, who do you think's going to take the rap? A rat like him?" I nodded in Runt's direction.

"You dirty bastard." He lunged off the couch, pulling the sap out of his back pocket with his left hand. He had trouble getting it out; he wasn't a lefty. When he finally did, he moved toward me.

I cringed, but before he could hit me, Scally Cap turned his gun on Runt and said, "Don't."

Runt froze, looked at the gun staring at him. "You gone shithouse? He's a fuckin' liar. I'm gonna bash his brains in." He turned back to me and looked like he was going to slap me with the ugly weapon.

"I'll shoot ya," Scally Cap said. "Don't think I won't."

Runt stopped, frozen like a statue. Slowly his hand with the sap lowered to his side.

The big man kept the gun on Runt, spoke to me. "What *exactly* has your cop friend told you anyhow?"

I just used common sense when I spoke. "Just that he's been informing on people he's been dealing with. People around him."

He turned to look at Runt. I could see the doubt on his face begin to clear, replaced by something closer to fear. Something that was good for me. Not so much for Runt.

Runt saw it, too, because he sounded desperate when he said, "Jesus Christ, can't you see he's lying? He'd say anything to get out of this." I didn't know if Runt was really a rat, but he looked like one now. His skinny face was drawn even tighter than usual and his black beady eyes looked around the room like he'd just nibbled poisoned cheese.

Scally Cap's face hardened. "I been wonderin' about you ever since you got cut loose on that dope rap. I thought you beat that too easy." His eyes narrowed and he jiggled the gun. "And when your buddy from Somerville got busted right after that? He was your connection. Yeah, I been wonderin' about that, too."

Runt was frantic now. He tapped the sap nervously against his leg. "That had nothin' to do with me. The jerk sold to some cop, that's how he got pinched."

"Maybe," the big man said. He licked his lips. "But I ain't takin' any chances right now. You probably think I'm a dumb immigrant. I ain't that dumb though. I ain't gonna whack nobody and have you give me up. That ain't gonna happen."

"I'm tellin' ya this is all a lie." The Runt's voice was loud now. He glared at me. "I'll kill you, you prick."

"If you do, I won't be here," the big man said. He began backing toward the door.

"Where are you going?" Runt whined.

"I ain't gettin' involved in any hit with someone who might be a stoolie."

"I'm tellin' ya, I ain't no stoolie."

"We'll find that out later. Now I ain't taking no chances." He reached the door, opened it, stepped outside, closed it behind him. I could hear him clomping down the stairs.

Runt turned toward me, started to raise the sap. I jumped to my feet, moved to the side, out of arm's distance. If he wanted to use the sap on me, he'd have to come closer. I balled my fists. Held them waist high. I could see the hesitation in his eyes. He was sizing the situation up—he had the sap, but I had two good arms. He probably figured it like I did— if he didn't put me out of commission with the first blow, then I'd have a big advantage. It was easy to tell when he'd made his decision. He began to inch toward the door.

"I'll get you for this someday, Marlowe. You dirty bastard."

He was going to leave. I couldn't allow that. The big guy might stay away from the Tide and any murder that was planned there, now that he believed Runt might be a police informer.

But Runt wouldn't. He'd be out the door and up to the High Tide faster than a speeding bullet. Not only to warn his buddies I was loose, but also to beat to the punch any talk about his loyalties Scally Cap might feel like sharing.

I couldn't let him leave. Couldn't let him warn whoever was holding Shamrock, and maybe Dianne, that I was free and probably on my way there.

I sprang at Runt and was all over him like a cheap suit. He looked as shocked as a million dollar lottery winner. He couldn't get the sap up all the way and kept banging me on the hip with it. I wrapped my hands around his neck and we both went down, landing against the edge of the couch. I was on top but I'd lost my grip on his throat. He had the sap up higher now and I used my right arm to fend it off, while I battered at his face with my left fist. I'm not a lefty and my blows weren't that good. He got a better angle with the sap and was hitting me at the base of my neck with the weapon. I used my arm to keep the number of blows and their force to a minimum.

Runt tried, but he couldn't connect hard with the sap. Still, it didn't take long getting hit with that blackjack before I felt a volcano of nausea erupt in my stomach, burn its way up my pipes and out my throat, showering Runt's face with a soaking bath of vomit. It didn't slow either one of us. We were in a fight for our lives. I could see the chunks of meatball sub from Gerri's and smell Heineken beer from the mess on his face. I was feeling light-headed and my head spun. I would've heaved again, except everything I'd had in my stomach was already dripping down Runt's face.

My punches were getting weaker and I could see Runt's wet face begin to smile. He must've seen my eyes going out of focus. That's when I noticed the eyeglass case on the couch where Runt had placed it earlier. I had time to make only one move.

I forgot about blocking the blows and stretched my right arm across Runt's chest, along the sofa. It was just enough. I pulled the case toward me, fumbling at it with my fingers. It popped open and the needle and syringe fell out onto the couch. I grabbed the spike, brought it toward Runt. He saw what I was doing and his smile turned to panic. He dropped the sap and tried to use that arm to keep me from raising the hypo over him. We struggled. He grabbed my wrist.

I had a good grip on the syringe. My fist wrapped around it, my thumb on the plunger. I maneuvered the syringe so it was over his face and used all my force to try to bring it down on him. He was struggling just as hard to keep it off. The look on his face was like someone pursued in a slasher movie.

I was using my right arm, he was using his left to hold me off. I had him, but people don't give up easy when they think they're going to die. I thought about Dianne and Shamrock and the fact that even a minute could make the difference between life and death for them.

I'd been using my left hand on his shoulder to hold his bucking body down. I let go, raised a closed fist as high above my head as I could, and brought it down with every ounce of strength I had left onto his injured arm. Runt screamed like an animal, released his grip from my wrist, and grabbed his damaged arm. I hesitated one second, saw the look of terror in his eyes as he realized what was about to happen. I brought the syringe swiftly down, stabbing him in the neck just above the collarbone. I drove the plunger home.

By now his hand was back on my wrist. It was too late; we both knew that. As soon as I saw the last of the liquid leave the syringe, I struggled up, stumbled backward. I stood there looking down at him. He pulled the hypo out of his neck, threw it aside. Then he got up. Gave me a look that was so fearful, I almost felt sorry for him. He turned, his good hand holding his neck and ran out the door.

Maybe trying to head for the nearest hospital. I wondered if he'd make it.

I glanced down at the floor, saw the sap lying there. I gave it a brutal kick toward the door. "Hey, you forgot something." I didn't have time to smile though. I only had time for Dianne and Shamrock.

Chapter 33

OCEAN BOULEVARD WAS deserted when I raced the Chevette along it. I didn't even see any cops. It was still dark out, no moon. When I got near the Tide I doused the lights and pulled down a one-way street a couple of blocks before the restaurant. I parked in an illegal spot, got out of the car, and ran through some backyards. I came to a fence that was shoulder high, boosted myself up and went over it. A dog started barking. He bounded toward me, snarling. I tripped over something in the dark trying to get away, stumbled, caught myself, and just kept going. I crossed another street, made my way through the backyards of that block. Finally I came out on the street I wanted.

Across from me was the High Tide. I was at the side of the building. I couldn't see anything except the glow of the lights that were kept on all night. I dashed across the street to the rear of the building. Quietly, I tried the door.

Locked.

I had my key and opened it gingerly. A sliver of dim light came out as I slowly pushed the door open. I could see all the way through the kitchen and up to the swinging doors that led into the dining room. No one.

I stepped inside, closed the door slowly behind me. It was then that Dianne came stumbling through the swinging doors from the dining room. I jumped to the side, behind the ice machine. Peeking around the corner, I saw Shamrock right behind Dianne. And behind him came what looked like a long-barreled .22 pistol. Holding the gun was one of the two look-alike muscle men I'd seen in Foley's office at the Silver Slipper. He was chewing gum like he was working on a fatty piece of steak. That was the only way I would've known which punk it was. I'd pegged them then as Foley enforcers. Apparently I'd been right.

He snapped his gum loudly before he spoke. "Get the fuck in there," he said, jabbing the gun into Shamrock's back, directing him toward the large walk-in refrigerator located in the kitchen near where I was crouched.

Those words sent a shiver of fear up my spine. I remembered what Runt had said about Dianne and Shamrock being killed in the walk-in cooler. My shotgun was probably stashed inside.

"Open the door," growled Gum Snapper.

Dianne opened the huge door, stepped inside. Shamrock went in after her and Gum Snapper followed. My breath was shallow. Still it sounded like a hurricane to me. And my heart beat raggedly. Once the cooler door closed, I raced to the kitchen. I didn't have time to think of what I was going to do. I didn't have any damn time period. He could shoot them at any second.

I reached up over the speed table and pulled down a wooden mallet hanging there with the other commercial utensils. Dianne used it to beat the steak tips senseless. I had the mallet in my right hand, stood to the side of the cooler, and tapped it lightly once against the door. I could hear a scuffling inside the cold box. I pressed my back against the wall, raised the mallet over my head.

It was probably less than a minute, although it seemed longer than an hour, before I heard someone push against the cooler door and it began to swing open. It opened toward me, so I was well concealed. I was holding the mallet as if it were my life savings and someone was trying to rip it from my hand. Beads of sweat tickled down my arm. I brought the mallet up even higher, ready to smash Snapper's head like a pumpkin on Halloween.

I was just about to come down with it, when Dianne stepped out of the cooler. She stopped. I could see her head and the side of her body. I couldn't see her back. Not until she was jabbed from behind and she jerked forward. That's when the .22 jammed into her back came into view. I was hesitant about doing what I did next, afraid that the gun might go off. But if I didn't act now, all three of us would be dead within minutes.

I came down hard with the mallet. It connected with the top of Snapper's forearm. There was a wail of pain and the gun went flying. Dianne was pushed out of the way and Snapper came stumbling out of the cooler. Shamrock was on the man's back, his one good arm locked around Snapper's neck. They banged against the speed table. Shamrock's face was red; he was straining to choke the man. Snapper was reaching back, trying to grab onto Shamrock. I moved from behind the cooler door, looked for a chance to clock him on the head. The way they were moving about, I couldn't get a clear shot. I would've been just as likely to hit Shamrock.

That's when Snapper got lucky. The two of them bounced around to the front of the speed table. Snapper threw himself backwards so Shamrock was slammed into the dishwasher opposite it. His head thudded against the top of the machine. That broke his one-arm hold and Shamrock slid to the floor. Snapper glanced up, and before I could stop him, he'd reached up to the hanging utensils and snagged an ugly looking meat cleaver with his right hand. Unfortunately he'd held the gun in his left hand when I'd whacked his arm. Shamrock was on his ass, half unconscious. Dianne was huddled in a far corner. Snapper turned on me. I took a quick step backwards. My huge mallet felt puny now.

Snapper looked around the floor, probably for the gun. He didn't look too upset when he didn't find it, more like a man who already had a gun at a knife fight anyway. I felt the opposite—like a man with a knife at a gun fight. I continued backing up around the rear of the speed table. He took slow steps after me. I was hoping for two things—one, to lead him away from Dianne and Shamrock, and two, to get out of these tight quarters in the kitchen. I don't know why, but I thought I might have better odds in the larger dining area. Maybe more running room?

I finally reached the swinging doors and backed hurriedly into the dining room. I made it just in time. Snapper was moving on me fast, occasionally shaking his injured left arm. I was lucky enough to get behind a table for eight, one of our largest, in the center of the dining room. That's where our game started. If the outcome, at least for me, hadn't had such deadly potential, it would have been funny. Like one of those old Three Stooges skits where they're chased around a table by some enraged stuffed shirt just before the pie fight starts. If Snapper caught me, however, I wasn't going to be hit with a cream pie.

We went around and around the table, me backwards, both of us stopping every so often, staring at each other, him faking which way he was heading, then moving again, both of us ending up at the same place we'd started.

"I could hit you with this, Marlowe," he shouted over the table as he shook the cleaver in his hand.

I was desperate, so I tried reverse psychology. "Go ahead," I said. I didn't have much of a chance against that cleaver in hand-to-hand combat, but he wasn't Tonto and that wasn't a tomahawk. I figured my odds of dodging it were pretty good. Then I'd be the one chasing him.

He must have come to the same conclusion because he suddenly faked a dash to his left and then ran right. We did a few more laps around the table. The whole routine from when we'd entered the dining room had only taken a few minutes. But he couldn't stay here forever. He must've realized that too. In one fluid motion he shot one foot up onto a chair and jumped up on the table. I was shocked. He may have had a very sore arm, but his legs worked well.

He came at me across the table. He held the cleaver shoulder high, a black look on his face. I had nowhere to run. Behind me was a wall of booths blocking any escape. If I made a run to either side, he'd leap off the table and whack me with that cleaver before I made three steps.

He moved to the edge of the table.

I backed up.

He jumped down and I stumbled backwards, landing in one of the booths. I was laid out on a bench, caught between the back of the bench and the table. Snapper came for me, raised the cleaver. I slid backwards as far as I could on the bench, my back jammed against the wall, my legs pulled up to my chest. At least he'd have to hack away at my legs to get to my upper body and head. That wouldn't take long though.

And it wouldn't be pretty.

He did a couple fakes with the cleaver and then was just about to deliver the first blow when I heard the gunshot. It wasn't loud but it stopped Snapper in his tracks. He semi-turned, keeping one eye on me. It was Dianne. She'd found his pistol and was standing there, pointing it at him. The shot she fired had gone over his head, probably ended up in the bar area somewhere.

Snapper took two steps away from the booth, faced Dianne. I was at his side, still on the bench against the wall. If I made a move, he could see it. I watched as he looked at Dianne and then at the gun, a smug expression on his face.

"Give me the gun, bitch."

"No . . . you get out of here." Her voice shook. She wiggled the pistol. She held it in both hands. As far as I knew this was the first time she'd ever fired a gun.

He had the meat cleaver at shoulder height. "You won't shoot. And even if you did, I'd be all over you in a second. Won't be pretty what this'll do to ya." He shook the cleaver.

Dianne held the gun straight out, with both hands. Still, I could see the barrel shaking. "Get out," she said again.

Snapper smirked. "You're shaking so bad, it's gonna fall out of your hands, girl." He took a step towards her, held out his empty hand. "Gimme the gun. I'll let youse all go. Honest, I will."

I looked around desperately for something, anything I might do. There was nothing. Snapper could still see me out of the corner of his eye. "Get out of my restaurant," Dianne said. Her tone was almost pleading.

Snapper wiggled one of his fingers like he was motioning her toward him. "The gun, girl. Gimme the gun and I won't hurt anyone. You don't want anyone hurt. Let me have the gun. I just want to take it with me. I can't leave evidence behind."

I saw a flicker of something cross Dianne's face. Did she believe him?

He took a step closer to her. "Don't believe him, Dianne," I shouted. "Don't give it to him. Shoot! Shoot!"

I hated saying those words. I knew what it might mean to her if she did shoot. But there was no other way out.

Snapper glared at me, then turned back toward Dianne. He smiled. A smile I prayed she could see through. "I just want to get out of here with my gun, sweetie. That makes sense, don't it?" He gave her a cheap imitation of a pitiful look. "Now hand me that gun and I'll go." He took another step towards her.

"No, no," she said. She sounded almost hysterical now.

He took another step, reached his left hand out farther. "Right here, sweets. Put it in my hand."

That was the last thing he said. His hand moved to within grabbing distance of the pistol, at the same time raising the cleaver just a whisper more.

"Dianne, look out," I shouted.

The pistol fired once. I knew instantly that it hit Snapper somewhere in his lower side. His free hand went to the spot where the bullet entered. He held it there for a long moment, then turned his palm up toward his face. I could see the blood on it from where I was. He looked stunned.

"Get out," Dianne screamed. "I'll shoot you again." Now she did sound hysterical. But I had no doubt she'd do it. He must've known that, too, because he took three steps backwards, frantically looking from side to side for a way out.

Dianne was blocking the kitchen door which led to the way he'd entered.

Before he could decide what to do, there was another gunshot, though it evidently missed. Snapper turned, ran toward the front door. He banged into a table and knocked over chairs as he went. When he reached the front door, he yanked on the handle like a madman. It was locked. Another shot went off. The bullet went into the wall to the side of the door. I took a quick look at Dianne. She'd fired with her eyes closed. She opened them. Snapper was in a panic, running back through the dining room towards me. He still held the cleaver in one hand. Dianne fired again. The bullet sliced through the front window and probably ended up in the Atlantic Ocean.

I balled myself up hard against the back of the booth, imagining what that first blow with the cleaver would feel like. As he roared towards me, scattering chairs as he went, his face looked like a man with starving cannibals just feet behind him.

I threw my arms up around my face and my eyes must've instinctively closed. The next thing I heard was glass shattering on the other side of the dining room. When I opened my eyes, I could see Snapper outside on the side street, getting up off the sidewalk. Then he stumbled down the street out of sight.

He'd crashed through the plate glass window, leaving behind an enormous ragged hole.

I struggled out of the booth and walked towards Dianne. "Dianne?"

She didn't answer, just kept holding the gun out straight. I wasn't sure if she even saw me, so I came up on her side, slowly. I gently reached for the gun, then brought it and her arm down to her side. That's when she let go and the gun clattered to the floor.

I pulled her close. I could feel her shaking. At least I think it was her. For all I knew it could've been me.

Chapter 34

"I WONDER IF it's from the bullet wound or the glass?" I said.

I was standing on the side street, looking down at the sidewalk beside the High Tide. It was littered with shards of glass from Snapper's escape. The sun was up now. My shirt stuck to my back with sweat.

"Both, I'd say." Steve Moore bent over, picked up a knife-like piece of glass. It was smeared with red. "Looks like the slug might have been the least of his problems."

"He was lucky Dianne hadn't thought of my shotgun in the walk-in," I said. "He'd be dead now."

The sidewalk we stood on was cordoned off with yellow police tape. A few uniformed cops lounged around near Steve and me. A police cruiser was parked beside us. Two cruisers and an unmarked car were up the street at the front of the restaurant. The always-present red rescue truck was up there also, along with a gaggle of spectators all looking our way.

"Maybe I better go inside and see how Dianne's doing," I said.

Steve frowned. "I'd stay here if I were you. She's with Gant. You going in there won't make her situation any better."

"Her situation? Steve, the punk was going to kill us. She shot him in self-defense."

Steve held up his hands. "I know, I know. And Gant does too. Don't worry. You going in there might poison the well, though. He doesn't think objectively when you're around." Steve looked back down at the broken glass on the sidewalk.

I didn't like it, but I knew he was right. "Yeah, I guess so," I said.

I looked in the direction of the crowd up on the corner at Ocean Boulevard. One figure caught my eye. It was the beard. He was staring in my direction. I turned toward Steve.

"Steve?"

"Hmm." He didn't take his eyes off the sidewalk.

"There's a guy up near the corner. Beard. You know him?" I whispered. I don't know why.

He slowly looked up over my shoulder, looking in the direction I'd indicated.

"Don't make it so obvious, will you," I said irritably.

"I don't see anybody with a beard. Who the hell you talking about?"

I looked toward the corner. The crowd was still there. The beard wasn't. "He's gone now. I've seen him around."

"Think he works for Foley?"

"I don't know, but he's up to something."

"Why do you say that?"

"Just a feeling."

"Yeah," Steve said. "A paranoid feeling. You're seeing things now." Steve ran his hand through his hair. There was sweat on his brow. "I don't blame you though. This has gone far enough to make anyone a little loopy."

"I'm not loopy."

"You know what I mean." Steve kicked at the glass on the sidewalk. "Anyway, we'll get this one at least. There's no way he isn't going to show up at a hospital."

"That won't do much good," I said. "Foley'll just send someone else. He's probably got an endless supply of thugs."

Steve shrugged. "I'm sure he does. If I were you, I'd go into witness protection."

I guess it was supposed to be funny, but I couldn't laugh. Not after what had almost happened to Dianne and Shamrock. And it was all because of me. "That's not funny, Steve."

He looked sheepish. "Sorry. But if I were you, I'd stay out of his way."

"He wants to take over Hampton Beach," I said solemnly.

"That's not going to happen, he's going to go down."

I did a double take. Had Steve said that just to make me feel better or had he let something slip? "What do you mean?"

Steve flipped his palms up. "Well, I know every time Gant tries to dig a little deeper into this Karnack-slash-Foley thing, someone upstairs puts the kibosh on it."

"Someone else investigating them? You didn't mention that before."

"There was nothing to tell you." He hesitated, then added defensively, "Besides it was police business. I can't tell you everything."

"Jesus Christ, Steve. Dianne and Shamrock were almost killed over this. You should've told me. Maybe it would've helped if I knew that. Maybe I wouldn't have gotten so involved. Maybe—"

Steve cut me off. "Woulda, shoulda, coulda. You'd have gotten involved anyway. You can't help yourself." His tone was still defensive and some red had crept into his face. "I had absolutely nothing to tell you except speculation. And you couldn't have done anything with that. It led nowhere. At least nowhere I knew about."

Of course he was right. Even if I had known there *might* be somebody else looking into Foley's activities on the beach, what could I have done with the information? Steve said he had no idea where the pressure on Gant came from. I certainly couldn't have found out. It would've ended up confusing me more anyway.

Then I had a thought. What if there was another reason Gant had been told to lay off looking into Red Foley? What if someone high up was on Foley's payroll? I realized instantly that any mention I made regarding police corruption had better be very diplomatic. "Steve, you don't think there's any chance Foley has anyone in law enforcement working for him?"

Steve looked at me like I'd just stepped out of the ocean in January. "Now you're being *too* paranoid. You may not like Gant, Dan, and vice-versa, but he's a pit bull when he smells something phony. And he would've smelled that. He's not stupid. Besides, Foley's a Boston hood. He doesn't have any pull in New Hampshire." Steve glanced up the street toward Ocean Boulevard and the crowd. "I got to get up there and get them moving."

He lifted some yellow police tape strung between two sign posts, crouched, and went under it. He held the tape up, looked at me. "Come on. You can't stay there."

I slid under the tape.

"I'll talk to you later," Steve said before heading up the street.

"Yeah," I muttered.

I stood there in the gutter of the side street like a dunce. I couldn't leave. I had to go back in the Tide, help with the cleanup. Again. But I didn't want to go in right now. It wasn't only that I wanted to avoid Gant, which I did, I also wasn't looking forward to facing Dianne. I'd led her to believe I was backing out of this Foley mess. I hadn't really promised that, I guess. But I couldn't kid myself—what I'd done was as bad as a lie. Maybe worse. I'd deceived her. Somehow I'd actually convinced myself that I could clear this whole mess up without endangering anyone else. I must've been delusional. Dianne was going to be furious and I didn't blame her.

Chapter 35

"YOU'RE FIRED, Dan."

I was shocked when Dianne said it. Not just what she said but that she said it in front of other people. Shamrock was still there and now the morning waitresses, too. We were all in the dining room. So were the emergency window people, who were installing temporary plywood over the hole where the plate glass window had been. The window people gaped in our direction. Not so the High Tide employees. They all became extra busy cleaning up the mess and getting ready for lunch, but doing a poor job of pretending that they weren't listening to the fireworks.

"Dianne, I . . ." I reached out to touch her arm. She pulled it away.

"Leave! Now! I don't want you here." Her eyes were slits and her face was red. She was as mad as I'd ever seen her.

I felt as low as a clam buried deep in the Hampton Beach sand. "Let's talk—"

"No! You're done. Go!"

She spun around, started moving utensils around on the table behind her. I watched for a moment. The setup had been perfect when she'd started, now it looked like something in the cafeteria of an insane asylum.

"I'll talk to you later, Di—"

"Like hell you will!"

I turned and walked toward the door. I felt like I'd lost six inches in height.

I DIDN'T DO much the rest of the day. I stayed in the cottage and somehow kept away from the beer, even though the bottles in the fridge called my name on a minute-to-minute basis. I did take a Xanax. The pill didn't do much good. I sat in front of a TV, watching I don't know what. I waited.

Eventually it was close to the time I knew Dianne would lock up the Tide and go home. I drove up Ocean Boulevard, parked in the lot across from the restaurant. I pulled into a vacant leased spot and watched the building. When I saw the last of the lights go out, I drove out of the lot, north on Ocean Boulevard. It was late, quiet. Even the shops in the Casino were shut tight. The only people I saw were a few groups of drunken twenty-somethings stumbling about.

When I reached Dianne's condo on Ocean Boulevard, I pulled into the lot across the street. I found a vacant parking spot with a meter. I waited until I saw Dianne pull into the parking area of her condo. I jumped out of the car, hopped a knee-high railing, and dashed across the street. A car just missed me, beeped. Dianne heard it, saw me, and hurried toward the front door of the building. I reached her just as she stuck the key in the door.

"Dianne . . ."

"Go away, Dan." She struggled with the key. I didn't know if it was fighting her or her hands were shaking. I'd never seen her have trouble with it before. Finally she made the key work and opened the door. I leaned against her, pushed in behind her. She shook irritably at my touch. I didn't know what would happen, but I followed her up the stairs to the second floor. When she reached her door, I didn't know what to expect. She stuck her key in the lock, fought with that one, too.

"Dianne, please can I talk to you?" I was desperate. She was all I had left to hang onto. Sure, I had Shamrock. But it wasn't the same. I'd really only made it this far because of Dianne. I knew that. I never tried to kid myself. And I wasn't now. She was the only thing that stood between me and that little coke den off of Ashworth Avenue. If this didn't turn out good tonight, that might be my next stop. Without Dianne, I was done for. And whatever she did, I deserved it.

So I was prepared to get slapped, punched, spit on, and yelled at. I wasn't prepared for what I saw when she turned to face me. Tears streamed down a face that was a mixture of frustration and hurt. A lot of hurt. For a moment I was relieved, but that relief was immediately replaced by an empty frightening feeling I'd never felt before.

She stared at me with green misty eyes. And now I could see something else in there too—pity. I didn't like that.

"Dan, you lied to me." She sobbed lightly between sentences. "Shamrock was almost killed. I was almost killed. You were almost killed. All because you lied."

She turned back to the door, got it open and went in. I followed her. She didn't try to stop me. It didn't make me feel any better. She turned on the light, walked to the couch, sat down. She'd stopped crying. But she looked washed out. I couldn't imagine what I looked like. I almost sat beside her, then thought better of it. I didn't know what to say; I had to walk on eggshells. I'd screwed up badly. But she wasn't throwing me out or calling the cops. At least not yet. That was something.

So I said, lamely, "Do you want a drink?"

She looked at me, pursed her lips, and nodded. I went to the kitchen nook, made her a Cape Codder. Dianne didn't drink much, Bud Lite sometimes. Vodka drinks even less. But it seemed when I was here, I'd always make her the same mixed drink. And I'd usually make it strong. I thought better of that this time. She'd cooled down since she'd fired me at the Tide. I could see that. I didn't know how much, but whatever it was I wanted to keep it that way. I made the drink weak. I gave it to her and sat with a bottle of Heineken in the chair opposite her. I watched her sip at the drink, waited for her to talk. It didn't take long.

"Why did you do it, Dan? You told me you were going to stay out of it and you didn't."

I wanted to ask her how she knew, but I didn't have to. She told me. "That muscle-bound goop who almost killed me and Shamrock told us you were causing trouble. Still poking around and I *believed* him. It's pretty bad when you believe a criminal and not your boyfriend."

Well, at least she was referring to me as her boyfriend. That couldn't be bad. "I'm sorry. I thought I was doing the right thing."

She took another sip of her drink, looked at me over the glass. "You always think you're doing the right thing. And that's not why I'm mad. You promised and you lied to me. And on top of that, people almost got killed because of what you did."

I set the beer down on an end table. "I screwed up. I know. I'm sorry."

She looked at me, shook her head. "What are you going to do now?"

I hesitated to say what I was thinking, but I wanted to lighten the moment, so I took a chance. "Do I still have a job?"

She set her drink down on the coffee table, wrapped her arms around her chest. "That's not what I mean, Dan. I mean what are you going to do about this Red Foley thing? I want to know. The truth."

And that's what I told her. "I'm done with it, Dianne. I'm going to give Cliff back his building and let the police handle the whole thing."

She looked at me doubtfully. "I wish I could believe that."

I put on what I hoped was an honest face. "I mean it. I'm done with it."

She unwrapped her legs from under her, put her feet on the floor, and leaned toward me. "Are you sure you can get out of it? It isn't too late, is it?"

I wasn't sure about that at all. But I couldn't tell her that. "All Foley wants is the property. Once he knows it's his, he'll forget the rough stuff."

"I hope you're right." She stood up, stretched a bit. "I'm tired, Dan. I'm going to bed." Then giving me a glare, added, "Even though I doubt I can sleep, thank you."

I stood. I didn't want to push my luck. I had Dianne back. And I wanted to keep it that way. "I guess I'll see you tomorrow." I took one step toward the door before she spoke.

"You don't have to go," she said. "I don't want you driving after drinking."

I glanced at the half-empty beer bottle on the end table. Then I walked over to her, put my arms around her waist. Her arms went over my shoulders, hung there limply. I put my face against her long black hair and breathed in. I could smell the fish she'd worked on all day. And I didn't mind it one bit. I tried to turn her face toward mine, but she held firm. I didn't push it. Neither of us said anything.

She felt so good against me. I just held her like that. Didn't do anything. I was going to follow her lead, whatever it would be. But she took her time. And I didn't care. I was holding the most beautiful woman in the world in my arms. Who'd want to give that up?

Finally, she looked up at me. Her full lips were slightly parted and her eyes were half closed. When I kissed her, our tongues darted together in a wild hot dance. I ran my hands up her sides, over her full breasts, pushed her hair aside and cupped her face in my hands as we kissed. She reached for me. We moaned in unison.

Her tongue left mine as she pushed my face away with one hand. I loved the feel of it on my skin. Those hands were as gentle as a leaf falling and as hot as magnified sunlight.

"Let's go to the bedroom," she said. Our noses were almost touching. Her breath was minty.

I just nodded like I'd been struck dumb. When I did speak, I wasn't surprised to hear my voice quiver. I don't know why but every time with Dianne seemed like the first time. So I was ready and anxious. "I've got to hit the bathroom."

We pulled apart. Dianne started to clear our drinks; I headed for the john.

I wasn't there long. I took a leak, swished mouthwash, and then I took the bottle of Xanax from my pocket. I looked inside, made sure the pills were still there. I don't know why, but I checked them every night. I guess knowing they were there was like a kid with a security blanket. I certainly didn't need one now. They didn't help sex, they did the opposite if anything. I put them back and washed my hands.

When I stepped out of the bathroom, I suddenly wished I had popped the little pill when I'd had the chance.

Dianne stared at me, her green eyes open wide. Beside her was Shamrock and he didn't look good. He looked like he'd taken a beating. Behind them stood Red Foley and Scally Cap. They both held guns.

"Dan, I didn't know it was them," Dianne said. "I thought it was just Shamrock."

"My . . . arr . . . fault, Danny," Shamrock sputtered. A little blood dribbled from his mouth and fell to the carpet. "If I didn't do it, they said they'd bust in and kill you both."

"Yeah, don't blame him, Marlowe," Foley said. "He did us Irish proud. Wasn't gonna help us no matter how many times we whacked him. I even put the gun up to his fat head and he wouldn't help. But when I said I'd kill the both of you if he didn't? Then he cooperated. Us Irish are tough." Foley let out a laugh. Scally Cap joined in.

"I'm sorry, Danny." Shamrock said.

"Forget it, Shamrock. It's not your fault." My heart was thumping now. "What do you want, Foley?"

Any remnant of humor left Foley's voice. "You. And you. And you." He nodded towards me, Dianne, and Shamrock as he spoke. "I've had it up to here with you, Marlowe. You've caused me a lot of problems. Now *I'm* gonna make sure those problems end tonight. Myself. Make sure it's done right."

"What about the deal we had?"

"Don't be stupid, Marlowe. I can read people. That's how I got where I am. And I read you the minute you walked in my office. I knew I couldn't trust you. So I told you what you wanted to hear, but I was just waiting for the right time away from my business. And this here's the right time.

My stomach collapsed. "What about the gift shop building? I won't sign it over."

"I couldn't care less," Foley looked at me like he wanted to shoot me right then, right between the eyes. "When you're gone, I'll deal with whoever. I'm sure they'll be a lot easier than you. You're the stupidest man alive."

I threw another pitch, hoped it didn't go wild. "You can't do it here."

Dianne whimpered. Or maybe it was Shamrock. Or maybe both of them.

"After what's happened, they'll tie it to you. Too many people know."

"Pretty good for the stupidest man alive. But who said I'm going to do anything here?"

"It doesn't matter. When they find the bodies . . ." Another whimper, ". . . they'll still come down on you."

"That's what you think." Foley motioned with his gun toward the door. "Here's what we're going to do. There's a car across the street. We're going to march over there nice and easy. Move."

Just as we started to walk toward the door, Foley added, "Oh yeah. And if anyone tries anything at all, I'm gonna put a bullet in the pretty broad's head first. Understand?"

I understood and it made me feel sick. We went out the door. Shamrock led the way, I followed. Scally Cap was behind me. Behind him was Dianne and then Foley. They both had their guns concealed under their coats. I could still tell where they were pointed. I believed what Foley'd said about shooting Dianne. Trying something didn't even cross my mind. I was hoping for a miracle now.

Across the street the three of us piled into the back of a blue Cadillac. Scally Cap drove and Foley sat in the front passenger seat. He sat facing us, his back pushed against the dashboard so he had plenty of distance. He had the gun in his right hand pointed directly at Dianne's head.

We didn't go far. And when we stopped and I saw where we were, I knew instantly what Foley had planned.

I had to give it to him. It wasn't a bad idea.

Chapter 36

IT WAS DEAD quiet at Hampton Harbor, still hours before dawn. Scally Cap pulled the car up to a series of docks and parked. Foley ordered the three of us out. Except for a couple of security lights it was dark. We were herded along a wooden walkway that jutted out into the water and led to a series of slips. Some were empty, some held boats of various sizes. I wondered if people were onboard any of the boats, asleep maybe. But I didn't hear anyone and apparently no one heard us.

We reached the end of the dock at what looked like a small fishing party boat. We went on board. When we were seated, someone we couldn't see started the engine up. Foley held his gun on us as Scally Cap threw the lines off and we pulled away from the dock.

It was low tide. We passed under the Hampton Bridge without it opening. No one spoke until we rounded the jetty and headed for open sea. I looked at Dianne. She was seated beside me on the forward side. We were on a bench that ran the entire rail of the boat. She was shivering. It wasn't cold. I glanced to my other side. Shamrock's face was pale and there were bruises and a small trickle of blood running down one cheek. He looked at me with dull blue eyes. I guess we all knew what was going to happen.

Foley and Scally Cap sat in deck chairs across from us. They both kept their guns leveled in our direction. Occasionally a wave would jostle them and they'd adjust to keep the guns on us.

Would one of those waves be the only chance I'd have? Maybe. It was better than nothing. But barely.

"Don't look so down, Marlowe," Foley said. "It won't be much longer."

Scally Cap grinned.

"You won't get away with this, Foley," I said. "They'll find our bodies eventually."

Dianne whimpered. Shamrock muttered, "Sweet Jesus."

Foley smirked. "They're not gonna find anything, smart guy. We're going to weigh you down nice. The fish'll have plenty of time to make you disappear."

"The cops'll still know it was you," I said. "Everyone knows what you've been trying to do. I've told plenty of people."

Foley stood up, took a step toward me, pushed the end of the gun's barrel against my forehead. "I'll have to take that chance, you motherfucker. It woulda gone smooth except for you. You probably thought I'd back off. But you didn't know I *can't* back off. You've made it so I have to kill you. If I don't, it'll probably be me." He stepped back, sat down.

I had no idea what he was talking about and I didn't have time to care. We were going to die if I didn't think of something. And like Dianne had said, it was going to be because of me. I couldn't let that happen.

I was trying to come up with that something, anything, when I felt Dianne's hand touch mine. I looked at it and then her face. She smiled at me. A forced smile. A smile that couldn't hide the fear underneath. But it was still a smile. She squeezed my hand. I squeezed back. We held each other's hands like that for the rest of the ride. I don't know how long it took. Not long enough.

"Turn it off, Captain" Foley shouted. The engine died.

"Should we drop anchor?" the captain shouted back.

"No," Foley said. "We don't need it. We won't be here that long."

Foley and Scally Cap both stood. They were swaying with the gentle rolling of the boat.

"Get up," Foley said, indicating the three of us. "Down there." He motioned with the gun toward the back of the boat. The three of us marched in single file to the back. Dianne was still holding my hand. I *had* to pull it loose. She didn't want to let it go, but finally she did.

When we reached the back, Foley said, "Turn around." We all did, facing him and Scally Cap. The captain, who I didn't recognize, was still up at the wheel, watching us over his shoulder.

"You want the chains on first?" Scally Cap asked. He motioned to a large pile of thick heavy chains curled like powerful snakes on the deck. They shone in the moonlight, obviously brand new. Brought along for the occasion.

"No. We'll do 'em first, then the chains. Easier that way."

Foley stood there, glaring at us, with one of those sick smiles I'd seen so much of lately. "I'm gonna do Marlowe," he said. His eyes turned to me. "Last," he added, spitting the word out. Then slowly, like he was enjoying it, he continued. "I want you to see your friends get it. What *you* did to them." He snorted. "And then after you've seen their bodies tossed in the drink, I'll do you. Not quick either, I don't think. I got a feelin' I'm gonna have a bad aim with you. A real bad aim. Might take a half-dozen or so shots to finish you off."

Scally Cap snickered.

"Shut up," Foley growled.

Scally Cap kept glancing at Foley, waiting for his orders. Finally, Foley said, "Take care of the Irishman first and . . ." Scally Cap didn't wait to hear the rest of what Foley was about to say. He crossed in front of Foley, heading for Shamrock.

I'd been on a trip wire since we'd first set foot on the boat. In that short second, when the big man crossed in front of Foley, blocking his gun, the trip-wire went off. I lunged at Scally Cap, shoving him aside, and barreled into Foley. He went flying backwards, me with him. We slammed against the galley door. Foley's gun went off so close to my ear I thought I'd been shot. Then what I assumed was Scally Cap's gun roared behind me. Dianne screamed.

Foley and I were face to face. I held his gun hand by the wrist above his head. He slugged me in the face twice with the other hand before I was able to get hold of that wrist, too. We did a little dance around the deck. Foley was as strong as he looked but I was fighting for my life, so I guess that made us even. Still he pushed me back. I lost my balance on the slippery deck and landed face up with half my body bent backwards over the waist-high rail, water below me.

I clung to Foley. He was above me, pushing his gun hand down, trying to get a shot at my head. I resisted with everything I had. But Foley was strong and had the advantage. The gun came closer to my head. Foley's face came so close to mine, I could smell his halitosis. He gnashed his teeth and he actually snapped at me like a rabid dog. I jerked my head to the side just before his teeth would have sunk into my cheek. I had no idea what else was happening on deck.

I turned back to look at Foley. His bared yellow teeth were inches from my face. So was the gun. My strength was ebbing and I could tell he knew it by the gleam in his eyes. That's when I did the only thing I could. I dropped all resistance and pulled on Foley's wrists with everything I had left. His eyes widened in surprise as we went over the side of the boat and dropped like rocks into the water. It was cold but strangely felt good.

It was just a last desperate act on my part and I'd expected it to do nothing but maybe delay the inevitable. That's why I was shocked for a moment when Foley and I surfaced for the first time. I was still holding his wrists but I saw right away that the gun was gone. He'd dropped it.

Foley flailed about, his arms pulling mine wildly. It took me a minute to realize he wasn't trying to hit me. The man was panicked; he was fighting the water, not me. I heard a loud engine in the distance and within a moment a siren. A boat's siren.

Foley grabbed at my shirt. He was trying to jump onto me. "I can't swim," he screamed. "I can't swim."

He started to go down, pulling me below the water with him. I fought back to the surface. Foley came along for the ride. A bright white light hit us and danced away. The siren sounded off and on and the noise of the engine grew louder. I could see the boat we fell from. It had drifted farther away. I couldn't see anyone onboard. A larger boat, the one the light had come from, bore down on it.

"Marlowe, help me," Foley said, spitting water. "Please. I'll let you all live. I'll . . . uggh . . . anything you want. Anything."

I thought about that and what Foley had almost done to Dianne, Shamrock, and myself. I couldn't be sure a man like Foley wouldn't try to do it again, no matter what he said.

And the next time he might succeed.

I could take that chance with myself, sure, but not with Dianne and Shamrock. Not with their lives. Foley clung to my shirt with both hands. I ripped the front and shook out of the shirt, breaking free. Foley's eyes widened in terror as he stared at the empty shirt he held in his hands. He flailed about and the shirt flew over his shoulder.

"Marlowe," he gurgled. His thin white hair was matted to his head. His hands grabbed for me like a madman. I paddled backwards, just out of his grasp. "Help me. Please, Marlowe, help me."

He went under. I didn't think he'd come up again. He did though, shooting water out of his mouth like a blowing whale. His arms whipped at the air and he made another move toward me, his arms splashing the water as he came. I back-stroked out of his grasp. He was breathing like an overheated dog and then he tried to scream but it came out a sputtering stream of water.

He looked at me like I was a life preserver floating just out of his grasp. For a moment, I almost reached out to him, but then I remembered Dianne and Shamrock. "Marlowe, please. For the love a god, man. I'll give you anything you want."

Then he sank and gave me what I wanted.

Chapter 37

BY THE TIME they fished me out of the water and hauled me on board the Coast Guard cutter, I was shivering like a naked Jamaican in Alaska. It wasn't just the cold water either, although that was part of it. I felt like a returning veteran with PTSD. I told myself to fight it, keep it under control. I did my best.

On board they threw a blanket around me and shoved a cup of steaming coffee into my hands. I gulped it, burned my mouth. I didn't care. Dianne came running over, threw her arms around me. I pulled her tight with my one free hand. Damn, she felt so good and she seemed fine.

"Dan, I was so scared," she started, then hesitated. I could see tears welling up in her green eyes. She fought them and when she'd gained control, she continued, "I thought you were dead."

"I'm okay. How are you?" I pushed her away from me, looked her up and down.

She just nodded, kept nodding. For a few seconds I didn't think she was going to stop. Finally she did. "Shamrock?" I asked.

She turned, looked toward the other side of the boat. Shamrock was seated in a chair. He had a cup of coffee in one hand and was looking up, talking to what looked like two civilians. They had their backs to me.

"What happened?" I asked.

"When you went after Foley, Shamrock jumped on the big guy. His gun went off. Thank god, Shamrock wasn't hit. He fought the best he could, Dan, but with just one arm? After a little bit, he knocked Shamrock down and held the gun on us again." She furrowed her brows. "You and Foley had gone in the water by then. Foley's men didn't know what to do." She let out a deep sigh. "When they heard the Coast Guard cutter's sirens and the searchlight found us, they gave up. Just like that. Shamrock and I ran to the side of the boat and yelled for the sailors to get you."

A Coast Guard officer interrupted us. "How are you feeling?" he asked.

"Okay, I guess," I answered.

"We're going to take you into Portsmouth. Have you checked out. It's summer, but that water can still be cold. " He studied my face. "You look like you have some bruises, too."

If I did, I couldn't feel them. I wasn't going to argue though. I had to go somewhere and a checkup at a hospital after what we'd just been through was as good as any place I could think of.

The officer patted my shoulder. "Just relax. It won't take long. We'll be leaving as soon as we secure that vessel." He pointed to the boat we'd arrived on. It was a hundred feet or so away. Dawn was starting to break and I could see Coast Guardsmen moving about on deck. "Glad to have you aboard," he said before turning and walking away.

"Thank you," Dianne said.

We stood there, holding each other's hand, looking around. I don't know what she saw or what she was thinking. I was thinking that it was over. And we were all alive. That was enough for now.

The two men who'd been talking to Shamrock turned. I was taken aback when I saw one of the men was the bearded guy who I'd thought had been watching me around the beach recently. Now I knew I'd been right. And maybe I was going to find out why, because they were walking our way.

When they reached us, the shorter one, clean shaven with blonde hair, spoke. "Ms. Dennison. Mr. Marlowe. I'm Special Agent Martin Van Deer with the Internal Revenue Service and this is Special Agent Steven Fisher, FBI." He pointed at the taller man with the dark beard, the one I recognized. "I'm glad you're both are all right. You are okay, aren't you?"

"We're fine," I said. "What's . . ." I stopped when I realized I didn't know exactly what to ask.

Agent Fisher spoke this time. His proper speech sounded like nothing you'd expect to hear from someone with a bushy black beard, dressed so casually. "I suppose you'd like to know what's going on?"

"I know you saved our lives," Dianne said.

"Ahh, yeah, thanks," I said. "But what *is* going on?"

The two men looked at each other. "With Foley gone, it doesn't make much difference," Fisher said.

Agent Van Deer nodded. "Let's go inside, get a little bit of privacy," he said.

The four of us headed for the cabin. Before we reached it, I called out to Shamrock to come along. Van Deer stopped. "I don't think—"

I didn't let him finish. "He's my best friend. He's been through this whole thing with us and almost lost his life more than once because of it. If anyone deserves to hear why he was almost killed, he does." Van Deer shrugged his shoulders. We all walked into the cabin. Shamrock was the last inside.

It was a very large area. We all sat around a cafeteria-type table. Fisher asked if we wanted anything. I didn't give anyone time to answer. "Tell us what the hell's been going on."

Fisher raised his palms off the table. "All right. I'll fill in the holes for you." He did. We asked some questions. Most they answered. A few, they couldn't or wouldn't.

It had all been about one thing—a gambling casino.

By the time we pulled into Portsmouth Harbor the sun was up and they were done with the tale. Everything made sense to me now. Or at least as much sense as it probably was ever going to make. That didn't mean I was happy with everything they'd told me. There were parts of the story I wasn't pleased with at all. Of course, those parts they apologized for. It didn't make me feel any better.

Epilogue

IT WAS AUGUST now and almost a month had passed since I'd killed Red Foley. The three of us—Shamrock, Dianne, and I—were seated on a bench at the Seashell stage facing the Casino building. We'd trooped up to meet Steve on his lunch break, after deciding not to get together at the Tide because of the lack of privacy and the interruptions we'd face. Dianne had left the restaurant in the hands of Guillermo, Ruthie, and the rest of the crew. Another bartender was standing in for me.

I was seated in the middle with Dianne and Shamrock on either side of me. It was a warm day. Dianne and I wore shorts. Shamrock had on his restaurant whites. Steve was standing in front of us. Chinos, sport shirt, gun.

"Sit down," I said to Steve, leaning forward and pointing toward an open spot beside Dianne.

"No thanks. Even though I'm on lunch, I don't want Gant to see me being too chummy with you." He glanced at Dianne. "Not you, Dianne." He shifted his gaze to me. "*You*, Dan."

I chuckled; I had to. Even after Gant had ended up with egg on his face concerning the Foley episode, Steve was still wary of the man.

"I'd think he'd be bending over backwards to make amends," Dianne said.

"Hah." Steve rolled his eyes. "You don't know Gant. He still thinks . . ." Steve waved one hand at us. "Never mind. I just wanted to touch base with you guys. I don't know if you've heard but the legislature's decided not to proceed with any casino bills."

"You mean that's it?" I asked. "It's over?"

"Yeah, it's over," Steve answered. "That's what I heard. And it's because of what happened with Foley. With the media playing it up so much, I guess the rats are scurrying for the exits."

Just then two skateboarders ollied in front of us—jumping off their moving boards, flipping them in the air, and landing expertly back on them when they landed. People jumped out of the way as they flew along.

"Hey, knock it off," Steve yelled after them. They ignored his shouts and disappeared into the crowd.

"Kelsey still skateboard?" I asked, referring to Steve's son.

"Oh, yeah," he answered. Then added quickly. "But not up here. Tournaments mostly."

"Is it true what the papers said?" I asked. "About Foley working for someone else?"

"It is," Steve answered.

"Who was it?" Dianne asked. She was looking up at Steve. She wore shades, but still cupped her hands to help keep the sun out of her eyes.

"Well," Steve began. "I guess it was Vegas money. Who exactly, I'm not sure if they know. Probably couldn't prove it anyway with Foley dead."

"One of the big casinos?" Shamrock asked.

"I'm sure," Steve answered. "They're the only ones that have the money and the incentive to try to make a move like this."

"I thought all the Las Vegas casinos were legitimate nowadays," I said. "Big corporations and all. Why the hell would they have anything to do with a gangster like Foley?"

Steve watched the bumper-to-bumper traffic crawling along Ocean Boulevard. "That's what they say. And probably ninety percent of the casinos are legit. But there's some that might still have ties to the old mobster crowd. And if billions are involved, and a guy like Foley can help them get that money in their pockets, it's naive to think they wouldn't use him."

"So Foley was only fronting for them?" I said. "Trying to pick up oceanfront property for a gambling casino?"

"That's right." Steve shifted his gaze back to us. "They couldn't have their own people up here buying oceanfront property. Christ, if word got out that a Vegas casino wanted in, prices would've skyrocketed. So while they had Foley and his lawyer picking up property, they had their lobbying people up in Concord trying to push a casino bill through the legislature."

"Spreading money all over the place up there, I'll bet," I said.

"I'm sure," Steve said. "That's just standard operating procedure for a so-called legitimate casino trying to get in somewhere new."

"And that would explain Foley and the Salisbury properties," I began. "A couple of years ago it looked like Massachusetts was going to legalize casinos. Then it just died."

"Bingo," Steve said. "They tried there too, but it didn't go through."

"Hmm," Dianne said. "So if gambling was legalized, they would have a place for a casino all ready to go on Hampton Beach."

"Not just any place either, Dianne." Shamrock leaned forward, his hands on his knees. "This is the best oceanfront property in New Hampshire." He waved his hand in a wide swath in front of him.

"And not only the best either," I added. "It's almost all there is. We've only got about thirteen miles of coastline in New Hampshire and most of it can't be used for one reason or another. Compare that to Maine with two hundred and twenty-five plus miles of coastline."

"That's right," Steve said. "They would've been in the cat bird's seat if they'd been able to push through the gambling bill. It would've been worth billions to them."

"I wonder how much they were spreading out to the politicians?" I said.

"Plenty," Steve said, wiping his hand across his forehead. "That's why they're all heading for the hills now. They don't want to get swept up in any fallout."

"Some of them might get arrested?" Dianne asked. She raised her shades for a moment to look at Steve.

"I doubt it," he answered glumly. "I've talked to the feds. They were counting on flipping Foley. Through him they were going to grab the Vegas people. From there maybe get the pols. But now that Foley's gone, there's no way to put the finger on Vegas. They probably have an idea which casino was behind it, but now they can't prove it."

"Foley?" Shamrock said incredulously. "They thought a tough Irish gangster like him would rat?"

Steve grinned. "You'd be surprised, Shamrock. They had a lot on Foley already, with tapes and informants who were going to turn on him. He would have flipped like a gymnast."

"Red Foley?" Shamrock said it like Steve had just told him there was snow predicted for tomorrow.

"Yes, Foley," Steve answered. "I guess I'm not telling tales out of school, what with the asshole dead, and it's going to come out in the papers soon anyway. But Foley was a long-time confidential informant. He'd been working off and on with different agencies for decades, I heard. And I guess the only reason he was keeping his mouth shut on this casino thing was that he knew how powerful the Vegas people were and what would happen to him if he opened his mouth. Like I said, some of those so-called legitimate businessmen still have very heavy connections. Also, Foley had a chance to make more money than even he'd ever seen. So he kept his handlers in the dark."

"Red Foley? A squealer?" Shamrock said. He pulled a cigarette pack from his shirt pocket, fired one up. "For the love a Mary. You never know, I guess."

"I thought your FBI friend said there was no investigation going on about Foley and the beach?" I said.

Steve shrugged. "Maybe he had to lie or maybe he was in the dark. What are you going to do?"

"What about the rest of Foley's gang?" I asked. "That little Runt and Scally Cap?"

"They're all going away," Steve said. "Their little sideline of shaking down Eddie Hoar is the least of their worries. They'll take a big rap." He hesitated, then said smiling, "You'll be glad to hear that Karnack copped a plea. I heard he's going to do ten years. Eight and a half with good behavior."

"Hmmph," Dianne said. "He deserves eighty and a half. He's a bad man."

"What'll happen to the Honeymoon?" I asked.

We all turned, looked north in the direction of the Honeymoon Hotel. Even from this distance I could see kids hanging over the balcony, waving beer bottles in their hands and shouting at passing cars.

"Maybe it'll be up for sale," Steve offered. "Want to get in the hotel business?"

"Nooo, thank you," I said. "Especially not with that dump."

"It is kind of a beach landmark, though," Dianne said.

"Not like that one," Shamrock said, pointing at the Casino.

We all turned, surveyed the length of the two-story, two-block long building directly across the street from us. A constant shower of noise poured from the shooting gallery inside. A horde of tourists and beach goers maneuvered along the Casino's walkway, trying to avoid hitting each other. Some shoveled french fries into their mouths while they walked, others devoured ice cream, fried dough, and a variety of fattening fast foods. People poured in and out of the many shops. Teenagers, of course, were everywhere. Hampton Beach was teenage heaven.

"You're right," Dianne said. "The Casino's special. It *is* Hampton Beach."

"Been here almost a hundred years," I offered.

"Looks it too," Steve said, shaking his head.

"That's part of the charm," I said.

"It could use a paint job," Shamrock said. "I wonder if they'd consider hiring anyone to take care of that?"

"Imagine if those Vegas people got their hands on *that*," I said to Steve, jutting my chin in the Casino's direction.

"They'd tear it down and build one of those monstrosities they have out there or in Atlantic City."

"No way," Steve said.

"Why not?" Dianne asked.

"You'll never see a gambling casino there," Steve said. "Won't happen."

"Why not?" I said. "With the kind of money casino developers could toss around to the local and state pols? The money local business people could make? Not to mention property owners. Christ, even the Tide would have a ton more business."

"I don't care how much more business *I'd* have, I wouldn't want to see a gambling casino on the beach." Dianne's tone was angry. "God, it wouldn't be Hampton Beach anymore."

"I wonder if card dealers get paid good?" Shamrock said wistfully. "I'm handy at that already."

"Shamrock!" Dianne gave him a cross look.

"I wouldn't leave the Tide." A little red crept into his face. "I was thinking maybe something part-time."

"I didn't mean that," she said. "I thought you loved the beach. Do you want to see it changed forever with a gambling casino?"

"Well, of course not," Shamrock answered. "But if people could make a little extra money, maybe it's not such a bad idea."

"See what I mean," I said. "If Mister Hampton Beach says that, watch out."

"I hope we don't ever see it," Dianne said. She crossed her arms across her chest. "I'll leave town!"

"Don't worry, Dianne," Steve said. "It ain't gonna happen. Never."

"I hope you're right," I said solemnly. "Still, ten or twenty years from now?" I shrugged. "It wouldn't surprise me. When big money's involved, strange things can happen."

We all turned to look at the Casino. The huge old wooden structure, the center of Hampton Beach, its heart. No one spoke. I think we were all lost in thought. At least I know I was.

Finally, Dianne broke the spell. "Hey, what about Bud Phillips? I haven't seen him around lately."

Steve chuckled. "He resigned as head of the Chamber. Back problems. So they say."

"Good riddance," I said. "It sounds like he's getting out of it easy."

"They might not have had much on him," Steve said. "Just enough to show him the door."

"Well, at least Cliff Ingalls has his building," I said. "That's another good thing. Maybe Peenell will come back. The government will probably seize his old building and put it up for sale too."

"Most likely," Steve said. "So at least everything's okay for now. And don't worry. That's the only casino we'll see on the beach for a long time." He pointed across the street. Then he looked at me, grinned. "And you, Mr. Lucky. You're cleared of everything."

"I don't feel very lucky," I said. That was because there was one secret I was going to keep inside me forever. Tell no one. And even though I didn't regret having let Red Foley die, especially when I had Dianne and Shamrock sitting beside me, healthy and well, I still wasn't sleeping good at night.

"Well, you should." Steve looked at his watch. "Got to get going."

"Us, too," Dianne said. The three of us got up from the bench.

"My car's up there." Steve pointed his thumb in the direction of a small area just beyond the Chamber office which was reserved for police cars and the like. "I'll talk to you all later. See you around."

Dianne and Shamrock said goodbye. I said, "Say hi to Kelsey and your wife."

The three of us started walking south. The sidewalk was crowded, we had to take turns stepping behind each other to let others pass. Most of the time I was in the middle with Dianne on the inside. We were all silent as we walked. The cars honked, teenagers yelled, and sirens sounded. When we reached the playground, I gazed through the chain link fence surrounding it. I thought of my two children. We'd spent a lot of fun time in there when they were younger. Good times. Wonderful times. Now I didn't have much time with them at all, good or bad. And that was my fault.

I pulled my mind out of those thoughts. I didn't want to go too far down that road. I couldn't afford to. If I did, I might never get back in their lives.

For now I had to be content with what I had. And I guess I was.

I looked down the boulevard, half the length of Hampton Beach. I could see the High Tide. We were getting closer. Almost home. I felt a smile start on my face. I let it grow. It felt good. I didn't smile that much anymore.

I took Dianne's hand, squeezed. She squeezed back and looked up at me with a smile that told me everything would be all right. I threw my other arm around Shamrock's shoulder, pulled him close as we walked. That was something I couldn't remember doing before.

"Danny boy," he said, accentuating his brogue, "I didn't know you cared."

"Oh, I do, Shamrock. Believe me I do."

About the Author

JED POWER is a Hampton Beach, NH-based writer and author of numerous published short stories. *The Boss of Hampton Beach, Hampton Beach Homicide,* and *Blood on Hampton Beach* are the three previous novels in the Dan Marlowe crime series.

The Combat Zone, the first crime novel in a new series, is now out. The series follows a P.I. who hangs his hat in early 1970s Harvard Square and roams the Combat Zone, Boston's red-light district. This novel was a finalist in the St. Martin's Press/Private Eye Writers of America "Best First P. I. Novel" competition. All books are available in both paper and ebook.

Find out more at www.darkjettypublishing.com.

23057949R00199

Made in the USA
Middletown, DE
15 August 2015